"Just how much do you know about horses?"

"Enough to know what I want to work with in front of the camera."

She could already see the headlines: Kelleran Killed By Kick To Head. Actor Dragged To Death. "And just what would that be?"

"An animal that's going to be still when I want it to be still. To respond the way I want it to, to move the way I want it to move."

He leaned forward a bit, not enough to make her feel as if he was crowding her, but enough to make her want to take a step back. She held her ground.

"Something with a little life in it," he said. "A little fire. A little backbone. I don't like things to come too easy."

Suddenly she wasn't sure they were still talking about horses.

Dear Reader,

The first time I saw a movie at the theater, I was six years old. I remember I wore my Sunday dress, and I got to stay up past my bedtime. As I sat in that dark, cavernous theater absorbed in Disney's *Sleeping Beauty*, I fell in love with more than the sparkling fantasy, the breath-robbing danger and the fairy-tale romance on the screen. I fell in love with the movies.

I simply adore watching larger-than-life characters live their larger-than-life stories, all played out on a larger-than-life canvas.

And I'm sure a nice, fat dollop of my film-fed dreams has dropped into this first of my BRIGHT LIGHTS, BIG SKY stories. I hope you'll find movie star Fitz Kelleran every bit as fun to know as he was to write.

And there's more fun coming in my next two stories which will blend a touch of Hollywood make-believe with a taste of Montana make-do. The rugged ranch land beneath that famous big sky makes a perfect larger-than-life setting for a love story, don't you think?

I'd love to hear from my readers! Please come for a visit to my Web site at www.terrymclaughlin.com, or find me at www.wetnoodleposse.com or www.superauthors.com, or write to me at P.O. Box 5838, Eureka, CA 95502.

Wishing you happily-ever-after reading,

Terry McLaughlin

MAKE-BELIEVE
COWBOY
Terry McLaughlin

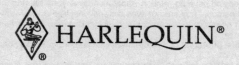

TORONTO • NEW YORK • LONDON
AMSTERDAM • PARIS • SYDNEY • HAMBURG
STOCKHOLM • ATHENS • TOKYO • MILAN • MADRID
PRAGUE • WARSAW • BUDAPEST • AUCKLAND

ISBN-13: 978-0-373-71372-1
ISBN-10:   0-373-71372-X

MAKE-BELIEVE COWBOY

This edition published by arrangement with Harlequin Books S.A.

® and TM are trademarks of the publisher. Trademarks indicated with ® are registered in the United States Patent and Trademark Office, the Canadian Trade Marks Office and in other countries.

www.eHarlequin.com

Printed in U.S.A.

ABOUT THE AUTHOR

Terry McLaughlin spent a dozen years teaching a variety of subjects, including anthropology, music appreciation, English, drafting, drama and history, to a variety of students from kindergarten to college before she discovered romance novels and fell in love with love stories. When she's not reading and writing, she enjoys traveling and dreaming up house and garden improvement projects (although most of those dreams don't come true).

Terry lives with her husband in Northern California on a tiny ranch in the redwoods. Visit her at www.terrymclaughlin.com.

Books by Terry McLaughlin

HARLEQUIN SUPERROMANCE

Don't miss any of our special offers. Write to us at the following address for information on our newest releases.

Harlequin Reader Service
U.S.: 3010 Walden Ave., P.O. Box 1325, Buffalo, NY 14269
Canadian: P.O. Box 609, Fort Erie, Ont. L2A 5X3

For the Wendys

CHAPTER ONE

FITZ KELLERAN WANTED TO VAULT over the side of his Ferrari 360 Spider convertible, the way a thirty-four-year-old movie star should, but all he could manage was a creaky-kneed wobble out the door. Had he ever been this tired? Oh, yeah…last night. Same time, same place, same worn-out reasons.

He braced himself against the leather upholstery for a moment and let waves of disgust break over him. Disgust with the rock music throbbing from the balcony of his Malibu mansion and the strangers framed in the tall windows, sipping his booze. Disgust with himself for the music, the moochers and his careless tolerance of it all.

God, what a mess. He sure had a talent for it. But someone had to keep the fast food on all those tabloid press tables. Might as well be John Fitzgerald Kelleran.

He straightened and winced at the catch in his lower back. Bucking hay wasn't the kind of exercise regimen Hollywood trainers recommended. A soak in the hot tub would loosen him up a bit, but he'd still be feeling some twinges come tomorrow morning.

Good. He welcomed the pain. The little creaks and cramps, the dried sweat and streaks of dirt, the specks of alfalfa and manure that clung to his work shirt and jeans made him feel somehow cleaner and more alive, more *real* than he'd felt in a long while. Gramps had always said there was nothing better for the inside of a man than the outside of a horse.

Samantha, his current lover, would hate it. She'd take one look, one whiff, and toss her $10,000 rhinoplasty in the air.

"No romp in the hay tonight for this cowboy," he muttered, shoving the car door shut.

And did he really care? Not anymore. She'd siphoned off enough celebrity from their relationship, and he'd satisfied his craving for her particular flavor. Time to rustle up the backbone to end the affair. Later tonight, when they didn't have an audience, he'd—

No, not tonight. She'd headed into the valley at noon to tape her guest spot on *The Tonight Show* and dine with her new agent, basking in the glow of her televised glory. No, he wouldn't dim her spotlight. Not tonight.

"Damn." Fitz angled his wrist beneath the beam of a security lamp and squinted at his Rolex. Too late to catch Leno's opening monologue, but he'd sure better catch Sam. If he didn't, there'd be hell to pay. Up-and-coming starlets demanded close-up focus on every detail of their self-absorbed lives. Tonight, for one last time, he'd play the supporting role.

He took a deep breath, chuffed it out and shouldered his way through the exotic tiled entry.

"Dude."

"Hey, Max." Fitz nodded a greeting at Sam's yoga instructor and edged past him, swinging by the wet bar to snag a Corona.

"Fitz. Finally." Burke Elliot, his personal assistant, perched on a bar stool, looking more stressed than usual. If Burke would ditch the type-A routine and the college prof glasses, his version of tall, dark and British would cut a wider swath through the single-and-available female population.

But Burke lived to nag, and he was just getting revved up.

"I was wondering when you'd get around to checking in," he said. "Greenberg's been calling, nonstop."

Myron Greenberg, Fitz's pit bull of an agent. Probably itching to crack a few bones and suck the marrow out of the Eastwood project. "I was out at the ranch."

Burke's nostrils twitched. "Something told me that might be the case."

Fitz had once passed an empty afternoon trying to imitate the precise level of disdain conveyed in Burke's nasal twitch, but had failed to perfect it. "Didn't want the cell phone to spook the mare I was working with. Guess I forgot to turn it back on."

"I'm quite sure I don't need to know the details."

No one knew the details, and that's the way Fitz wanted to keep it. His ranch, his legacy. His escape from reality and his link to the past, all tangled up in a few tumbledown acres near Thousand Oaks. He wasn't sure why Gramps had hung that millstone around his neck when he'd died last year. But because it had been Gramps's place, and Gramps's doing, Fitz would likely drag it around until the day he died.

He took the edge off his exhaustion with a swig of cold beer before facing the news. Burke had slipped off his stool to hover, so it was probably bad.

"What's up?" Fitz asked.

"You can see for yourself after the next commercial break."

Fitz followed him through the house, past the clink of ice in cocktail glasses and the clack of billiard balls on felt, past wafting perfume and drifting cigarette smoke. He didn't recognize too many faces. This was Sam's set, Sam's friends and hangers-on, come to watch her go shoulder to chin with Leno.

He slipped into the crowded media room behind Burke and sank into an empty spot on one of the oversize sofas. Before he could draw his next breath, surgically enhanced cleavage pressed against his arm. The blond head above the bosom purred. "Hi, Fitz."

"Hi." He took another sip of beer. "I'm sorry...you are...?"

Collagen-stung lips pouted. "Sunday? The barbecue?" A fingernail dagger stroked down his shirt front. "You told me to be careful of the sun."

"Oh, yeah." He'd made the mistake of mentioning sunscreen and had been roped into smoothing a bottleful on several bathing beauties. Nameless, numberless, interchangeable beauties.

One of Sam's fans across the room called out, "There she is!"

Fitz glanced up to watch Samantha Hart, the former Miss Venice Beach currently tempting James Bond in wide release, saunter across *The Tonight Show* set. Air kisses for all, myopic wave to the studio audience. A tug at the too-short skirt to draw attention to the gorgeous crossed legs. Wet the lips, flash the dimples, giggle for Jay.

Down to business, baby: promote the movie, promote yourself. Wait for Jay's cue for a quotable sound bite. Here it comes: your *special relationship* with Fitz Kelleran, Hollywood bad boy and box office superstar. What's he like at home? Does he do the dishes, or just hurl them against the wall the way he did in *The Madison Option?*

Another pretty pout. God, did they teach that at the starlet studio? Fuss with the necklace—great delaying tactic, and draws attention to the cleavage. Tongue against the upper lip, slight frown between the perfect waxed brows.

Come on, Sam, what game are you playing now? The question wasn't that hard.

"Actually, Jay, things at home haven't been all that...well, you know," she said. "Fitz just doesn't...do it for me anymore, you know? Like, we're not together now. I walked out on him. A couple of days ago."

Fitz glanced at the occupants of his media room. Predatory consideration gleamed in the eyes staring back at him from the flickering semidarkness.

"I can't believe she dumped you, man. On the freakin' *Tonight Show*."

"That's so like, whoa, you know?"

"Cold, man. Subzero."

"Dude."

"Sam's always been such a bitch," said Fitz's sofa mate. She ran her French manicure over his hand in sympathy and pressed her advantage. He wondered if her nipple would leave a permanent dent in his arm.

Then he wondered if Sam's PR bomb would leave a permanent dent in his offscreen image. As messes went, this one was Oscar worthy. Greenberg was probably hunched over his calculator at that very moment, running projections and figuring percentages.

Fitz was surprised he didn't feel something. Betrayed, relieved, angry, set free to go forth and sin again. *Something.*

Something other than this emotional flatline.

Burke's cell phone chirped. He checked it, frowned and shoved it back in his pocket before standing to shoo Sam's leftovers out the door. "Okay, party's over."

Fitz waited, calmly sipping his beer, while Sam's people scattered into the Malibu evening. He waited until the big front door slammed shut and the thumping music switched off, until the only sounds he could hear were the whispers of the surf beyond the windows and the echoes of Burke's shuffling steps coming down the hall. He waited until his assistant—his friend—came back into the darkened room and sank into a nearby chair, and then he said, "You knew about this."

"Yeah." Burke pinched the bridge of his nose. "Greenberg's been on my back all night. And Sam's new agent called after the taping. What a bastard."

"Because of the call, or because he took her on?"

"No, he really is a bastard. A twenty-four-karat bottom feeder. Those two deserve each other."

"Speaking of people who deserve each other…" Fitz stared at the bottle in his hand. "What were all her fair-weather friends and slight acquaintances doing here? Helping her pack?"

"Making the scene, raiding your bar." Burke picked up a magazine and rolled it tight. "Watching the train wreck, up close and personal. I thought I'd keep them here, liquored up, away from the press. Postpone the collateral damage for a while." The magazine tapped a nervous staccato against his leg. "I seem to be doing a lot of that lately."

"Yeah." Fitz pulled up short of a shrug. "I know."

Burke leaned forward, elbows on knees. "You okay?"

"Yeah."

"I thought you'd be." He started to say something else, but nipped it off. Instead, he wound the magazine more tightly and squeezed.

Fitz tilted the bottle toward his mouth, hesitated, lowered it. "Okay. So, things have gotten a little out of control lately."

Burke lifted one skeptical eyebrow.

"*And*," Fitz added, "I should keep my name out of the tabloids if I'm going to get anyone with serious clout in this town to executive produce. I won't let this…this kind of thing happen again. I can't. I want to see this deal come together. I want it, bad."

He set the bottle on a table. "But it's not just the deal. I'm getting too old for this, Burke. God knows I feel too old tonight." He scrubbed his hands over his face and let them fall in his lap. "From here on out, the only offscreen role I'm playing is Boy Scout."

He angled his head back against the sofa and closed his eyes. "So, has she packed yet?"

"Not that I can tell."

Fitz sighed. Suddenly he was too tired to climb into the hot tub. Maybe he'd just sleep here for, oh, twenty years or so.

Burke was tapping again.

"Relax." Fitz stretched out on his side, crunched a throw pillow under his head and tried to burrow deeper into the leather. "I can deal with it."

"You won't have to deal with it. You won't be here." Burke cursed and threw the magazine down on the coffee table. "The scheming shrew had perfect timing."

"What do you mean, I'm not going to be here?"

"There's been a schedule change on the location shoot. We leave for Montana on Monday. Bright and early."

Bright and early. An extra-loud alarm and extra-strength caffeine. LAX and paparazzi on an empty stomach. "Aw, shit."

Burke sniffed and twitched. "You got it."

ELLIE HARRISON REINED IN her mare on the bank of Whistle Creek and frowned at the construction project turning the facade of her family's Montana ranch house into Hollywood's version of a Montana ranch house. Saws shrieked, air compressors whumped, dust whirled, cords twisted, crew members swore. So much money to waste, so many people to waste it. Seemed like everyone had a tiny slice of some ridiculous job, and each of those folks had an assistant.

As long as a fair share of all that money trickled into her pockets, she'd keep her mouth shut and her opinions to herself. Except for sharing her disgust with Will Winterhawk. She'd shared that and plenty more with the ranch foreman over the past twenty years, while she was growing up and he was helping to make sure she did it right.

She shifted in her saddle and glanced over her shoulder at him. "Wonder what Tom would have thought about what's going on up there."

Sometimes it seemed she spent most of her waking hours second-guessing what her dead husband—or his dead father—would have done with the family's land. The weight of all that responsibility to do things the Harrisons' way wore her down more than the job itself.

Will fingered the rope slung over his saddle horn and squinted at the scene across the creek. "I'm thinking he might have appreciated the irony of it. All that fuss and bother to make things look pretty much the way they looked before all the fuss and bother."

"Well, all that fuss and bother is helping me pay the bills."

"Yep." He nodded solemnly. "There's that, too."

"Meaning?"

"Meaning…another kind of irony, maybe. Keeping up appearances, keeping up the ranch." His squint narrowed, and the wrinkles at the corners of his dark eyes deepened. "Maybe using Hollywood like this'll keep Hollywood out."

Too many of her neighbors had already sold out to L.A. millionaires, turning productive ranch lands into extravagant wilderness playgrounds. She wasn't going to let that happen to Tom's inheritance—or to his daughter's future.

Will was right. Every bit of the sawing and hammering and painting, the electrical wiring and the headphone yammering, the helicopters swooping and the trucks lumbering back and forth, the dust and the noise and the confusion—none of it was anything to get herself in a twist over. Every bit of inconvenience meant dollars in the bank.

If everything went well and on time. If nothing interfered too much with normal ranch business. If no one got hurt.

She pulled herself up and out of her slump in the saddle, straightening her spine and ignoring the stitch between her shoulder blades. This phase of the filming of *Wolfe's Range* would be finished in six weeks, and then the cast and crew would head back to California for the studio work. Life could get back to normal, with fodder tucked away for gossip during long winter nights and a tidy sum tucked away for making the balloon payment on the mortgage and the next round of taxes.

Debt, and the means of easing out from under it, made her stomach churn and her head pound. Sometimes it seemed financial concerns had dogged her every step for the past thirty-one years.

Thirty-one. She was still a young woman, but today she felt as old as the land she managed. "Best get on over there and play wrangler for a couple of hours," she said.

"Don't think they see it as much of a game."

"I know. All that make-believe is serious business."

"Why, Eleanor Louise," Will said, tipping his hat back with his thumb to squint at her. "Just when I thought you didn't have an ironic bone in your body."

"You may be a dozen years my elder and the closest thing I've got to an uncle, Will Winterhawk," she said, "but you don't know every little thing that goes on in here." She pointed at her chest.

"Don't want to, most of the time. I like keeping things clean and simple."

"Meaning?"

"Meaning I know when to shut the hell up and make my exit, stage left." He kneed his piebald down into the creek bed and splashed across into Montana Movieland.

Ellie sighed and followed. She'd busied herself with early summer chores to put off an afternoon check-in with Trish Cameron, the young production assistant in charge of making things difficult. Might as well get it over with. She dismounted and carefully led Tansy, her mare, into a circus campground of big white vans, through a tangle of cables and wire and people scurrying about on mysterious tasks.

"Ellie!" Trish raised her clipboard in greeting as she approached. "There you are."

Ellie nodded. "Just wanted to let you know we're all set for that sunrise scene tomorrow. Got the extra stock in and a temporary corral set up for the second unit folks."

"Uh-huh, okay, I... No, damn it," Trish snapped at some invisible person over her headphone set. "I said— What does he mean, we're— Oh, right, like I give a shit what he— Okay, good."

Trish fiddled a bit with the little gray ball stuck at her ear and checked the gizmo clipped to her waist and then flipped the clipboard over to slap another scrawled sticky note on top of a wad of fluttering litter before smiling at Ellie. "All set, huh? Good. That's great. Only now they want ten more."

"Horses?"

"Yeah. And make 'em, you know..." She waved her hand in tight, tense circles. "Mixed."

"Mixed?"

"Like, different colors." Trish pulled a cell phone out of a back pocket and frowned at the screen. "More white ones. A couple of those spotted ones. Some lighter browns. You know—something that'll be a stronger contrast on film."

Ellie's stomach turned to battery acid and flowed into her boots. Ten horses, in some crazy crayon assortment pack, to beg and borrow from her neighbors, round up before dark, settle in the paddocks tonight, and then move before dawn to a pasture fifteen miles, one river and a tricky stand of timber away.

Piece of cake.

Probably the piece she wouldn't be eating for dinner tonight. No time for dinner when there was stock to wrangle for idiots who couldn't make up their minds from one minute to the next what in the hell it was they wanted.

She bared her teeth at Trish in something resembling a smile, only because the production assistant looked slightly more harassed than Ellie felt at the moment. "Okay. Anything else?"

"Yeah, I— Shit." Trish slammed her clipboard under one elbow and cupped her hand over the headphone at her ear. "No, Frank, he said—no, Friday, latest. Whatever it takes, man. Fitz is here."

It took Ellie a second to realize that last bit had been addressed to her. "Fitz?"

"Kelleran? The lead?" Trish headed toward the barn, scrawling another note. "He got here earlier than we expected. He's asking about his horse."

Ellie tugged at Tansy's reins and followed. "His horse? What about it?"

"I don't know," said Trish. She jerked her thumb over her shoulder. "You'll have to ask him."

And there he was, leaning against a nearby van with not a care in his millionaire movie star world, his chambray shirtsleeves rolled back and his hands shoved into his pockets: Fitz Kelleran.

Ellie simply couldn't prevent the shock to her system, the stagger in her step, the sudden intake of breath. He was taller than she'd expected, and leaner, his face more angular, his features more chiseled. He was much, oh, so much more handsome than the movie-screen Fitz—and that should have been an impossibility. She'd assumed the make-up, or the lighting, or the magic and mystery of film would make reality disappointing.

But the reality of Fitz Kelleran was that no human being should look that good. It was impossible for one head of thick hair to contain so many variations on the theme of blond. It was impossible for two eyes to match the kind of perfect blue that nearly hurt to look at when it blazed overhead.

It was impossible not to stare, not to study each feature, not to commit to memory the fascinating slide of expression over bone and muscle and skin. She tried not to stare, in that first breathless moment. She swore, in the next, that she'd defy his threat to her composure.

But then he smiled, all even white teeth and craggy edges and hollows, all sexy crinkles and teasing eyes, and another thunderbolt streaked through her.

And in that final moment of her first impression, she decided Fitz Kelleran was going to be a pain in the ass.

She knew it wasn't fair, but the conclusion bubbled up through a stew of resentment and basic animal attraction. And—God help her—there was a dash of infatuation, slapping her upside the head and stinging her private parts with little needle pricks of desire.

Yep, a literal pain in the ass.

"Fitz Kelleran," Trish said. "Ellie Harrison. Damn it, Jeff, I told you—" She stalked off, waving the clipboard.

Ellie looked up—way up—and hoped the flutter in her middle wouldn't spread to her lashes. She stuck out her hand, and he took it in one that was big and warm and rough with calluses.

"Welcome to Granite Ridge," she said. "I'm head wrangler."

"So I hear."

His voice was more than it was in the movies, too. Deeper, smoother. It rumbled right through her, from her tingling scalp to her twitching toes.

Damn him for that, too.

"I've got a nice gelding picked out for you, Mr. Kelleran."

"Fitz."

"He won't give you any trouble."

"I don't expect any."

"Okay, then."

"But I'd like to pick out my own mount," he said with that teasing smile, "if it's all the same."

Ellie stiffened and scrambled for patience. "I chose that mount for you. Specifically."

"I'm sure you did an excellent job."

"He was approved by the art director."

His smile widened.

"And he's already been okayed by the director," she added.

"I'm sure he has. But Van Gelder wouldn't know a Morgan from a mule."

"And you do?"

A shadow flickered over his smile, a tiny hitch of his jaw. "You shouldn't go making assumptions about people based on appearances, Ellie."

"Looks like you're making one of your own," she said. "About mine."

His eyes took a leisurely tour of her face. "You got me there."

She battled back a blush. "Tell me, Mr. Kelleran—"

"Fitz."

"Just how much do you know about horses?"

"Enough to know what I want to work with in front of the camera."

She could already see the headlines: Kelleran Killed by Kick to Head. Actor Dragged to Death. "And just what would that be?"

"An animal that's going to be still when I want it to be still. To respond the way I want it to, to move the way I want it to move."

He leaned forward a bit, not enough to make her feel like he was crowding her, but enough to make her want to take a step back. She held her ground.

"Something with a little life in it," he said. "A little fire. A little backbone. I don't like things to come too easy."

Suddenly she wasn't sure they were still talking about horses.

CHAPTER TWO

FITZ THOUGHT ELLIE HARRISON could stare daggers with the best of them. Her eyes were interesting, an earthy mix of brown and green and gold. He could almost feel them gut and fillet him. It was an intriguing sensation, sort of like being carved up by the critics.

She shoved her freckled nose up toward his chin. It was small and sharp and pointy, just like the rest of her. "You seem pretty sure about how you want things, Mr. Kelleran."

"Now that's one assumption you'd be safe to make, Ellie. And it's Fitz," he added, because he could see it annoyed her.

"All right. Anything you say. You're the boss. *Fitz.*"

His name sizzled like a curse across her lips. Lips that looked a little chapped from the sun and a little tight with anger. Lips that still looked plump and spicy enough to nibble. Sort of like those dark red chili peppers that gave him heartburn.

And then she turned on her boot heels, tugged at her pretty little mare and stalked off toward the barn. He stood there for a while and watched her tight butt swivel with every tight, ticked-off step. Hm. Nothing pointy there.

Fitz grinned. He probably wouldn't be receiving an invitation to rub sunscreen on Ellie Harrison's compact derriere any time soon. What a shame. This was one time he didn't think he'd mind playing Boy Scout, especially if the good deed involved getting his hands on some of that sass and spit.

Burke stepped from the van and scrunched his features against the late afternoon sun. "Making friends already?"

"Heard some of that, did you?" Fitz took the bottled water his assistant offered and twisted the cap. "I saw her first."

They watched Trish jog around the corner of the barn and trip over a cable. Her clipboard flew into a water trough.

Burke sighed and shook his head. "You should steer clear of that one."

"Don't worry." Fitz pointed the bottle at Trish. "I wouldn't let that one anywhere near the family jewels, especially with a sharp object."

"Not the accidental castrator." Burke hooked a thumb toward the barn. "The premeditator."

"Ms. Montana?"

"She's a widow," said Burke. "And a single mother."

"God." Fitz's scouting fantasies faded to black. "Sounds like a movie of the week."

"Just so you know what you'd be getting into."

Fitz emptied the bottle and swiped at his mouth with his sleeve. "Deep shit."

Burke's twitch and sniff were Montana-size. "Plenty of it to go around."

The last thing Fitz needed was a new set of complications with a new woman. He turned his back on the barn, and on the intriguing but sharp and pointy woman inside. "You know one good thing about shit, Burke?"

"No." He sighed. "But I suppose you're going to mend that minor lapse in my education."

"If you don't step in it, it doesn't stick to your shoes."

ELLIE HASTILY GROOMED TANSY and released her in the south paddock. She made half a dozen phone calls from the barn office and hitched the trailer to the truck before notifying her small grains farmer that he'd be working through the night on the stock roundup. While she dealt with a swollen tendon and medicated a case of mastitis, she fretted over the possibility that too many more unexpected expenses might nibble all the profits from this film deal.

By the time she headed home to check her messages and pack a sandwich for the night's work, she was in a foul mood. She hiked up the gravel road and stomped up the back porch steps, muttering a string of her favorite cuss words all the way.

Slamming through the screened mudroom door, she yanked off her hat before Jenna Harrison, her mother-in-law, could get after her for wearing it into the house. And then she stopped dead in her tracks.

Lasagna. She closed her eyes and breathed it in, tangy and garlicky and just about finished, and her stomach twisted into one big hungry knot. Heading toward the deep kitchen sink to wash some of the grit and stink from her hands, she hollered for her eleven-year-old daughter. "Jody!"

No answer. Probably upstairs, gossiping on the phone with a girlfriend. Might as well get her one of those headsets Trish wore—it would free Jody's hands so she could get something done besides talking the whole day and half the night away.

At least she wasn't talking to boys yet.

Ellie glanced at the ceiling. She wasn't talking to boys yet, was she?

And what if she was? What was Ellie going to do about it?

Should she do anything about it?

Jenna swung through the door with a laundry basket of tea

towels and table linens. Character lines bracketed her blue-bell-colored eyes and a few silvery strands wove through her corn-silk hair, but she was still as willowy and graceful as the Texas debutante she'd once been. "Heard you calling," she said. "Jody's in her room, on the phone."

"I figured." Ellie opened the refrigerator door and reached for the heavy cut-glass pitcher filled with lemonade.

Jenna dropped her load on the kitchen table and took a seat. She pulled a napkin out of the basket and snapped it into a neat square. "Wayne called. Says he's got two grays he can loan us."

Ellie poured a glass and sipped, wincing at the cold, tart shock to her taste buds. "Good."

"He'd like to come watch, if you don't think he'd be in the way."

Too bad Ellie couldn't sell tickets to the set to offset expenses. "Don't see how he could. I'll call him back in a bit."

Jenna shot her one of those mild looks, the kind that asked when Ellie was going to start using the manners Jenna had drilled into her. "Dinner'll be ready in half an hour."

"Sorry," said Ellie. "I'm not going to be here."

Jenna crumpled a napkin into her lap. "Oh, Ellie."

"Can't be helped." She finished the lemonade and turned to rinse the glass in the sink. "Got to get some more horses out to Cougar Butte by dawn."

"Is that why Wayne called?"

"Yep."

Behind her, she could hear Jenna's long suffering sigh. She opened a cabinet door and reached for the aspirin, battling back a fresh layer of guilt. Pleasing Jenna was one of life's priorities, and it stung every time she failed.

Twenty years ago, Jenna had taken one look at undersize, underweight eleven-year-old Ellie Connors and had simply taken her in, into her life and into her heart. When Ellie's nomad of a father had packed their bags after a six-month stint at Granite Ridge, Jenna had quietly pulled Ellie's duffel from the back of his truck and carried it through the front door of the big ranch house.

Ellie had known what that meant—she'd likely never see her real father again.

But she'd also known it meant no more aimless searching for an easier life over every horizon. No more switching towns in the middle of the school term and falling another grade behind. No more standing off to one side in the school yard, afraid to make a friend she'd soon part with. She'd stood dry-eyed in the wide, dusty ranch yard, watching her old life disappear down the road as her new mother's hand had fallen, soft and steady, on her shoulder and her new father's voice, just as soft and steady, had asked her to come in to dinner. Her new sister had grinned at her from the front porch and, inside the tall white house, a handsome college-aged brother had grinned at her from family photos.

She'd traded up that day, gifted with a permanent foothold in a shifting world. But she'd also traded up to an adult's set of worries and an adult's burden of guilt. The worries varied from day to day, but the guilt was a constant, gnawing ache.

She shook a couple of aspirin into her palm and hoped they'd work off some of today's sore spots before she started working on tonight's. "I'll go say good-night to Jody before I head out."

"Is Will going with you?" Jenna waited for Ellie's nod. "Then I'll pack a sandwich for him, too."

ELLIE STOOD IN JODY'S DOORWAY for a minute. The sight of her long-legged daughter draped over a pink and ruffled bed made the stresses and strains of the day slip away. She sure took after her father—coltish and confident, as foamy and fun as cold beer in a tall glass on the Fourth of July. She was every bit as impulsive and trusting as her father, too, just as quick to gift a stranger with a piece of her heart and just as likely to see it tossed aside or trampled. Dreamers, the pair of them.

Ellie had always been the one who soothed the pain and patched up the pieces. But knowing that Jody would always have a home, that she would always be secure in her family's love— that's what made the work and the worries worth the effort.

The phone was getting its battery recharged in the cradle on the nightstand, and Jody was sprawled on her back with her nose tent-poled up inside some newsprint tabloid. Teen magazines were strewn across the spread. Wasn't it just last week she'd been working her way through Jenna's collection of children's classics?

Ellie studied the nearest magazine cover, searching for a conversation topic in one of the neon-print headlines. "So, who's hot and who's not?"

"Oh, you know—the usual." Jody dropped the gossip paper on the floor and scrambled to her knees to gather the mess on her bed into a neat pile. She clutched it all to her chest with a defensive glance at Ellie. "Gran bought these for me."

"That's fine, hon."

Ellie shifted from one foot to the other, feeling as uncomfortable as her daughter looked. She didn't like the idea that Jody might want to hide things from her. And worse, she didn't know how to talk to her daughter about the need for deceptions. It was as if she and Jody were slipping away from each other, too fast, too far, as if the same mysterious metamorphosis that was turning Jody into a grown, independent woman would also turn her into a stranger.

Ellie grasped at the few moments she could spare for her

daughter tonight, longing to share a sliver of whatever Jody thought was important. She walked into the room and sat on the edge of the bed. "Is there anyone in particular who's hot right now?"

Jody hesitated, and then pulled a tabloid from the middle of the stack and set it on the bed. Fitz Kelleran's handsome face grinned up at them both. "Is he here yet?"

Ellie nodded. "Yep."

"Oh, my God." Jody edged closer. "Have you seen him?"

"Talked to him just a while ago."

"Oh, my God." Jody stared at the cover. "What does he look like? I mean, you know, does he really look like this?"

"I'll tell you exactly what he looks like." Ellie lifted a hand to fan her face. "Oh. My. God."

Jody shrieked and flopped across the bed to sweep the tabloid off the floor. "Listen to this," she said, flipping pages until she found what she was looking for. "'Bond Bombshell Samantha Hart gave live-in boyfriend Fitz Kelleran a kung-fu kick in the teeth when she announced on nationwide television that she was leaving him. Fitz heard the news on *The Tonight Show with Jay Leno* while sitting at home in his TV room, along with several million of his fellow dumpees. Samantha's been spotted in several Hollywood hot spots, with several Hollywood hotshots, while Kelleran's howling his Hart out with the coyotes, shooting on location in the Montana wilderness.'"

Jody glanced up. "This isn't exactly the wilderness."

Ellie picked up the magazine with Fitz's cover. He suddenly seemed a little more interesting—and a lot easier to deal with—now that she knew that spectacular exterior masked a dumpee's interior. Still, it was a bit unsettling to be staring at this glamour shot of the flesh-and-blood man she'd been speaking to an hour or so ago. "You believe everything you read in these things?"

Jody rolled her eyes. "No."

She leaned over Ellie's shoulder and pointed to a photo of Fitz in his *Justice, D.O.A.* attorney's suit—tie askew, hair falling over his forehead, a briefcase dangling from one hand and a gun clutched in the other. "Are his eyes really that blue?"

"Bluer."

"Whoa. Does he look, you know—" Jody wrinkled her nose. "Kind of mean?"

"Like in this picture?"

"No, I mean, like, *mean*. Scary."

Ellie remembered that smile searing a hot trail through her midsection and felt another blush coming on. Oh, yeah…*scary*. She shook her head at her foolish reaction and handed the magazine to Jody. "No, he doesn't seem that way at all."

Jody smoothed her hand over the cover. "I can hardly wait to meet him."

"Jody, we talked about this." Ellie shoved to her feet. "You know I don't want you bothering those people."

"I wouldn't be, honest. Trish even asked me to help."

"I especially don't want you getting in Trish's way. She looks like she's got more than she can handle as it is."

"Aw, Mom—"

"I really don't want to have this argument again." Ellie closed her eyes for a moment to block out her daughter's mutinous glare. "I came up to say good night. Will and I are heading out to round up some more stock for the second unit work in the morning."

Jody tossed the magazines on the nightstand. "Gran made one of your favorites."

"I know. Lasagna." Ellie bent down to smack a loud kiss on Jody's head. "Have seconds for me, okay?"

"All right. Night."

"Night." Ellie hesitated in the doorway, knowing she'd mangled another moment and wishing she could start fresh. There was one edict she could reconsider: her ban on movie meddling. Keeping Jody away from the film crew made her a virtual prisoner in her own house. "Tell you what. If you can haul your butt out of bed in time, I'll take you with me to watch them film."

"Really?"

"You have to promise to stay close and do exactly what I tell you."

"I promise." Jody jumped off the bed and threw her arms around Ellie's waist. Her scent was powdery cologne and bubble gum, and her head bumped Ellie's chin. So tall, so soon. So *scary*. "Thanks, Mom."

Ellie wrapped her arms around her daughter. "You won't be thanking me when I wake you up before the crack of dawn."

"Yes I will."

"We'll see." Ellie squeezed her tight. "Gotta go."

"Bye, Mom." Jody squeezed her back. "Love you."

"Love you, too." Ellie held her breath and held on tight. She didn't want to be the first to let go.

JENNA TUCKED THE TEA TOWELS neatly into the proper drawer and sighed with satisfaction as she glanced around the tidy space. Her kitchen, her refuge, done up in cheery yellows and warm, honey-toned woods. She spent her days keeping her little family and her small corner of the world just as tidy, just as cheery. The soothing routines had been her salvation since her husband had died, and she clung to them still.

She moved about the room, pulling supplies out of storage, and then eased into the familiar routine of fixing one of Will's favorites: roast beef on sourdough with plenty of plain yellow mustard.

She'd tried one of those gourmet condiments once, about a year ago, to spice up his fare. He'd bitten into his sandwich and chewed for a while, his face creasing in that slow smile of his. "Pretty fancy stuff for a fellow like me," he'd said. "My taste buds don't quite know what hit 'em."

"Don't you like it?" she'd asked, more anxious than a change in mustard merited, her anticipation squeezing her heart tighter than one of Will's smiles deserved.

"Didn't say I don't." He'd taken another bite, chewed and swallowed. "Didn't say I do." And then he'd winked at her, and Jenna had fled into her kitchen to hide a blush and promised herself the fancy mustard would get used in some other way.

It was still sitting there, tucked away in the back of a refrigerator shelf, taunting her. Just like Will's presence in her life—his slow smiles, his sly winks, his yearning glances. She was a widow three years past the worst of the grieving, a woman twenty years past the peak of her potential, and she had no business being taunted by anything, or anyone, at all.

Especially not by a younger man, a man who had been her son's best friend. A man young enough to be wanting children, young enough to raise a family of his own. Or so she told herself when those warming, softening, liquid sensations flowed through her body.

Just another form of taunting. Just another set of those cruel tricks nature liked to play on women of a certain age.

Well, she was too smart to fall for a menopausal malfunction like temporary insanity. She had plenty of chores and plenty of responsibilities—with a few extra duties tossed in, what with that film crew camped outside her front door. There were too many truly important things crowding into her life these days for her to spare one moment daydreaming over the ranch foreman's flirting.

She reached into her tin bread box for some extra-wide slices of sourdough. The back door opened and she heard a familiar heavy step behind her. "Jenna."

He stole her breath with the way he said her name. She glanced over her shoulder at him, at his rangy height and his rugged features, and waited for the tingly pressure in her chest to subside. "Will."

He removed his hat and dropped it over one of the ladder-back chairs clustered around a scarred oak table, and she turned back to her task. The solid thumps of his boot heels drew near, and his leathery scent competed with the tang of the mustard, and his warm, moist breath washed across the nape of her neck. She bit the inside of her lip against the shock waves that rolled through her and leaned a bit away from him to keep her knees steady against the cabinet.

A big, warm hand settled on her shoulder. "Is that for me?"

"Heard you were going to be out late."

His hand slid down her arm to rest over hers on the bread knife, and oh, my, that slow stroke cut right through her best intentions, settling in deep and smoldering in hidden places. But her hand was no longer that of a young girl. And she shouldn't be experiencing the feelings and flushes of a young girl, either. She didn't understand how she could be, when her body was drying up inside, when she was as emptied out and brittle as an old corn husk. She was a fragile, arid, fifty-five-year-old ghost of herself.

"Jenna," he whispered.

She closed her eyes to shut it all away. "It's just a sandwich, Will."

"If you say so. But you know me and my notions. I like to think some things are more than what they seem. Like that sandwich. It could be so much more. Everything could be so much more." He turned his head, a fraction of an inch, so his lips brushed at her hair as he spoke. "Just say the word."

CHAPTER THREE

YES, WHISPERED A GIRLISH corner of Jenna's heart. *It's too soon*, nagged the doubting voice in her mixed-up mind. She froze, afraid to shatter the moment or upend the fragile balance of her ambivalence. The tiniest motion, the merest notion might tip the scales too far to ever get her life on the level again.

She sucked a deep breath into her hollow, brittle core and shoved it out with an empty, stilted cheerfulness. "I made some cookies today. Cinnamon oatmeal. I'll pack some of those in with the sandwich."

He laced his fingers through hers and squeezed her hand with the gentleness that was as much a part of him as the bronzed skin that stretched over his prominent cheekbones and the blue-black hair that brushed along his shirt collar. "Thank you, Jenna," he said and stepped away.

The gap between them yawned wider than mere inches of space. "You've nothing to thank me for," she said.

Nothing. It seemed that was all she ever offered, and yet he took it. He lapped it up, every stingy drop of it, and waited and watched for more of the same. She wanted to curse him for his patience, and curse herself for her cowardice while she left him in limbo.

She busied herself arranging slices of beef on slabs of bread. "How are things going?"

"Ellie's doing fine," he said, answering another question Jenna had meant to ask. "Maybe you could talk her into going to town with you sometime next week, to get her out of here and get her mind off her troubles for a few hours."

"And get her out of your hair?"

His low, throaty chuckle seemed to tickle up her spine. "That, too," he said.

She worked in silence for a few moments, and then he shifted behind her. "Jenna—"

Ellie rushed into the room. "Better get going."

"Just about finished here," said Jenna. She picked up the knife and quickly, cleanly sliced Will's sandwich in half.

FITZ SPRAWLED ON THE THIN slice of burlap-covered foam that passed for his trailer sofa, thumbing through the latest draft of his script. *His script.* Optioned and paid for. One more step toward his dream of creating the definitive remake of the Cooper classic, *The Virginian.*

Outside the living area's low-slung metal window, the whumps and whines of power tools faded as the swing gang broke for dinner. They'd start up again in less than an hour and keep at it under the lights until midnight. He'd seen the second unit loading up gear for a dawn shoot out at some place called Cougar Butte. If he wanted to get any sleep tonight, he should head back to town.

Burke's familiar four-beat rap sounded at the trailer door.

"It's open."

He stepped in and closed the door behind himself. "How are the accommodations?"

"Not bad. The electricity's on, the plumbing works and the bed's tolerable."

"You didn't mention the kitchen."

"I didn't want to hurt your feelings."

"Am I fired?"

"Nope." Fitz smiled at the slightly hopeful note in his assistant's voice. Burke hated location work. "But you're not going to get fed until I can get into town to shop for some decent supplies."

Catering fare on film sets didn't interest him, as a rule, and he liked to cook. He spent most of his days being what other people wanted him to be. When he dabbled in the kitchen he could relax, and be himself, and please himself.

Hell, in that respect, cooking was more relaxing than sex.

"So?" he asked. "What's up?"

Burke hesitated. "Stone called."

"Damn." Fitz didn't need to ask what the producer had called about, or what the message was. "No deal."

"He says he's not fond enough of the script to take a chance on a western right now."

"We're not asking him to put up any money." Fitz stood and started to pace, but there wasn't enough room in the trailer to get up to speed. "All we need are some connections. A nudge here or there."

He grabbed a Corona from the tiny refrigerator and offered another to Burke. "What is it he's not saying?"

Burke avoided the question with a long, slow sip of beer.

"Samantha Hart." Fitz twisted off the bottle cap with a little more violence than necessary. "Leno."

"He did mention it." Burke shrugged it off. "You knew going in on this a western was going to be a tough sell."

"But not impossible." He tossed out his arms. "Hell, I'm surrounded by the evidence."

He stared at the view outside the window, looking past the base camp of white vans clustered in raggedy rows, past the tidy nineteenth-century farmhouse on the slight knoll behind them. When his gaze lifted to the jagged silhouettes of the mountains sprouting from silver-green pastureland, his pulse kicked with anticipation.

Maybe he'd read one too many Louis L'Amour novels. Maybe it was genetic—his grandfather had lassoed the family's Hollywood connections working with John Ford on *Stagecoach*. Maybe he was just a sentimental fool. Whatever the reason, he wanted a chance to make *The Virginian*, and to play that role, with a passion he hadn't felt for anything else in his adult life.

It was a huge gamble, but if he wanted to win big, he had to bet big. Myron Greenberg had howled with rage and expanded his cursing vocabulary when Fitz had signed on for this relatively small Van Gelder film. But there was a lot more riding on this Montana location shoot than the filming itself. If he could pull this off, if he could prove to the studio heads that audiences would pay to see him on horseback, he could make his movie the way he wanted it made. Big, and bold, and packaged with the best a production could have.

All he had to do over the next few months was focus on *Wolfe's Range*—act his heart out, promote it until he was ready to drop and then keep all available appendages crossed that it made a profit.

That, and keep his nose clean and his name out of the tabloids.

He settled on the sofa and glanced at Burke. "So, what's the next step?"

"Word's out you've been talking to Stone." Burke squeezed into the compact dining booth and folded his legs under the miniature table. "Seems that brought another interested player out of the woodwork."

"Funny how that works." Fitz took a drag of his beer. "Give me the edited version."

"Lila Clarkson likes the story."

"The Lila Clarkson who produced *Virtual Indemnity*?"

Burke nodded. "That's the one. She's working with a hot new script doctor. Says he's a whiz at punching up visuals and dialogue. Can make any project more marketable."

"Doesn't she have a first-look deal with Warner?"

"Yes. Yes, she does. But if the Warner execs like what they see, they'd come in on the financing."

"Or they could tie it up for years." Fitz set the bottle aside. "Hell, I might never get it back."

"There's always the other option."

Fitz set his jaw to stubborn. "I've done everything on this I'm going to do."

"Look, Fitz." Burke spread his hands on the table's surface. "You're already doing everything an executive producer does, anyway. You've optioned the script. You've put up the initial financing. You're trying to get some of the players in place. Hell, you did the whole Cannes scene last month."

"Don't remind me."

There were few things Fitz hated more than Cannes. The tedious glitz, the shallow glam, the deals bubbling underneath it all like brewer's yeast in a septic tank. He'd gone over early to set up his office, and he'd made his pitch to the international investors, mucking around in the filth along with the other beggars. It had taken a week for him to wash off the stink. But he'd do it all again, and more, if it meant he could make this film his way.

"It's your deal," said Burke. "Why not see it the rest of the way through? Why not take the credit?"

"I don't need to see my name up on the screen more than once."

"That's not what I meant, and you know it."

"Burke." Fitz shifted forward. "Can you honestly see me setting up and running a production company? I barely manage to do the one job I've got."

Burke pushed his glasses higher on his nose. "Yes, you somehow manage to do as little as you possibly can. And brilliantly so, in my humble but expert opinion."

"Besides," said Fitz, ignoring Burke's sarcasm, "I'm just not convinced I can do it up right. The way it needs to be done. And I want this done right. I want—"

He held out his hand, grasping for an eloquence worthy of the scenes and emotions in his head, but they slipped away yet again. All he had was his idea, his vision—and his faith in both.

And determination. He'd dredged up plenty of that, for once in his life. He curled his fingers into a fist and brought his hand down, slowly, firmly, on the sofa arm. "I want this done right."

"Then do it," said Burke. "You've already got everything you need. The name, the connections, the clout."

He probably did. His mega-paychecks automatically translated to mega-power. But Hollywood loved to watch the mighty fall. He'd done plenty of tripping over the years, but so far he'd managed to keep his balance by keeping to his one small place in the shuffle.

He was an actor, plain and simple, not a hyphen director, a hyphen producer, or a hyphen screenwriter. He'd leave the hyphens to the people with the dual and triple ambitions. One ambition at a time was enough for Fitz Kelleran.

One ambition. To make one film. One perfect, classic version of a perfect, classic novel. To play the role of his lifetime, a part that would require all his talent and ability. He didn't want to dilute that effort or diffuse his concentration, to ruin his vision at the very heart of its creation. "No," he said.

"It isn't the money."

"No. Though a hell of a lot of it's already tied up in this, with a nice, neat bow."

"You know you could get more if you needed it." Burke stared down at his hands. "Kruppman says he's got a buyer who'll take the Thousand Oaks place as is. And it would be one less distraction, a distraction you don't need right now."

Fitz sank back against the stiff cushion. The reminder of his financial adviser's pressure to dump Gramps's ranch had him feeling mulish again. "My grandfather's ranch is not for sale."

"It's your ranch, now."

Fitz shrugged, acknowledging the slip.

Burke shrugged, too, and stood. "Do you want me to set up a meet with Lila?"

"Let me think about it."

"Don't take too long to make up your mind. She wants to move on this."

"If she's really interested, she'll still be interested when I'm ready to discuss the deal."

"All right." Burke slipped his sunglasses out of their case. "If that's all for tonight, then, I'm heading back to town."

"Thought I'd head in myself." Fitz stood and stretched. "Maybe pick up a few groceries."

"Are you cooking tonight?" Burke tried unsuccessfully to downplay his interest, but Fitz knew his cooking was one reason Burke tolerated his abuse.

"Yep. Want some?"

"Sure." Burke started out the door ahead of him. "What are you making?"

"Montana grub."

Burke halted at the bottom of the trailer steps and turned to face him. "Grub?"

"Buffalo steak. Venison stew." Fitz locked the door behind them. "We'll see what the locals have that's fresh."

Burke paled a bit beneath his California tan. "You're kidding, right?"

"About my dinner?" Fitz shoved his hands into his pockets and led the way to Burke's rental car. "Never."

IT WAS JUST PAST NOON the following day when Ellie staggered up the house's back steps behind Jody. She was dragging with fatigue, her caffeine overload nudging her closer to cranky than alert.

Her eyes narrowed to slits at a series of hoots and whistles from the direction of the outbuildings. "You go on in," she told her daughter. "Think I'll check out the cause of all that ruckus."

Jody grinned. "Must be the day for it."

"For what?"

"For checking things out." Jody sneaked a peek through the screen door and then leaned toward Ellie. "Like the way Mr. Hammond was checking you out."

"What? Who, Wayne?"

"Yep." Jody fluttered her eyelashes. "Mr. Wayne 'Anything I Can Do for You, Anytime' Hammond."

Ellie's cheeks stung with what was working up to be a champion blush. "I don't know what you're talking about."

"Mom." Jody reached into her pocket and pulled out some change. "Here's a dollar. Buy a clue."

Ellie hid her hands behind her back. Wayne Hammond? No. It couldn't be. The very idea was…mortifying, to say the least. "You don't know what you're talking about."

"Well, one of us better figure out what I'm talking about," said Jody, "or this conversation's going nowhere fast."

Ellie pulled the stern parental routine. "This conversation has nowhere to go."

Jody tugged at the screen door. "All I'm saying is, it's, like, totally obvious Wayne Hammond has the hots for you."

"Jody?" Jenna called from deep inside the house. "Ellie? You coming in for lunch or not?"

"Coming!" Jody stepped inside and held the door. "Mom?"

Ellie shook her head and backed away. "I've got things to do."

"Okay." The door slammed shut, and Jody grinned through the screen. "We'll talk about this later."

"God." Ellie turned and fled from the porch.

Wayne Hammond. *Wayne Hammond.* She groaned as she swung down the gravel road. Probably looking at her and thinking it would be a fine and sensible thing to tear down some nice long stretches of fence between his ranch and hers. Well, hell, he could look and think all he wanted. She was done with giving folks around here reason to think she was marrying for a place to call her own.

She slowed her pace, tripped up by needle-sharp guilt. She'd loved Tom Harrison, surely she had—she'd matched him leap for leap through a carefree, rollicking courtship. He'd been six years older, the wandering prodigal son returned to aid his ailing father, a dashing college graduate with big ideas he'd developed working on bigger ranches. She'd been fresh out of high school and reluctant to leave the only home she'd ever known. So unsure of her footing, so quick to tumble in over her head. And when the daydreams had faded, they'd settled down in comfort and contentment and had made their beautiful daughter.

Maybe neither of them had been built for a deeper passion. Nothing wrong with that, she thought with a hitch of a shoulder. It was the safe and sensible way to go about living a life and sharing a love. Passion could suck a person into a world of pain.

Or so she imagined.

But oh, just once in her life—just for a moment or two, nothing too risky—just once she'd like to know what it felt like. Just once she'd like to be swept up in something dark and reckless and intensely, wickedly thrilling.

None of those adjectives could be applied in any stretch of her imagination to a relationship with Wayne Hammond, but that was probably a good thing. At least she'd keep her wits about her if he started sniffing around.

She set her chin and picked up her pace. She was doing okay these days taking care of herself and her own. Better than okay, once the extra money from this film started rolling in. She had plans—expanding the herd, replacing some of the equipment with new. Adding to Jody's college fund, sending Jenna off on one of those cruises she was always talking about.

Maybe her dreams weren't as audacious as Tom's, but perhaps she had a better chance of making them come true. And she didn't need a man to help her do it.

Another round of laughter sailed in on the languid afternoon breeze. Ellie pinpointed its source—the sand arena down along the creek. She hiked the short distance from the calving barn to the stables, and then skirted the low-slung building and headed for the open area beneath a row of cottonwoods.

One of the temporary hires trudged up the path, lugging an armful of bridles and saddle blankets. He nodded politely. "Hey, Ellie."

"Hey, Nudge." She tilted her head at the arena. "What's all the excitement?"

"Fitz is giving ol' Noodle a try."

"Noodle?"

"Yeah. You gotta see this, Ellie. It's quite a show. He already put Pete through his paces. It was something, I'm telling you."

She snorted. "Pete could make anybody look good." She tucked her hands in her back pockets and kicked at some loose gravel. "So, why's he trying Noodle?"

"That gal with the clipboard liked Noodle's looks. And Fitz said he didn't want Pete." Nudge rolled a wad of tobacco from one side of his jaw to the other. "It's okay to let them check out the stock, right?"

"Yeah, it's okay. Anything they want, within reason." Ellie sighed. "But there's nothing wrong with Pete. He's a good pick for this job. The director liked him well enough."

"Oh, Fitz liked him well enough, too," said Nudge with a shrug, "but he said he was hoping for something a little more quick on the draw."

"Pete's okay."

"Pete's pokey, Ellie. Everybody knows that."

"Yeah, but he won't shy, and he won't throw some Hollywood dude on his million-dollar ass."

"I don't think Fitz is worried about that."

"I'm sure he's not." She rubbed at a tight spot on the back of her neck. "That's why I get to do it for him."

"I don't think you're gonna have to." He nodded toward the arena. "Go take a look."

"I just might."

"Okay, then." Nudge lifted the bridles. "Better go get these cleaned off and hung up before the spit dries on 'em."

By the time Ellie claimed a viewing spot among the crowd hanging on the arena rails, Fitz was switching mounts again, pulling a saddle off Noodle. Brady Cutter, the ranch's bowleg-ged stable hand and farrier, was standing to one side, smooth-ing a blanket over Hannibal, her oversize sorrel gelding.

Not Hannibal. Not my boy.

CHAPTER FOUR

ELLIE TENSED, READY TO CALL out and put a stop to the proceedings, but she bit her lip.

Why not Hannibal? Sure, he was a little green and more than a little headstrong, but if Fitz knew anything at all about horses, it'd only take a minute or two for him to figure it out. And if Fitz didn't know as much about horses as he claimed, it would only take Hannibal a minute or two to figure *that* out—and then Fitz would be getting an education, fast and hard, down on the ground.

She watched Fitz sling the saddle over Hannibal's broad back and then step aside to take the reins while Brady fussed over the cinch. The actor stood just to one side of the horse's head, a serious and solemn look on his face, but whatever he was murmuring to Hannibal must have been amusing enough to have Brady throw his head back with a bark of a laugh.

And then Fitz stepped up into the saddle with the ease of a lifetime of practice and wrapped those long legs around Hannibal's ribs, and the horse began to move. A leisurely walk, a smooth slide into a slow jog, a sudden turn to the center of the arena followed by a stiff-legged stop.

Ellie's chest squeezed in suspended panic as she waited for the big horse to shimmy or break. But through the next few minutes of shifting gaits and motionless pauses, though she studied the way the actor's boots rested in the stirrups and the way his fingers curled around the reins, she couldn't fault his style. Heck, she couldn't even catch half the cues he was giving. The gelding had never looked so good with someone on his back.

"Whoo-ee," said Nudge, clambering up beside her. "Will you look at that?"

"I'm lookin'," called Milo from another side of the arena. "Not believin', but lookin'."

"Hey, Ellie," Jake shouted from his perch next to Chico, "Whad'ya think?"

"I think I'd better get back to work," she answered.

Her comment cleared the hired hands off the rails faster than the dinner gong. Soon only a few film crew members remained with her to watch the rest of the show.

There wasn't much left to watch. Fitz took Hannibal over a couple of low jumps and let him stretch his legs in another set of loping circuits, but soon he reined the horse into the center of the arena, where Brady waited with a halter and lead.

Will ambled over from behind the stables and headed toward Ellie. He waited for her to climb down, and then handed her half a sandwich and a bright red mug full of lemonade. "Heard Hannibal finally found himself a match."

"Hmph." Ellie bit into the sandwich and ripped off a satisfying chunk. "Probably having an off day," she muttered as she chewed.

"Maybe he liked the signals he was getting." Will turned his back to the arena, resting his elbows on the rail behind him. "Sounds like Fitz knows how to give 'em."

"Maybe." Ellie started to take another bite, but hesitated with the sandwich halfway to her mouth. "I wonder what

Tom would have done about this, whether he would have put a stop to it. I mean, that crazy actor could have had a fall and broken his leg, and then where would we be? Maybe I should have done something. Tom would have, don't you think?"

"I don't spend too much of my time wondering what Tom would have thought or done about this or that. He's not here, Ellie. You are. And you did the right thing. No broken leg today." Will glanced over his shoulder. "That crazy actor could still break something, though. There'll be plenty of chances."

"Yeah." She took a smaller bite as the first one tossed around in her stomach. "That's what's been keeping me up nights."

Will gazed up into the cottonwood trees, squinting at the glare of the sun where it peeked through the fluttering, shimmering leaves. "You don't like him much, do you, little girl?"

"Who?"

"Fitz."

She shrugged and took a sip of lemonade. "What's not to like?"

"Nothing much. Maybe that's the problem." Will shot her one of his painfully neutral looks and then climbed over the rail and dropped into the arena.

FITZ SWUNG DOWN from the big horse and rubbed a hand along its neck. "I've got a few minutes to kill," he told Brady. "I'll take him in, if that's okay."

"Sure." Brady handed him the tack. "I'll set his things out by his stall."

As Fitz looped the halter around Hannibal's neck, he noted Ms. Pointy Nose watching him like a hawk from her perch on the rail as her sidekick made his way across the arena. He'd been pushing his luck, waiting for the two of them to be occupied elsewhere so he could take a closer look at their stock.

He stood his ground as the ranch foreman approached. "Afternoon, Will."

"Afternoon." Will lifted his elbows and arched his back a bit with a groan. "Is that all the later it is?"

Fitz smiled. "Heard you had an early morning."

"Yep. Too early for these creaky bones." Will glanced at the stable entry. "Brady comin' back out?"

"Nope." Fitz slowly ran his hand down Hannibal's face, tracing the thin white blaze. "I'm going to take him in."

"Mind if I tag along?"

Fitz glanced over Will's shoulder at Ellie. "Figured you might."

Trish jogged out of the stable and into the arena. "Fitz! Burke's looking for you. Nora's here, and Mitch wants to get some publicity shots of the two of you. And Van Gelder's got some rewrites for tomorrow's scene."

Rewrites. Damn. He tightened his grip on the lead as he guided Hannibal past her. "I'll head back in a while."

Trish hesitated before ducking into the breezeway behind the men. "How's it going?" she asked.

"Fine," Fitz said. "If I get the okay from the people in charge, I'd like to work with Hannibal here."

Trish frowned. "He certainly is...big."

"With a big, easy way of moving." Fitz poked the lead through a ring on the wall near Hannibal's stall and glanced at Will. "Maybe I could work with him whenever I had some free time. Off the set."

Trish looked from Will to Fitz and back again, her pen hovering over one of her little note papers.

"I s'pose he could be made available on that basis." Will

bent down, pulled a hoof pick out of Hannibal's bucket of brushes and handed it to Fitz. "He's sort of Ellie's boy. She likes to keep him close to home."

Fitz pressed his shoulder against one of the horse's hind legs and pulled his foot off the packed-dirt floor. From beneath Hannibal's belly, he could see Trish shift impatiently from one foot to the other, waiting for information she could process and file.

"So, are we going to use the horse or not?" she asked.

Fitz finished cleaning the hoof and straightened. He looked to Will to make it official. The foreman tipped his hat back to scratch at his head. "I s'pose we should check with Ellie first."

"I'll take care of it," Trish said. As she scrawled a note across her clipboard, she glanced at Fitz. "Burke said he'd meet you at Nora's trailer."

"Got it." Fitz unleashed his do-me-a-favor smile. "Oh, and Trish?"

"Huh?" She blinked once, twice, and then she stilled.

He kicked it up a notch. "I'd appreciate it if you'd call him on your phone, let him know I'll be there in twenty."

"Oh. Okay." She backed out of the breezeway, into the sunlight.

"Thanks, Trish."

"Uh…sure." She tripped over a dip in the ground. "Anytime."

Will glanced at Fitz as he tugged a curry comb through Hannibal's long mane. "Wonder if someone'll want this trimmed up a bit."

"We'll find out the first time the wind blows all that hair up into my face and ruins a shot."

"Must be something, a face like that." Will tossed the comb

into the bucket and moved out of Fitz's way as he bent to check a front hoof. "Using a smile to get pretty young things to do what you want."

"It's something, all right." Fitz stood and rested an arm across Hannibal's back. "It's also a target for every camera in zoom-lens range and for boozed-up jokers in late-night bars."

Will grunted. "Gets in the way sometimes, I imagine."

"Sometimes. And sometimes people forget there might be something going on behind the smile, too."

"Seems a clever fellow could take advantage of that."

"Seems so, doesn't it?" Fitz traded the hoof pick for a brush. "So, this is Ellie's horse."

"His dam was Ellie's. She handpicked his sire, was there at the foaling. She's the one who lead broke him." Will gave him a friendly slap on the hindquarters. "Rides him, too, every now and then. But he's a mighty big boy. Last time she took him out she told me she felt like a no-see-em up on his back."

"A no-see-em?"

"One of those little gnats you swallow before you know they're there."

"A no-see-em." Fitz smiled and shook his head. There was something seriously twisted about the way his gaze kept settling on the pointy little woman with the big brown eyes. She wasn't much of a looker, and he usually didn't do much looking unless a woman was.

She had a way about her, though, that prickled like a case of poison oak. Hot and tingly, and begging to be scratched, even though he knew he shouldn't. "I have a hard time imagining Ellie Harrison fading into the woodwork, even if she is a bit of a gnat herself."

Will chuckled. "She's always been on the small side. But she does tend to make her presence known."

Fitz worked the brush along the horse's hide. "Do you think she'll loan out Hannibal for the duration?"

"She wants things to go well."

"But she won't be happy about it."

Will shoved his hands in his pockets. "I don't know that Ellie puts all that much stock in happiness as an end product."

Fitz's brushing stilled. "Tough life, huh?"

"Don't s'pose life is meant to be easy. Just lived." Will stepped aside as Fitz swung under Hannibal's neck. "I'm thinkin' you've lived part of yours around horses."

Fitz grinned at Will's matter-of-fact change of subject and mosey into an interview. "S'pose I did, yes."

"Ranch work?"

"Some. More than I cared for, at the time." Fitz started in on Hannibal's thick tail. It needed some trimming, too. He'd check with Ellie before he hunted up a razor. "My grandfather was raised on a ranch not too far from here, as a matter of fact. Big Hole country."

"Imagine that."

"I'm trying to imagine it, now that I'm here. Nice country, from what I've seen. Wouldn't mind seeing more." Fitz gave up on doing anything more than a basic job on that tangle of a tail. He dropped the comb into the bucket and opened the stall door to lead Hannibal inside. "Gramps saved up enough to buy himself a ranch in Southern California. I spent most of my summers there. Most of the year, sometimes."

"It's a good life."

"It can be. If it's what you want."

Fitz stood in Hannibal's stall for a moment, feeling the warmth radiating off his big body. He inhaled the blend of manure and wood shavings and horse, and listened to the snuffles of that big sorrel nose at it poked through the hay net hanging in the corner. He soaked up the simple, earthy atmosphere, waiting for the high he knew would come, riding it like a hit from a drug. He knew what to do around horses, how to work with them and tend to their needs. He knew who he was when he was on a ranch and understood his place in the simple scheme of things. This life, this place was real, unlike the make-believe and special effects that filled most of his days and nights.

The echo of his own words bounced around inside his brain and tickled through his gut. *If it's what you want.*

He had what most people wanted—talent, money, success. Just because he hadn't chosen those things for himself didn't make him value them less now that he had them. Life didn't always hand a man what he wanted, but it was his job to make the most of what he'd been given. Most people thought that's exactly what Fitz Kelleran had done—made the most of the talent, the money and the success.

He was an actor, after all.

Most people probably thought a profitable acting career was enough, too. He just wasn't sure he was one of them, not anymore.

EXACTLY TWENTY MINUTES LATER, showered and changed into comfortable khakis and a linen shirt, Fitz knocked on the door of Nora's location trailer. She opened the door herself and, with one of her trademark lusty laughs, launched herself off the top step and into his arms.

Delighted to see her, he swung her around in a big, wide

circle. "Darlin'," he said, "just when I think you could never look better, you go and prove my imagination is a weak and pitiful thing."

"Oh, you old smooth talker, you." She pressed a loud, smacking kiss against his cheek.

He gave her one last squeeze before setting her down on her own feet. "It's not just flattery. You look…"

His gaze swept over the dark, lush features that were such a stunning contrast against her ivory skin. There was something new here, something softening. "Wonderful," he said, for lack of anything more precise.

"Well, there's a wonderful reason for it." Her smile spread, wide and defiant and a little terrified. "I'm pregnant."

Fitz whooped with joy and stooped to sweep her up again, but changed his mind at the last moment and settled for a gentle, rocking hug. "Congratulations, little mother."

"Oh." She shoved him away as her eyes filled with tears. "Look what you made me do. It doesn't take much to make me tear up these days, so don't. Just don't."

He tucked her thick, wavy black hair behind her ears and leaned in close. "What does Ken think about fatherhood?"

"Not much." Her lower lip trembled, and one tear escaped to slip along an extravagantly curved cheek. "He says he needs some time to think about the whole thing. And he moved out to do his thinking alone."

He brushed a thumb over her cheek and clamped down hard on the impulse to pound something, anything that could serve as a substitute for Nora's selfish bastard of a husband. Speaking of bastards… "Does Van Gelder know?"

"No." She ran her hand down his shirt front. "I've got such rotten timing, Fitz. Ken, the film, everything."

He clasped her fingers in his and curled them against his

heart to comfort them both. "Babies choose their own timing, from what I've heard."

She squeezed his hand. "I want to do this movie, Fitz. I've been waiting so long for a chance to work with you again. And I need to hitch a ride on a Kelleran vehicle right now, especially after my latest disaster limped straight to video. I just hope I—we can all get through it in one piece."

He lifted her hand and kissed her knuckles. "You know I'll do what I can to help."

"I know." She sniffed and smiled up at him. "I'm counting on you."

"Who else have you told?"

"Sasha in wardrobe. Marlene in make-up."

"The first ones who'd guess."

"That's what I figured." She sucked in a deep breath. "They're sworn to secrecy, of course, but you know how things are on a set."

He wished he could reassure her on this point, but she knew the score as well as he did.

"Oh," she said, "and I told Burke, because I figured you'd tell him eventually, anyway."

"You told Burke before you told me?"

"Well, I wanted to tell you first." She slipped her hand out of his to scrub at her lipstick smudge on his cheek. "But you were busy playing cowboy."

"Well, I'm here now." He looped his arm around her shoulders and turned them both back toward her trailer.

"Yes, you are," she said, leaning her head against his chest with a sigh. "The Fleischners send their love, by the way, and Harry says if you don't behave yourself, he'll hunt you down and cut out your liver, since you don't have a heart."

"I need to find some new friends."

She laughed and wrapped her arm around his waist. "You better just hold on tight to the ones you've got. No one else would want you."

They paused at the foot of her trailer steps. "Van Gelder's fighting with the screenwriter again," she said.

"I heard a rumor to that effect." He ground his teeth in frustration. The last thing Nora needed after a long day of travel was stress over last-minute script changes. "How many new pages do we have to learn?"

"I haven't looked yet."

"Well, let's not look for a little while longer. Let's find something cool to drink, put our feet up and have ourselves a nice visit. I'll send Burke out to find something to eat, and we can have a rehearsal party over dinner."

"Oh," she said with another sigh, "that sounds perfect."

Fitz helped her up the steps and opened her door while he treated himself to a string of silent curses over his multiplying problems: a shaky movie deal, a costar with a crumbling marriage and a secret pregnancy, a neurotic director with delusions of literary talent.

What else could go wrong?

Burke handed Fitz a cell phone the moment he stepped inside. "Greenberg wants to talk to you. *Now*."

Stupid question.

CHAPTER FIVE

"EXCUSE ME, DARLIN'," said Fitz.

Nora waved him toward the back of her trailer. "I'll get those drinks."

He stepped into her tiny bedroom and closed the door. "Howdy," he said. "That's Montanish for 'What's up, doc?'"

"Did you read Barton's script?"

He tried not to muss Nora's spread as he perched on the edge of her bed. "Hello, Myron. How are you? How's the weather? Not as hot as it is here, I bet. I could—"

"Cut the crap, Kelleran."

"Sure. I can do that. But it's so much fun to steal pieces of your valuable time." He and his agent had scrambled their way up Tinseltown's ladder of success in a snarling symbiosis, clawing each other bloody in the process. Harassing Greenberg when he was in cardiac-arrest mode was one of life's small pleasures. "I read it."

"Tell me you're going to do it."

"Can't do that, Myron."

Fitz pulled the phone from his ear while his agent spewed a loud and violent stream of obscenities. "Kelleran!" a tinny, long distance Greenberg screamed at last. "Kelleran!"

"I'm still here."

"What the hell's the matter with you? You need to stretch

as an actor. Everyone says so. You need to show the money in this town you can bring more than charm and good looks to a role. This is it, Kelleran—your ticket to an Oscar."

"The problem isn't the role. It's the scheduling." He wanted to shoot *The Virginian* next summer, not some other film.

Greenberg steamrolled over the objection. Time didn't exist in the agent's universe, not if it conflicted with the bottom line. "Do you know what a nomination would do to your asking price?"

"Increase it to ridiculously unheard of levels?"

Greenberg launched into another tirade about Montana and westerns and the idiots who wasted their time on them— nothing Fitz hadn't heard a dozen times before. "Give Barton the stall treatment," he said. "Tell him I'm interested in his project, but I need a little time to finesse my schedule."

"Are you interested?"

Fitz hesitated long enough to keep his agent wriggling on the hook. Greenberg wasn't the only one who knew how to play out a stall. "It's an interesting script."

"I'm telling you, it's your ticket to the number one slot."

"I thought I was already there."

"You think everyone else in this town is going to sit back and let you keep it?"

One corner of Fitz's mouth tipped up in a grin. So, he was number one. For the moment, at least. He hadn't been paying attention to the dollars and the deals lately—a mistake for someone trying to finesse an executive producer for an optioned script. He'd have Burke make some calls tomorrow morning, bright and early, plant a few rumors in a few fertile spots.

"You're right," he told Greenberg. "I'll give it another look and get back to you."

"What is this? The 'don't call me, I'll call you' crap?"

Fitz stood and placed his thumb over the disconnect button. "Why, yes, Myron. I believe it is."

ELLIE RESTED HER ELBOWS on the back porch railing after dinner and stole a moment simply to let herself be. Meadow grass and cinquefoil blazed like gold, banding rosy shreds of prairie smoke with the mauve of the foothills and the violet of the Tobacco Root Mountains. The scent of wild strawberry rose from the lingering warmth of the earth, and the keening notes of a red-tailed hawk's cry echoed like Taps over the dying day.

She stepped off the porch and headed out into the twilight. There was one last chore to do before she could turn in for the night.

She took a shortcut through the temporary trailer park and swung around the humming power vans. Grips and cameramen waved at her as they loaded cameras and dollies for tomorrow's work. The next few scenes would be filmed at the makeshift town they'd built down the trail beyond the stables. Kelleran getting tossed out of a saloon, Nora's confrontation with a store owner. Jumbled bits and scraps that someone would stitch together later, like the pieces of a quilt.

She flipped a switch as she entered the stables and stepped into the pale yellow oval of light cast across the breezeway floor. "Hey, Hannibal."

An answering nicker followed a rustle of shavings, and the gelding's head shoved over the top of the half door. Big brown eyes locked on hers, and long reddish lashes held steady against dust motes drifting on invisible currents. Her heart easing at the sight of him, she grabbed his lead and slipped into his stall. "Gonna make you even prettier than you already are, big boy."

She leaned against the warm, solid body and smoothed a hand over his neck. So soft, so supple and powerful. So gentle, with her. "Come on out and let me fuss over you a bit."

She soothed them both with pieces of a song as she secured him with leads fastened to both sides of his halter. Hannibal enjoyed a good grooming, but he could get ornery about the application. He didn't much care for getting his mane or tail trimmed or his whiskers shaved, and he'd been born too big to wrestle.

She ducked into the tack room for supplies. When she emerged, electric razor kit in hand, Fitz Kelleran stood at Hannibal's head, sneaking him an apple. He flashed one of those movie-star smiles, and she braced to take the hit to her equilibrium.

The fact was, he was simply stunning to look at, and having all that male beauty aimed in her direction was something akin to intoxication. Those looks of his, and the liquored-up sensations they induced, were a monumental inconvenience. But she had to look at him, and accept the tongue-tying, spine-tingling impact he had on her, because they had a job to do.

He'd changed his outfit, though somehow the pleated slacks and stylish shirt didn't seem any more out of place than the work clothes she'd seen him wear before. It struck her that he always seemed to fit, always seemed the same. Must be some actor's trick.

She rolled her shoulders and started toward Hannibal, feeling slightly off balance and a little resentful because of it. Why should she stumble over a disadvantage in her own place? Someone like Kelleran was bound to pick up a kind of polish when he spent his life in the kinds of places that layered on the shinola. She'd never been to those places, didn't even know the way. All she knew was the more his smooth, easygoing way bumped up against hers, the rougher she felt by comparison.

But not so rough as to forget her manners. "Evenin', Fitz."

"Evenin', Ellie." He waited for Hannibal to lip the last bit of apple off his palm and then wiped his hand across his pants. "I understand this horse is sort of special to you."

"He's stock." She set the razor down on the grooming bucket and picked up a wide-toothed comb to tug through Hannibal's mane. "Good stock as it turns out, and that's the sum total of his value. Sentiment's got no part of it."

"Still, I suppose it might sneak up on a person, sometimes."

"Yeah, I guess so." She was surprised by his diplomatic approach to the request that had already filtered down through Trish. More evidence of those smooth ways of his, she supposed, but…considerate. He didn't have to be concerned with her feelings in the matter or take the time to pry them out of her.

She shoved her confusing thoughts aside and concentrated on her task, combing Hannibal's mane and gauging where to make her first cut. The moment he felt the tug of the razor, she'd have to work fast.

"Tell me about his name." Fitz tucked a shoulder against a support post and slipped his hands into his pockets, looking as if he were settling in for some conversation. "Hannibal. Not a typical name for ranch stock."

She shrugged. "Not much to tell."

"Why Hannibal?"

Keeping one eye on her horse, she made a swipe at the edges. Hannibal flinched, but didn't seem to mind the tugging—for now. "I had to name him something. That's the first thing that came to mind."

"Hannibal?"

She shrugged again and hoped he wouldn't read too much into her embarrassed blush.

"Most people might think of the Hannibal in the movies," he said. "You know, the cannibal."

"Is that your only frame of reference?" She couldn't resist the urge to tease at him, just a bit. "The movies?"

"I wasn't including myself in the 'most people' category." He shoved away from the post and stepped in close to run a hand down the horse's face. "Besides, you're here to do that for me."

She slanted a narrow-eyed glance at him over her shoulder, annoyed that he wasn't taking offense or her hints to back off. And that he was getting to her. "Another item on my job description?"

The smile that spread over his features was positively wicked. "Care if I add some more?"

If this were any other man, she'd think he was flirting. But this was Fitz Kelleran, one of *People's* Sexiest Men Alive. And she was…nobody a man like him would ever flirt with. She turned back to her task.

"Wasn't Hannibal an ancient general?" he asked.

"A Carthaginian. He fought the Romans."

"And lost, right?"

"Yeah."

Fitz rubbed his knuckles over Hannibal's nose. "Sorry, fella. You're named for one of history's losers."

She smiled and realized she was enjoying herself, enjoying the company and the conversation. Maybe she was a sucker for that notorious charm, after all. Or maybe her relatively mellow mood on this pretty evening was smoothing out some of her rougher edges. Or maybe, just maybe, she was starting to like Fitz Kelleran. Just a fraction of an inch's worth. It was hard holding petty grudges against someone who seemed to appreciate her horse as much as she did.

"Hannibal wasn't really a loser," she said. "Well, in the end, maybe. But he was a brilliant tactician, one of history's best. A dreamer and a fighter. A powerful combination. Anyone determined enough to take elephants over the Alps— now that's someone with a whole lot of spirit."

She evened up another section of mane, and then swept her hand along her horse's long, warm neck. "This Hannibal's got a whole lot of spirit, too."

"Why, Ellie Harrison." He shifted to stand behind her and lowered his voice to a seductive singsong of a whisper. "You're a romantic."

"No, I'm not." Another wave of warmth crept across her cheeks, and she hunched her shoulders in mortification. She hoped he couldn't see the pink creeping over the back of her neck. She suspected the man saw too much for comfort.

She sensed him leaning in closer, closer, until his breath washed the scents of coffee and mint over the side of her face. "Yes," he said. "You are."

She was on fire, trapped between two large, warm bodies. She swallowed and steadied, and then tugged again at Hannibal's mane. The horse quivered and snuffled his impatience with her clumsy moves, and her elbow accidentally connected with Fitz's surprisingly solid midsection.

"You don't know me well enough to say something like that," she said.

"I know you're a romantic. That's a start."

"A start off on the wrong foot, maybe."

"I like that 'maybe.' It's full of possibilities. Like taking elephants over the Alps." He moved away, and a chill raced down her spine in the cooling night air.

She sucked in a deep breath and turned for the comb. Fitz was still there, standing too close, studying her face with those sky-blue eyes, famous eyes she'd sighed over on the screen a dozen times. Eyes that locked on hers and darkened in pure and potent male consideration.

Oh. My. God.

She swallowed a fizzy brew of disbelief and panic and primitive female response. "Excuse me."

He stepped back and shoved his hands into his pockets, and then whistled some tuneless nonsense as he strolled down the breezeway. He paused in the wide doorway, turned and flashed her one of his dazzling smiles. "Elephants over the Alps, Ellie. Elephants over the Alps."

THREE DAYS LATER, Fitz launched himself from a rickety set chair to stretch his legs. It wasn't the acting that wore him down and got him in trouble. It was the waiting around, the inactivity that made his legs twitch and his hands itch and his mind the devil's playground.

Surely it was the stop-and-go boredom that kept these vaguely impure thoughts about their no-nonsense saddle boss oozing and bubbling in the sewer of his subconscious. It couldn't be her stop-right-there scowl. Or those slitty-eyed glances she shot him every so often.

He thought he'd had her pegged—the uptight widow saving herself and the family spread for the guy with the whitest ten-gallon hat in the local cattlemen's association. But then he'd caught her crooning a silly lyric to that big red horse of hers, and watched her eyes drift soft and dreamy over some ancient, ill-fated hero.

Something had been tugging at him since that night, something other than an urge to tease her cross-eyed and wipe the smug off her face, or loosen up her thick reddish braid and stick his tongue down her throat. Whatever it was, she'd sure thrown him off balance.

"Fitz." Burke stepped into his path. "Nora's looking a little pale."

Fitz turned to see Marlene clucking at Nora and dabbing a foundation sponge along her forehead. The endless delays, combined with the day's heat, were beginning to take their toll.

"Think I might be a bit temperamental about my lunch hour today," he said. "You get her out of the sun and off her feet while I clear things with Van Gelder."

A few minutes later he found his leading lady collapsed in a chair beneath a van awning. "Can I get you anything?"

"No, thanks. Burke went for some water." Nora sighed and let her head fall back against the chair. "I saw you pulling strings for me just now. Thanks."

He swung another set chair around and lifted her feet onto it. Where was Anna, her assistant? "How are you doing? Any morning sickness?"

"Not yet." She smiled and smoothed her hands over her stomach. "Just more tired than usual. This break will help."

He ran a finger along the back of her hand. "You let me know whenever you need to take another one. I can come up with enough excuses for both of us."

"Thanks, hon." She sighed and settled more comfortably in the chair and closed her eyes. "You're a real gentleman."

"Yeah, that's me all right." Knowing Burke would be back soon to play mother hen, he dropped a kiss on the top of her head and strolled off in the direction of the catering truck.

Across the open area behind the set, he spied a battered wooden lawn chair tilted at a crazy angle, one of its wide legs bumped up against the roots of an oak tree umbrella. The scene had a kind of Norman-Rockwell-does-Montana rustic appeal. He made a mental note to stake out some territory in the dappled shade for a post-lunch nap.

There were two chairs, he discovered as he drew closer, and the second was occupied by a scrawny kid with Ellie's fly-speck freckles and sorrel-red hair. The moment she spied him headed her way, her nose dive-bombed into the fat book spread across her lap.

"Hi," he said as he stretched out on the long grass near her feet. He looped one arm beneath his head and set his hat on his chest. "Are you Ellie Harrison's kid?"

"Yes, sir." She flashed a shy smile in his direction, and then stood and gathered a camera and a pile of library books into a tidy stack before starting off toward the ranch house.

"Hey, don't let me run you off," he said.

She hesitated, glanced at the big white house perched above the creek and bit her lip.

"What's your name?" he asked.

"Jody Harrison."

"Come on, Jody Harrison." He sat up and waved her back to her chair. "Keep me company. That is, if you don't have anything better to do."

Still worrying her lower lip, she accepted his invitation. "You're Mr. Kelleran, aren't you?"

"Yep. But I like it better when people call me Fitz." He raised his knees and rested his elbows across them. "Okay?"

"Okay."

"Fitz," he said with a grin.

"Fitz," she said, and smiled back.

So far, the kid was a whole lot easier to get along with than her mother.

He snapped off a piece of long grass and stuck it in one corner of his mouth. "What are you doing out here, Jody Harrison? Besides enjoying this fine day."

"Watching. Reading."

"Hm." Fitz held out his hand. "Let's see."

She passed him a book from the top of the pile. *An Introduction to Photography*. Pretty boring stuff—technical terms, black line drawings, shaded shot angles. "You like photography?"

"I don't know yet." She frowned at the camera in her lap. "I'm just learning."

"Don't you think you'd learn better by taking some pictures, trying stuff out? See what works, instead of just reading about it?"

"I guess." She glanced at him from under her lashes. "Do you like photography?"

Press flashes blinding, Steadicams angling in close, tabloid zooms clicking like scuttling cockroaches. "I'm not sure."

He spit out the grass and returned the book. "Let me see your camera."

She handed him a cheap model. He lifted it to his face and snapped a shot of a startled young girl in a lemon-yellow tank top, rumpled denim shorts and dusty athletic shoes. "Okay," he said, handing it back. "Your turn."

"What?"

"To take my picture."

"Can I?"

"Sure." He stood and squinted up through the tree branches. "But I don't know if this is the best kind of light for a picture." He looked down at her. "What do you think?"

She hitched up both shoulders. "I don't know."

"Guess we're not going to learn much about photography

by talking to each other." He swept his hat off the grass and settled it back on his head. "We could talk to Krystof."

"Krystof?"

"Krystof Laszlofi. He's a kind of photographer—a cinematographer. Come on," he said, plucking the books off her toothpick legs. "Let's go."

He headed back to the set, pretending he didn't notice her attempts to stare without actually staring. Pretty polite, for a kid. He couldn't remember the last time he'd been called Mr. Kelleran by someone who didn't have an angle.

"So, Jody Harrison," he asked, "have you been studying photography a while?"

"No. I just got interested from, you know, watching some filming last week. And Jason—he's a Steadicam guy—he told me some stuff and let me look through the lens."

"It's pretty cool stuff."

"Yes, sir."

Krystof climbed on the camera dolly to make an adjustment as they approached.

"Hey, Krys," said Fitz. "Got a moment?"

Krystof peered down with his pouchy, basset-hound eyes. "Yes, I can make a moment. I am learning to make many moments, and to have much patience these days."

Fitz shot a glance over his shoulder at Van Gelder, who was harassing a grip. "You ought to be a real pro in a couple of months."

He reached behind him and dragged Jody forward. "This is Jody Harrison, a student of photography."

Krystof nodded slowly. "How do you do, Miss Harrison?"

"How do you do, Mr. Lazz—"

"Laszlofi. It's Hungarian. All the best cinematographers are Hungarian," he said before launching into a discussion of shutters and settings. Jody nodded at the appropriate moments and asked the right questions, but she sneaked a cross-eyed glance Fitz's way to share the pain of the technical tedium.

He grinned back at her. Cute kid.

Damn if he didn't feel that funny tug in his chest again. He tipped his hat back a bit. "Lunch break. Coming, Krys?"

"In a minute."

"Jody?"

"Me?" She pointed at her bony chest, and then at Fitz. "Eat lunch with you?"

"If you don't have any other plans." He shoved his hands in his pockets and angled his head back toward the white vans. "Come on. Keep me company, Jody Harrison."

CHAPTER SIX

FITZ HAD SECOND THOUGHTS about the cute-kid impression as Jody grilled him over barbecued chicken and potato salad.

"Why does Mr. Van Gelder ask you and Nora for so many takes?"

"How come it's 'Mr. Van Gelder' and 'Mr. Kelleran,' and Nora gets to be Nora?"

"It's a girl thing," she said, licking sticky red sauce off her thumb. "She likes to hang out at the house. Gran's teaching her to knit."

"Nora? Knitting?" Leave it to Nora to use the Method to prepare for the role of motherhood.

"She says it gives her something to do. You know, with her hands."

Idle hands. Devil's workshop. Maybe he should take up needlepoint. He'd keep his hands full of sharp, pointy objects to help keep his mind off a certain sharp, pointy woman.

"So, what's up with all these takes?" Jody persisted. "What's he looking for?"

"There are two kinds of directors." Fitz rested his elbows on the table, ready to share the wisdom he'd acquired as a child actor learning his trade in television commercials. "There are the ones who know exactly what they want, and keep you trying to give it to them. And then there are the ones who aren't sure what they want, and keep you trying to help them figure it out."

Jody chewed silently for a moment. "So, which kind is Mr. Van Gelder?"

"The third kind. The kind that doesn't know what in the hell he's doing, and keeps us all busy trying to cover his ass. Pardon my French."

"French?"

"*Ass*."

"*Ass* isn't French."

"It is the way I just used it."

He grinned at Jody's laugh, surprised to discover he was having a good time. The best time he'd had with a female outside of the bedroom since...since the last time he'd gotten a rise out of her mother.

"Why did Mr. Van Gelder get this job?"

"Probably because the producer's married to Van Gelder's ex-wife," he said. "I'm thinking it's some kind of twisted Revenge on the Range."

"Cool." She took another bite of chicken. "This is, like, movie gossip, right? The kind of stuff that's in those supermarket magazines."

"God, I hope not." He forked up some salad, determined not to let the tabloids put a crimp in his appetite.

"So, if Mr. Van Gelder is such a bad director, why are you working with him?"

"I like westerns, but they don't make many of them any more. I took a chance on this one."

"You seem like a real cowboy." Jody chugged from her milk carton and wiped her mouth with the back of her hand. "I mean, you know, like you're not acting or anything."

"Thanks."

She waited until he swallowed his bite of salad. "Will told me you grew up on a ranch."

"Sort of." Fitz shifted on the picnic bench. "My grandfather had a ranch, not too far from Hollywood. He knew horses, and he did some wrangling for the movies."

"Like, with Kevin Costner?"

"No." He shook his head with a smile. "With John Wayne."

"Whoa. That was a *long* time ago." Jody dropped a cleaned bone on her plate and dug into a small mountain of salad. "So, did your grandfather get you into the movies?"

"No." Fitz pushed the lumps of potato around on his plate. "My parents did. They were actors."

Memories flickered through him like a damaged reel through a projector. His father sitting in the dark, watching himself walk on and off the screen in bit parts. His mother tossing her head in a shampoo commercial, all suds and teeth. Drink-slurred shouts, shattering glass, the stale stench of the morning after a party. The heavy, pressing atmosphere of not enough luck, not enough money.

"They got a few parts," he said, "enough to keep us fed, most of the time. And when they didn't, they shipped me out to my grandfather's place. As soon as I was old enough to memorize a few lines, they started dragging me around to auditions, too."

"Didn't you want to be an actor?"

"I never took a chance on being anything else. I don't know what that 'anything else' might have been, but I do wonder sometimes."

He toyed with his drumstick. "Do you ever wonder about an 'anything else' in your life, Jody Harrison?"

"You mean, anything else besides living and working here? Yeah, sure. Sometimes," she said, and reached for a second piece of chicken. The kid sure had a healthy appetite.

"What do you think about doing?"

"I don't know." She shrugged and stripped a hunk of meat off the bone. "Most of the time I get the message I'm supposed to stay right here."

"Nothing like a little parental pressure to mess up your life."

She grinned around a mouthful of chicken. "Only if you let it."

"Smart move."

"I know."

He grinned at her smug reply and shoved his salad across to her. She picked up her fork and started in on a second helping.

"Speaking of parental pressure..." he said, "your mom's a pretty scary lady."

Jody shook her head. "She's not that bad. She just works too hard, and it makes her crabby. Me and Gran tried, like, talking to her about it, but that only made her worse."

Fitz hid his smile behind his napkin. "I could see where that might happen."

"She wasn't always crabby. Just since my dad died."

She washed the salad down with the remainder of the milk. "It was a plane crash. Grandpa didn't want to buy a plane, and after he died, Mom argued with Dad about it, too. She didn't think we needed something that expensive to keep an eye on the herd. But he bought one anyway, and the first time he went up in it by himself, he crashed."

"God," said Fitz. "I'm sorry."

"Thank you," she said politely, and then redirected her attention to the rest of her lunch.

"So," he said, "your mom wasn't so scary before your dad died?"

"All moms are scary sometimes, if you're their kid." She glanced up at him. "Why are you scared of her?"

"I'm not scared of her, exactly. She's just…scary. A real ball buster."

Jody's eyes widened.

"Shit," he said. "I didn't mean to say that. And I didn't mean to say *shit*, either. Sorry. For both. For *shit* and…for the other thing I said."

"You can say *shit* around me. Brady and some of the other guys do it all the time, and Mom doesn't bust their balls." She hit him with another smug smile.

"God," he said. "It's genetic."

The two of them chewed in companionable silence for a while, and then he leaned across the table. "You're not going to tell your mom I said that, are you?"

"Why?" She tipped forward and lowered her voice. "Are you scared?"

"Shit." He shoved another milk carton into her hand. "Drink your milk, kid. It's good for you. Helps you grow up straight and tall, so you can torment old folks like me."

"Jody?"

He winced at the sound of Ellie's voice behind him. Across the table, Jody looked like her lunch was curdling in her stomach. "Uh-oh," she said.

Fitz grimaced and dropped his chicken. "Busted."

Ellie circled the end of the table and slipped into the empty space next to her daughter. "Been looking for you," she said. "Gran wanted to take you to town with her."

"Sorry, Mom."

Ellie handed her a napkin. "Better run up to the house."

Jody quickly wiped her fingers and jumped up, ready to leave immediately. When she moved past him, Fitz reached out to grab her wrist. "Wait a minute."

The look on Ellie's face made him drop Jody's arm.

"It's my fault she's here," he said. "We were in the middle of a discussion about...lots of different things, and I asked her to join me. Look," he pointed out, "she hasn't finished her lunch yet."

Ellie transferred her Go To Your Room glare to him. *Uh-oh.*

"That's okay," said Jody. "I don't want to keep Gran waiting. Thank you for lunch, Fitz. It was delicious."

Ellie waited until her daughter was out of range before rising from the table, the better to let him have it from both barrels at chest level. "I'd appreciate it if, in the future, you'd avoid undercutting my parental authority in my daughter's presence."

Fitz swallowed. It wasn't much of stretch to turn in a performance as a chastened man. "Yes, ma'am."

Ellie shot him a sharp, scary nod and stalked off to the big main barn. Something about the slight swagger in those subtle hips of hers had him twitching and itching again. Damn if she didn't have the strangest way of getting under his skin.

It wasn't infatuation, not with her bee-stung boy's shape and her sweat-stained western wear. It wasn't fascination, not with her stuck-up nose and her snippy attitude. It was...something else. Or everything else. He couldn't figure it out, and the mystery was making him reckless.

Good thing reckless was one of his best moves.

"Ooooh!" ELLIE CURLED her fingers into tight, vibrating fists and wished she could punch something without doing herself an injury in the process. Losing her temper was always a dangerous proposition, with her pride sustaining most of the heavy damage.

She shouldn't let Fitz Kelleran get to her like that. She didn't know why he did, and that bothered her most of all. But when she'd seen that actor—that party-cruising, bimbo-chasing, tabloid-magnet actor—cozying up to her innocent, trusting daughter, her blood pressure had spiked. Little white sparks had shot through her vision, and she wouldn't have been surprised if smoke had come pouring out her ears.

And then he'd had the nerve—the umitigated gall!—to argue with her about a private family affair in front of her daughter.

"*Ooooh!*"

Well, that was the end of that. Unless she could be there to keep an eye on things, Jody was banned from the set. Ellie may have invited the serpent into paradise, but that didn't mean she'd sacrifice her daughter's happiness for a chance to pay the bills. With Tom gone, Jody couldn't help craving an older man's attention, but a here-today-gone-tomorrow actor was the wrong candidate for a stand-in father figure.

Boot steps. Someone had followed her into the barn. It couldn't be Kelleran. He might be crazy—she didn't think he was suicidal.

"Ellie. Wait up."

Guess she'd thought wrong.

Ducking into the temporary tack room, she grabbed a bucket, some oil soap and a handful of rags. Her temper was still bubbling, and all she wanted was a little time to simmer down in private. When a tall, broad figure darkened the doorway behind her a moment later, she realized she wasn't going to get it.

"You're not so tough," he said.

She turned to face him. He stood with his legs spread in a gunfighter's stance and his hands shoved into his pockets, blocking her way out.

"Scary, maybe," he added, "but I could take you in a fair fight."

He'd been poking at her like this for days. Every time she

turned around, there he was, flashing a grin or winking at her, or pressing in close to whisper something outrageous. She couldn't figure out why he'd waste his time on someone like her, someone who wasn't drop-dead beautiful—just drop-dead uninterested.

He was probably so accustomed to having an audience he didn't notice when one of the front row seats was empty. Ignoring him may have been a useless exercise, but it was safer than giving him a taste of her temper.

And first she had to get past him. "Excuse me."

He didn't budge. He just turned one of those lethal smiles loose to slide across that heart-stopping face. She waited him out, her pulse pounding with something that wasn't temper, exactly, but had her just as hot and all stirred up. When he finally moved to one side, she released a silent sigh of relief and angled past him.

"You know," he said, "she's a great kid."

It would be a big mistake to let him see that his opinion mattered, so she donned her poker face and tossed him a careless shrug. "Of course she's a great kid."

"Looks like we finally found something we can agree on." He plucked the bucket out of her hand and motioned for her to lead the way. "Could be the start of a beautiful friendship."

"Don't hold your breath, Kelleran."

"Don't worry. I won't." He bent down moved in a bit, with that way he had of scrambling her thoughts and making her female parts stand at attention. "But thanks for the concern over the state of my respiratory health. I'm touched to know how much you care."

Damn, he really had that charm act nailed. It was a big part of what made his millions for him—that devilish twinkle in his eyes that canceled out anything angelic in his intentions. On-screen, it was pure seduction. Up close, it was…well, whatever it was, it was far more effective.

And damn, he'd used that charm to slither around her yet again. She yanked the bucket from his hand and headed down the passageway. "You're touched, all right."

"Curious, too," he said as he tromped along behind her, too close for comfort. "I wonder which bothers you more—the fact that I like your kid or the fact that we have something in common."

She stopped, closed her eyes and took a steadying breath—and then another—before giving up and turning around to face him. Deep breathing and counting to ten were pitiful defenses against the tide of indignation roiling through her. There wasn't enough patience in all of Montana to keep her from saying what needed to be said—in exactly the manner she planned on saying it.

She stepped to a spot where they stood practically toe-to-toe, and then she looked up at him, straight into those dazzling eyes. She resented the way her neck nearly kinked because he was so tall, and she resented the way his long, amber-tipped lashes curled up in the kind of evenly spaced, sexy spikes she could never achieve with her mascara wand, and most of all she resented the way her pulse tripped when the crinkles at the edges of his eyes deepened with amusement.

She started to shove aside the thought that this was Fitz Kelleran, cinema superstar, and then she realized that was exactly the fact she needed to focus on. His presence here was a scoop of Hollywood make-believe plopped à la mode on top of her everyday reality—a garnish that would melt away soon enough.

"Get this through your head," she said. "What you think or do means nothing to me. If I do happen to notice what you think or do, it's because it's part of my job. That's all. Just one of the dozens of tiny, inconsequential tasks I deal with every day."

"Like shoveling manure?"

"Exactly."

He shoved his hands into his pockets and rocked back on his heels. "Wouldn't want to end up buried in the stuff."

"Probably not."

He leaned in a bit. "Good to know where I stand."

"That's right."

"In deep shit."

"You got it, Kelleran."

He shifted closer, crowding her. "I'm a quick study."

She took a half step back, cursing herself for it, and cursing her erratic pulse even more. "Good for you."

"Just one question."

"Make it fast," she said. "I've got things to do."

He cocked his head toward hers and grinned. "More shit to shovel?"

She narrowed her eyes and held her ground.

"If I think Jody's such a great kid," he said, "—and I do, by the way—why do you think I'd mind spending time with her? Hm?"

He pointed a finger at her, right between her breasts. Her nipples tingled and puckered up so hard she was afraid they'd pop right through her shirt front.

"And if you agree she's a great kid," he continued, "why do you think she'd bore anyone?"

"I don't. That's not what I meant." She swatted his hand aside, annoyed with his logic and her physical response to his pointing, annoyed with his nearness and his potent masculinity. "I just don't want her getting in the way."

"If that happens, I'll take care of it. We'll take care of it." He gestured toward the movie crowd outside. "Those people are professionals, working eighteen hours or more a day on a tight schedule and a tighter budget. They're not going to allow some preteen girl to get in their way or muck it up."

"Then I'll make it easy on them. By keeping her out of their way entirely."

"That's the simple solution," he said with a nod. "But there's a better one."

His arrogance stole her breath for a moment. "That wasn't a 'simple solution' I came up with, Kelleran. That was a decision." She aimed her thumb at her chest. "My decision."

"I still say there's a better one."

The little white sparks danced across her vision again, and she waited for them to clear. She shouldn't let him rile her up like this. He didn't matter. Not at all.

"You're entitled to your opinion." She waved it away and moved down the passageway with Fitz dogging her steps. "You're entitled to speak your mind. But the decision's mine to make."

"I don't mind you thinking the worst of me and my motives," he said. "But I do mind you selling Jody short."

She spun around to face him, mad enough to spit. "That's not what I'm doing."

"Okay, let's say you're not."

Now he wanted to theorize over something that wasn't his business to begin with. She'd seen day-old ticks that were easier to dig out from under the skin. Too bad she couldn't pinch and twist half his head off—although with her luck, his mouth would probably keep working away, burrowing in deeper, even without the brains attached.

She rolled her eyes and turned away. He followed her to the hose bib, where she dropped the bucket and snatched the soap and rags out of the way before twisting the tap.

"But here's one more fact," he said. "Jody seems to enjoy my company, too. For her sake, I hope you can deal with it."

"For her sake?" Ellie aimed the hose's spray nozzle at the bucket and took guilty delight in watching water slosh over the rim and douse his pants leg. "Even I didn't think you could sink so low you'd use a little girl to get what you want."

"And just what is it I want, Ellie?"

"I don't know, and I don't want to."

She bent down to turn off the tap, and when she straightened she nearly collided with his chest. He grabbed one of her arms and pulled her closer.

"You don't always get what you want," he said.

His eyes locked on hers, dark and intent with something that had nothing to do with Jody or any of those other things they'd been discussing. Things she had trouble remembering when his other hand lifted to wrap around her other arm and his kneecap prodded suggestively against her thigh, when his breath washed over her lips and tickled her nose. He smelled exotically of movie-set makeup and expensive cologne, and she could see the beat of his pulse at the base of his throat, right above the reddish-blond hairs that curled around the top of his shirt placket.

She knew it was her turn to toss out the next line, some snappy comeback to keep him at a safe and proper distance, some little barb to let him know he wasn't getting to her.

And he wasn't getting to her. Not at all, not really. Not with his ready wit or his steady logic, with his subtle humor or his outrageous charm. And not with his to-sigh-for good looks. She wasn't going to let any of that have any effect on her, not anymore, because even though he was a woman's film fantasy, he was also just a man. An ordinary man. A man who was worming his way into a place he had no right to be.

And to prove he wasn't getting to her, she raised her chin and leveled her haughtiest stare at him. "Let go of me."

A little muscle twitched at one corner of his mouth in something that looked suspiciously like the start of another smile. He wrapped his long, lean fingers more securely around her arms. "In a minute."

She tried to tug loose, but he had a grip like iron shackles. "What the hell do you think you're doing?"

"Getting this out of our systems."

He yanked her up against him and slowly lowered his face toward hers.

Oh. My. God. Fitz Kelleran, big and warm and solid where he'd plastered his front to hers, dropped his sky-colored eyes to her mouth, angled his beautiful head to one side, parted his perfect lips and prepared to kiss her. *Her.* Ellie Harrison of Granite Ridge Ranch, Montana.

The air seemed to vibrate between them, humming along her skin and setting off an echo deep within her, a hot and sluggish throb that settled low in her gut and turned her limbs to rubber. Her heart tripped into overdrive, but it was too late to pump any life into her limbs. She was mesmerized, caught up close and helpless in his arms, just the way she'd been captured and suspended in his spell in the darkness of a movie theater.

She struggled for control, for a way to find her balance as reality wobbled. This wasn't happening. Couldn't be happening. And yet his mouth was softening, opening a little wider as it dipped closer to hers. He didn't want her. Couldn't want her. And yet his eyes darkened to cobalt in the instant before they fluttered closed.

She was losing her battle, collapsing against his broad chest and losing herself in a fantasy, spiraling down, down into a dream. So she did the only thing she could.

She kicked him in the shin.

CHAPTER SEVEN

"*Ow!*"

Fitz jerked back and swung his injured leg out of range. He hadn't seen that move coming, but he kept his grip on her arms when she tried to escape.

The little minx. God, she was something else. Something entirely outside his sphere of experience with women—and he hadn't thought that was possible.

"Sorry," she said, mashing her lips together in a pitiful attempt to suppress one of those smug smiles.

He set his foot down gingerly. "No, you're not."

"Yes, I am," she said as she shoved against him. "Believe me, I am."

"Why? Because I'm still standing?" He took a chance and shifted his hands to a slightly more romantic wrestling hold. "Lady, you've got one hell of a way of puckering up."

"I don't want to pucker up." She twisted and managed to dig an elbow into his gut. "I don't need to get you out of my system. And even if I did, the only thing that might make you go away, or make me feel better, would be to pop you a good one."

"I'll let you take a swing at me later." He tightened his embrace. "But first I think you'd better give in and let me kiss you."

"Why?"

She'd stopped her wriggling, and he began to appreciate what he'd caught up in his arms. It was nowhere near as sharp and pointy as he'd been thinking. He leaned in closer and savored a whiff of oil soap and wildflowers, a scent as subtle as her curves.

"Why not?" he whispered against her mouth.

"Please, don't," she said, and there was a quaver of panic in her voice.

He pulled his head back far enough to gaze down into her eyes. Had he thought they were a muddied kind of brown? They rioted with color—shards of amber, flecks of jade, streaks of silver. And they were filled with confusion.

The confusion appeared to be contagious.

"Please," she said again. "I'm no good at this kind of game."

"Believe me, this is no game." He loosened his grip, slowly, cautiously, and then slipped his hands into his pockets. Things had gotten a little intense there for a moment, a little out of control.

"Why should I trust anything you say or do?" she asked. "You're a professional actor. You get paid to make people believe your lines." She turned on her heel and headed toward the wide barn opening.

"Wait a minute." He jogged past her and cut off her retreat. "Give me a chance here. Ellie. Tell me what to say to make you believe me."

"Why?"

Because I want to kiss you more than I want to take my next breath. Because I don't want to mess up whatever it is that's going on between us before I have a chance to figure out what it is.

A dozen other options raced through his mind, but none of them sounded like anything he wanted to say out loud at this point—if ever. So he said the next closest thing to the truth: "I have no idea."

She raised her stubborn chin, and he reached out to stroke a finger down her sleeve. "All I know," he said, "is that I'm finding you more and more attractive, though I can't for the life of me explain why."

She snorted an unladylike response. "If this is how you get a woman to kiss you, you're lousy at it."

"At least you know that was my lousy line, and not something out of some script."

Her expression turned downright mulish, and his pulse kicked into triple time. God, she was delectable when she was being difficult. The more those plump lips of hers pursed in annoyance, the more he wanted to nibble away the puckers.

"This is just me, Ellie. Just Fitz. Not the actor, just the man." He took a deep breath. "And I wonder if you find me attractive, too."

She rolled her eyes. "Have you looked in the mirror lately?"

One corner of his mouth quirked. "I'll take that as a 'yes.'"

He shifted closer. She arched back to keep her mouth out of kissing range, but she held her ground.

"Is that a yes?" he asked.

"Yes."

"Well." His gaze lowered to her lips. "That's something, then."

"But not the kind of yes you're looking for."

"Lady, you are one tough customer."

His next step brought him close enough to slip an arm around her waist. She spread her hands over his chest and shoved against him, letting him know he'd moved in as close as he was going to get, but close enough for him to appreciate the allure of the slightly foxy arrangement of her features. Not classic beauty, not exactly. Something more…fascinating. Intriguing.

He concentrated on her woodsy, witchy eyes and her plump chili-pepper lips, while her compact curves tortured him with a preview of the havoc she could wreak on his twisted wreck of a libido. "What kind of a yes am I looking for, Ellie?"

Her cheeks flooded with a dusty pink, and her eyes widened with a lost and baffled expression he hoped was one step away from surrender. "I—I don't know."

He skimmed one hand up her slim back and fingered the warm, moist hair at the base of her heavy braid. "I think you do."

"I know it's not real." She trembled beneath his fingertips. "It's just another kind of make-believe."

"Make-believe may be how I make my living, but…" He moved more slowly this time, gathering her in with a gentle insistence. "Tell me if you think this is just an act."

He parted his lips, and she sucked in her breath, and he hesitated at the brink. Their mouths nearly met and then barely parted, dancing an erotic shift and retreat played out in fractions of inches. But finally her eyelids fluttered shut, and he closed the last, minute space between them and touched his lips to hers. Slightly, softly, the merest of samples, teasing them both with hints of more, oh, so much more to come.

"Ah-hm-hem."

Fitz glanced up to see Trish silhouetted in the barn's doorway, and then he cursed and dropped his arms when Ellie flinched. Her back was ramrod straight as she stepped aside and marched back toward the abandoned bucket of suds and rags.

"Excuse me," said Trish. "Sorry. They're ready for you on the set now."

"Nothing to apologize for." He took a deep breath, battling his way out of the spell he'd been under. "I could use a stiff dose of reality."

A FEW HOURS LATER, Ellie slapped her red film gimme cap against her jeans to shake off some of the dust before she pushed through the back door. She tossed the cap over one of the mudroom hooks and plopped her rear on the bench seat. Maybe she could talk Jenna into delaying supper, so she could run upstairs to jump in the shower. She could use a quarter of an hour to stand under the spray and try to steam the insanity out through her pores.

What fool notion had crept in and taken possession of her long enough to let Fitz Kelleran kiss her?

She'd kissed Fitz Kelleran.

Ellie Harrison, average-looking nobody from nowhere, had kissed outrageously handsome and sexy movie star Fitz Kelleran.

And oh, if they hadn't been interrupted, it would have been *good*. Better than good. Like nothing she'd ever experienced. She could tell—in that one second of contact—the man could kiss.

Of course he could kiss, she reminded herself with a scowl as she tugged off her first boot. He'd been practicing with every available starlet and model on five continents for years.

But did she really care, if all that practice had been distilled, just for her benefit, into one miniscule moment of pure, unadulterated bliss? She slumped, spineless, against the wall, floating on the memory of silky, heated, breath-robbing contact.

"Ellie?" Jenna called.

"In here."

Jenna stepped into the mudroom, twisting a dish towel in her hands. "You've got a visitor."

Ellie shoved the boot under the bench and started wrestling with the other one. Something about the way Jenna had said *visitor* made it sound like supper was a ways off and the conversation at the table was going to be difficult. "Who?"

"It's Wayne." Jenna gave the towel another squeeze. "Wayne Hammond. He's waiting for you out in the front parlor."

"What's he doing in there?"

"Ellie." Jenna unfurled the cloth and snapped it straight. "He's been waiting for a chance to talk to you."

"Why's he still in the parlor?" Ellie jerked at the boot with a grunt. "He could've come out to the set. I know he's been wanting to watch some more of the filming."

Jenna shot Ellie a bland look and began to fold the towel into neat squares. "I don't think it's that kind of talk he's after."

Well, hell. Ellie popped off her second boot and stared at it in her hand. What was it with the men around here? Couldn't they leave a female alone for one day? And what was so different about her today that had them sniffing around?

She nearly took a whiff herself to try to figure out what all the excitement was about. But she knew she'd smell the same as she always smelled this time of day—like horse, feed and sweat.

She nudged the boot out of sight and leaned back against the wall, her hands dangling between her knees. "I'll just take a minute or two to freshen up, and then I'll be right there."

"I'll tell him. And then I—I think I'll take Jody into town for a burger at Walt's. She's been wanting to go."

Ellie shot her mother-in-law a suspicious glance. "I thought you two went into town this afternoon."

Jenna puffed up with indignation. "Is there some law against making the trip more than once a day?"

Ellie sighed. "No."

"There's ham left over from the other night. And some cold corn-and-pepper salad I made up fresh today, and some sour-dough rolls ready for the oven."

"I'll manage."

"There's more than enough for two," said Jenna.

Ellie knew a setup when she saw one. And if it was Jenna doing the setting up, there was no getting out of it. "Isn't that convenient," she muttered.

"Wayne's a good man, Ellie."

"I know he is." She frowned at her mother-in-law. "Maybe I just don't want to feel so grateful for it."

"What do you mean, grateful?"

Ellie wished she could take back the words. She knew she'd be in for a scolding if Jenna thought she still felt, deep down inside, that she owed any of the Harrisons a debt she could never repay. "Grateful a good man would be showing that kind of interest in me," she said.

"You've got nothing to be grateful for, other than good looks and good health. But Ellie, honey..." Jenna perched next to her on the edge of the bench. "You've got much, much more than that to offer. So many fine qualities. You had some good years with Tom. Happy years, full of happy dreams. You've got so many more years still ahead of you. Don't you want to share them with someone special?"

"I'm doing okay. I don't need anyone." She rubbed her hands over her knees. "And I don't think I want anyone, at least not right now."

"I didn't mean to imply that you aren't doing just fine on your own," said Jenna, "and I hope you didn't take it that way. I'm real proud of all you do around here."

Ellie reached for Jenna's hand and gave it a squeeze. "I know."

"But don't you want to share all that with someone? Someone who cares just as much as you do about what's important to you? Someone who cares about you?"

"I guess so." Ellie shoved a stray wisp of hair behind one ear. "I just don't want to feel like I owe him for it."

"Oh, Ellie." Jenna shook her head. "Aren't you ever going to learn that love doesn't require a payment for feelings rendered?"

"That's not what I meant."

Jenna's shoulders lifted and fell with her sad, resigned sigh. "I surely do wish I could be certain of that."

"I always figured I'd start looking for that kind of companionship again some day." Ellie straightened away from the wall. "I just didn't figure it would come looking for me first, in my own parlor."

Jenna laughed and wrapped an arm around Ellie's shoulders in a quick, light hug. "There's never a good time for things like this. They just happen."

Ellie shot her a sideways glance. "You don't have any reason to feel grateful, either."

Jenna angled her head to one side. "And just what is it I have to be feeling grateful about?"

"You've got Will."

Jenna's cheeks turned positively crimson. "I'll go tell Wayne you'll be out in a minute."

ELLIE SMOOTHED HER HANDS over her dress and tried to ignore the draft blowing up her rear end. The feeling that something essential was missing on that particular part of her anatomy—

something like pants legs—didn't exactly add to her feminine confidence. In fact, she felt damned ridiculous. But she figured that wearing a dress would be a kind of apology for keeping Wayne waiting.

An apology, not some kind of courtship costume.

God. Maybe she should change.

Before she could change either the dress or her mind, she raced down the main stairway to the entrance hall and scooted around the corner into the front parlor.

"Hello, Wayne. Sorry to keep you waiting." Her voice sounded a little breathy, but she managed to cover her wince with a casual smile.

"Hello, Ellie." He rose, slowly and carefully, from the fussy little chair where he'd parked his big, square frame, and his eyes lowered to the spot where the hem of her dress riffled and settled against her shins. "A man doesn't mind waiting for a woman who ends up looking like that."

Then his gaze dropped lower still, to the toes of his boots, and his weathered face flushed a ruddy tone beneath the tan. Good ol' Wayne—always a touch bashful around women, though that had never prevented them from flocking around him. Of course, those soulful brown eyes of his might have played a major part in the attraction. Though he hadn't dated while he was in school, his quiet, steady ways had earned him the captain's spot on the high school football team. And later, a county supervisor seat.

"Thanks." She tried to think of something to jump-start a conversation but came up empty. Too bad the two of them couldn't borrow some clever Hollywood scriptwriter to get them through all the awkwardness this evening promised. "Jenna told me she left some of her famous corn-and-pepper salad for the two of us. Would you like to stay to supper?"

He followed her through the second parlor and into the oversize dining room beyond. Jenna had set the table for two with the good china before she'd left. Now it was Ellie's turn to blush a bit as she lit the candles standing sentry near a clutch of lilacs in a glittering crystal vase.

She carried the food to the table, and Wayne pulled out her chair. As they tucked into their dinners and settled into the familiar routine of ranch talk and community news, the stiff formality between them began to fade. He told her about tracking a grizzly up the ridge and chuckled over Tom's grand scheme to import exotic cattle breeds.

She slipped into familiar patterns, too—rancher, neighbor, friend. And if stubborn, steady Wayne had never understood Tom's driving ambition to improve on things, it wasn't a failing. She and Wayne shared a world that was real and right—right for her now, anyway.

That's what she told herself, even in the moments that made her stomach clench, moments when the grandfather clock in the parlor marked the length of the odd silences that fell between them, or when she picked up her napkin and touched Jenna's special-occasion linen to her lips. Moments when she caught Wayne staring at her in a peculiar fashion, the way he was staring at her right now.

"Can I get you anything else?" she asked.

He shook his head. "I'm full up. Thanks."

She rose from the table, and he came halfway out of his chair, blushing again at the Sunday manners on a midweek evening. Then he settled back and waited in silence as she bustled about, clearing the dishes and pouring the cup of coffee he agreed to.

She rejoined him and sat with her chin in her hand, watching him sip his steaming drink as slowly and methodically as he did just about everything. Behind him, through the lace curtains that swooped and draped to the dining room floor, the shadows climbed the mountain slopes and the setting sun gilded their peaks.

He finished and pushed himself back from the table with a satisfied sigh. "Jenna's one hell of a good cook."

"Always has been." She decided to be up-front about the issue. "Me, I'm lousy at it."

He started to make a response, but dropped his eyes and stared at his empty cup.

Tick, tick, tick, tick.

Suddenly Ellie couldn't figure out what she dreaded more—the end of this evening or its continuation. She decided to get it over with and make a judgment after the fact. "Well," she said, rising from her seat, "we've got an early call tomorrow."

"Is that movie talk?" Wayne followed her through the dim parlors to the entry hall. "Those folks seem to have an odd phrase for just about everything."

"No more odd than our ranch talk seems to them, I s'pose." Ellie handed him his hat and stepped to the door. "It's been a pleasure. Good night, Wayne."

He hesitated, turning his hat in a circle, and then he reached out to close his hand over hers on the door knob. "Ellie, I…"

"Yes?"

"I…"

The skin above his collar darkened. It was difficult to see his blush in the shadowed entry, but Ellie imagined it must be an impressive lobster-red. She held her tongue and let him struggle, thinking it was fair payback for this impromptu date.

Lady, you are one tough customer.

No, she wouldn't let herself go there. It wasn't fair to

compare Fitz Kelleran and Wayne Hammond. It wasn't fair to them, and it wasn't fair to her. Fitz was pure fantasy. Wayne was reality.

Her reality.

Wayne might not be as exciting to talk to and spar with, or to think about kissing, but then reality rarely was. "Would you like to come to dinner again?" she asked.

"Yes, I would. Thank you."

The abject relief and gratitude in his voice melted away her impatience with him, and she stepped closer, into kissing range. She waited for him to make a move, but he seemed to be paralyzed. Or maybe he was moving so slowly his progress wasn't visible, like some big, broad, cowboy-shaped glacier.

"Well…" She moistened her lips, as much of a nudge as she could manage without losing her self-respect. "Good night, Wayne."

He lowered his head, finally, and she caught a whiff of horse, and feed, and sweat in the moment before he pressed his lips to hers. His mouth was firm and warm and tasted of ham and coffee. Familiar scents and tastes.

She waited for the familiar to enfold her, to seep into her and draw her to this man with the power of shared memory, with comfort and warmth. But the fit was off, somehow, as if some tiny but essential element of the familiar had gone awry.

The parlor clock ticked off a handful of seconds—an eternity of seconds—and then he slowly pulled away from her with a frown. "Good night, Ellie."

She closed the door behind him and sagged against the solid wood. "Oh, God," she whispered into the gloom, and her shoulders shook with a silent laugh of despair.

CHAPTER EIGHT

HALFWAY THROUGH THE SIX-WEEK location schedule, Will was enjoying a morning of muscle-straining, mind-clearing labor. The late-June sun baked his bare shoulders and bleached the green out of the meadow grass. He tugged and strained at the loose strand of barbed wire and grunted as he clipped the line to the fence post. Grunting went with the work, kind of like the underbelly beat of a bass guitar.

Working with the *Wolfe's Range* folks was interesting enough, but it interfered with the comfortable rhythm of his regular chores. He was looking forward to the day they packed up their mess and moved on. Especially that flirty little production assistant, Trish. Those come-and-get-it looks she aimed his way were raising a rash on his conscience.

Ghost, his edgy piebald, lifted his head and snorted at something to the east. That was another indulgence of the day: saddling up some companionship for the long, lonely hours on the fence line instead of riding a more practical ATV. He'd had his fill lately of trailers and vans and four-wheelers, the whines of engines and the stink of exhaust.

He looked off toward the mountains, stretching another grunt into a groan while he rubbed at his lower back muscles. From behind a rise in the dirt track, a dust cloud boiled up against the noon blue sky. "Car's coming," he told Ghost as he slipped his shirt from the saddle horn.

A moment later one of the ranch trucks rose into view. It rumbled and bumped to a stop beside the fence line, and dust flowed over the tailgate and the cab hood like a river in reverse. Will poked his arms into his shirtsleeves and debated doing up a few buttons, but it was too danged hot to fuss.

He stooped and stepped gingerly through the clawed wire lines as the driver emerged. "Hey, Jenna."

"Hey, Will." She brushed her gold-and-silver hair from her forehead and left her hand in place as a visor. "Thought you might like some chicken and some cold lemonade."

"Well, now." He pulled off his hat and took a moment to drink her in. She was as every bit as sweet and refreshing as what she offered. "I was just thinking how fine it might be if you showed up like this."

Uncertainty—and something that looked like unhappiness—flickered across her features, and her hand dropped from her face to smooth over her slacks. The shadows disappeared, and she turned toward the tailgate. "You can have the rest of what's here. I've already passed by Jake's crew, and I found the others out near the river bar. You're the last of the hands I thought to look for."

"Hope there's something left after those hyenas picked over the bones."

"Don't worry. I saved aside a couple of drumsticks. And look." She tossed back the lid on her enormous picnic basket and lifted out a cloth-covered plate. "Sugar cookies."

"Hope you didn't have to take out your shotgun to defend those."

"Nope." She grinned up at him. "I just told everyone Ellie was waiting for the rest."

Lord, she was beautiful when she smiled like that. It sucker punched him, and he took it right in the belly like the sucker he was. "That would do it," he said. "Nothing quite so mean as Ellie scrappin' over one of your sugar cookies."

She laughed and snagged a drumstick from the cooler, placing it on a bright blue checkered napkin. "Get started on this while I pour you some lemonade."

"Yes, ma'am." He tossed his hat into the truck bed and scooted up on the tailgate, knowing Jenna couldn't drive away while he perched there.

He bit into the chicken and chewed, gazing out over the silvery range grass. "Going to be a dry summer."

"That's what they're saying in town." She coaxed a thin stream of lemonade from the thermos into a small plastic cup. "Good for the filming, I guess."

"How's all that going today?"

"Loud." Jenna sighed. "Hard to think with all that hammering and hollering going on outside my front porch. Speaking of my front porch," she said as she handed him the cup, "Trish was by this morning. They're going to film a scene there next week. Right there on the porch."

"You don't say."

"Isn't that something? My very own front door, larger than life on movie screens across the country."

"Imagine that."

"They'll probably decide it's the wrong color," she said.

"Or the wrong size."

"Or in the wrong place."

"Or the wrong door altogether. Maybe they've got a front door stunt double ready to fly in from California and do the job the right way."

She laughed again. "Imagine that."

He knew her well enough to read the tension beneath her breezy chatter. Something was bothering her, and she'd headed out into the ranch land, armed with sugar cookies and looking for some kind of solace. He reached behind him to snag a folded horse blanket, pulled it up next to him and patted the scratchy wool. "Hop up here and keep me company for a bit."

She glanced at the space on the blanket beside him and then back at the empty road.

He slowly extended his hand, trying not to spook her, waiting for her eyes to settle back on his face. He held himself steady under her considering gaze, letting her see what she needed to see and know what she needed to know. "I'll share one of my cookies with you," he said.

She worried her lower lip with her teeth, and the moment spun out, hovering, wavering in the air like the ripples of a mirage. A bead of sweat snaked its way down his backbone and was absorbed into the waistband of his jeans. His arm stayed suspended between them, a flesh-and-bone bridge. He let the silence work on her and counted on her manners to nudge her into acknowledging his invitation.

"Just one?" she asked at last.

"Come here, Jenna."

Slowly, in halting increments, she reached up and placed her palm in his. So soft, so delicate. He stared at her glossy pink nails and thrilled to this one small victory. It was the first time she'd chosen to touch him like this.

A sudden, fierce yearning roared through him. He wanted to watch those hands, pale in the moonlight and gentle as a breeze, smooth over his skin. He wanted to wrap his arms around her, rise above her, sink into her, pleasure her, love her. Soon. He wasn't sure how much longer he could go on like this, waiting, hoping, marking progress in smiles and touches. His fingers wrapped around hers and tightened.

"Here," he said and kicked out a foot bent stiffly at the ankle. "Careful now, it's a bit hot to the touch."

She stepped on his boot, and he hauled her up and onto the blanket and gave her a moment to settle. "What's wrong, Jenna?"

She shot him a disapproving look from beneath her lashes and smoothed her hands over her slacks. "A lady doesn't appreciate hearing that her feelings are so transparent."

"Changing the subject?"

She sighed and reached for a plastic cup. "Maggie called."

Maggie Sinclair, Jenna's daughter. Like her older brother, Maggie had turned her back on Granite Ridge when she'd left for college, and her visits home in the dozen years since had been few and far between. Only the adopted child, Ellie, had truly taken the land to her heart.

"Is her divorce final yet?"

"We can pry all the nasty details out of her soon enough." Jenna sighed again—Maggie tended to have that effect on people. "She's coming for Jody's birthday party. And she says she's thinking about staying a while this time."

"That'll make Jody happy." The young girl idolized her aunt's Chicago-ized style and big-city ideas.

Jenna tipped the thermos to pour herself some lemonade. "Wayne Hammond called for Ellie this morning."

"I'll tell her when I see her."

"Oh," said Jenna with a flap of her hand. "It wasn't anything like that."

"Anything like what?"

"Anything like what you're thinking."

He frowned at the plate of cookies. "Just what is it you think I'm thinking?"

"That he wants to talk to her about ranch business."

"Why else would he call?" he asked, though he had a

feeling he wasn't going to like the answer. He picked up a cookie and took a big bite.

"Why else do you think an eligible man might call an eligible woman?"

Cookie crumbs stuck in his throat like sawdust in sap. "Eligible woman?"

Jenna sighed. "It's been nearly three years, Will."

Three years. A little more than that since Ben Harrison had suffered a final, fatal heart attack. And a little less since Tom had crashed his plane into the side of a mountain, shattering so many dreams.

Will set the plate behind him and collected the rest of his lemonade. "It's only been a year or so since Wayne's wife ran off and left him."

Jenna frowned. "You aren't going to hold that against him, are you?"

"Haven't so far." He stared into the distance, past Harrison timber and foothills pasture, in the direction of Hammond's sprawling acres of lush valley land. "No one who knows him would find cause to."

"He's a good man, Will."

"Didn't say he wasn't."

"That ex-wife of his—she always was a flighty one."

Alicia Hammond had caused quite a stir when she'd arrived in town with a broken-down Trans Am and a synchronized sway to her hips and bosom. She'd managed to keep several men dangling on her line before reeling in Wayne. "He knew that going in on the deal."

Jenna straightened her spine with an exasperated little huff. "So it was his fault?"

"I don't know whose fault it was, and I don't need to. Only Wayne and Alicia need to know, and I figure they do."

"So, what's the problem?"

"Did I say there was a problem?"

"You didn't need to."

He grabbed his cup and slid off the tailgate. He wished there were something a little stronger than lemonade in that thermos, but he'd settle for anything to get him through this conversation in one piece.

"Well," said Jenna, "aren't you going to ask what he wanted?"

"Who?"

"Wayne."

He shot her a bland look. "I thought you already had that figured out for everyone involved in the matter."

"Ooh." She hopped down from the tailgate and stepped in close, impatience humming around her like a rattled-up nest of hornets. "I'm wondering why it is you asked me to keep you company, Will Winterhawk, if you're not willing to participate in a decent way in a decent conversation."

"I've been participating as best I know how." He twisted the knob on the thermos and shoved it back against the side of the truck bed. "I guess I'm just not aware of the rules in this particular instance."

"Aren't you curious about Wayne and Ellie?"

"I don't think there's a couple there yet to be curious about."

Jenna threw her hands up in the air. "My point exactly!"

Will drank his lemonade and hoped it wouldn't add more sour to the churning in his stomach. Wayne Hammond? Setting his sights on Ellie?

It made sense, if a person considered the situation with a lazy kind of logic. Wayne and Ellie shared experiences and values, a world and a social set, not to mention a long fence line. She'd only been a class or so behind him, all those years they'd been in school together, all those years Tom had locked himself away in self-exile. All those years when it would have been so simple to get together, if getting together had been something Ellie or Wayne had wanted to do.

But Wayne was a stolid, settled man, conservative in his plans and his needs. And Ellie was a whirlwind, a powder keg with a tall stack of short fuses. Will had watched her wrestle with her nature and tamp down her flights of fancy these last three years until he feared she'd shrink and wither into a desiccated dust mote before his very eyes.

She was as much a dreamer, in her own quiet way, as her late husband had been. Will always figured that's what they'd recognized in each other. But where Tom's plans had been bigger than life and breathtakingly ambitious, Ellie's were whimsical and personal—wishes of the heart. Will was still holding out hope she'd find someone who could love her for her imagination as well as for her strength, someone who could bind her to him with promises of laughter and adventures instead of the sobering weight of shared responsibilities.

Wayne Hammond wasn't that man.

Jenna stood before him with her arms crossed over her chest, expecting him to respond in some sort of preconceived manner. But he wasn't in the mood to go along just to get along. He was of a mind to shake things up a bit. Some things in this withering landscape could use a good, strong jolt.

"How do you feel about Wayne and Ellie making a match?" he asked. "How do you think Jody would handle it? How would it affect the future of Granite Ridge?"

He read her confusion and struggle in the series of expressions that flickered over her features, and he knew she was second-guessing some of her own desires in the matter. The fight leaked out of her stance by degrees, and her mouth worked its way into a thin-lipped frown. "I don't know," she said at last. "I don't know how I'm supposed to feel."

He stepped closer, awkward and oversize before her, longing to offer some comfort. "Guess you'll have plenty of time to get used to the idea, if the situation's what you think it is."

"Oh, it's what I think it is, all right." She brightened a bit. "I can tell."

"What did Wayne say?"

"It's not so much what he says or doesn't say. It's the way he looks at her."

"How's that?"

"The way a man looks at a woman when he's thinking about her in a certain way."

His pulse kicked up in a throbbing beat. "Wanting her?"

"Maybe." She blushed and sidled away. "I don't know him well enough to be guessing about things like that."

"You can just tell?" He closed the gap between them. "Just by looking? Just by the way he looks at her?"

She glanced at him and then gazed out at the field. "You know what I mean."

"Maybe I do. But I want to hear you say it."

"Why?"

"I want to make sure we're looking at things the same way." He hooked her chin with a knuckle. "Look at me, Jenna. Tell me what you see."

"I don't need to look at you to know what you're thinking, Will."

"Look at me, Jenna." He kept a steady pressure under her jaw, holding her in place with that one small touch as he moved still closer. "Tell me what you see when you look at me."

"I—" Her lids fluttered down, shutting him out. "I can't."

"Can't see? Or won't?"

"Please," she said. "I can't deal with it right now."

"I'm not asking you to deal with it all at once." He lifted his hands to frame her face in his palms. "Keep your eyes closed, then, and deal with this one small, simple thing."

He lowered his head toward hers, slowly, savoring the anticipation, imagining the moment he'd feel that soft, moist contact. He brushed his mouth against hers, once, twice, before he surrendered to the sheer joy of communicating his feelings in this way, and he settled his lips over hers with a low sigh. His fingers strayed into her hair, tangling in the silky strands, grasping her warm scalp to tilt her face up to his. She lifted her hands to his shoulders, and she opened her mouth to take him in. And he was lost in sensation, suspended in time.

She tasted of lemons and sugar and homecoming. He floated on her scent, her unique essence of roses and warmth and woman. Her fingers crept over his shoulders, tracing a path toward his collar, circling behind his neck to hold him, ever so lightly. The soft gust of her breath whispered in his ears like a siren's song.

He lowered his hands to her waist and took a chance on drawing her closer. She didn't skitter away.

Lord, it was sweet, sweet torture holding himself back at that moment, while she trembled beneath his fingers yet pressed her mouth to his, while she shivered and shuddered yet touched her tongue to his. He was sinking, drowning, losing his grip on his self control. So he struggled back to the surface and grasped for reality's substance.

A slight breeze filtered through his shirt, and he heard Ghost wade through the grass and swish at flies. He seized on that, on his awareness of time and place and the sweat-streaked skin beneath his clothes, and he drew back before he could brush up against her fresh pink blouse. "Jenna," he said, and then again, after another soft, brief taste of her, "Jenna."

"I wish you wouldn't do this," she murmured beneath his lips.

"Kiss you?"

"Yes."

"Why?"

Her hands drifted down to rest on his arms. "It's no small thing when you kiss me, Will. And it never makes things simple."

Her words moved through him, swelling his heart until it squeezed up against his rib cage with bright, hopeful pain, and the dazed look in her eyes and the rosy moistness of her lips nearly undid him. His hands tightened on her waist, and another tremor ran through her.

No. She'd lingered in his company longer than ever before, admitted to more than ever before. She hadn't cringed from his embrace. He told himself to be grateful for that, to settle for that—for now—and he backed off.

He didn't trust himself to speak, and he couldn't think of anything to say, anyway. So he collected his gloves from the back of the truck and tipped his hat at her before shoving it back on his head. He walked back to the fence and stepped through, and then he turned to watch her secure the picnic items and climb back into the truck.

She paused and looked at him, just as he'd asked her to, for one long and eloquent moment before she started up the engine and pulled out onto the dusty track. The truck rolled back over the hill, churning up a cloud of dust that drifted down to smother the still, dry grass.

FITZ OPENED HIS EYES to the uncertain light of predawn and wondered why. Then he heard his cell phone's trill. "Fitz," he said.

"I'm bleeding." Nora's voice quavered on a sob. "Oh, God, Fitz, I'm bleeding."

He sprang out of his rumpled trailer bed and rifled through his things for a pair of jeans. "Are you at the ranch or in town?"

"Town."

"Have you called Ken?"

"He said to call you."

Damn him. "Are you hurting?"

"No," she said in a strained whisper. "Just bleeding."

"Have you called your doctor here?" Nora's assistant should be handling details like this right now. "Where's Anna?"

"I gave her some time off to go to Butte."

He flung a shirt from the tiny closet to his bed and rammed the phone under his chin so he could button his jeans. "Okay, darlin', you've done everything just right so far." He used his actor's skills to keep his tone casual and soothing. "I want you to get back in bed, if you're not there now."

He switched hands to wriggle into his shirt. "Call your doctor and tell him you can meet him at his office or the hospital in—" He tucked the phone back under his chin to strap on his watch. "Forty minutes. I'm on my way to town now, and I'll take you."

"Burke, too?"

"He'll be there. You'll have two big guys watching out for you."

She sniffed. "Thank you, Fitz."

"See you in a little bit, darlin'. Now go get horizontal and make those calls, and I'll be there before you know it."

Nora needed a woman—a friend—to be with her now for

moral support, and he had an idea which woman would be good in a situation like this. He tugged on his grubby sports shoes, and then sprinted out of his trailer and raced up the short path to the main ranch house. He pounded on the massive front door and paced from one side of the deep front porch to the other before pounding again. "Jenna! Jenna Harrison!"

A moment later, Ellie opened the door. Her hair was damp, and she gripped a white cotton robe closed at her neck. "What do you want?"

He shoved past her and strode through the entry to a massive newel post at the foot of a paneled oak stairway. "Mrs. Harrison!"

"Yes, I'm here." Jenna leaned over the railing from a second-floor landing, her gown billowing between the balusters. "My goodness! Mr. Kelleran! What is it?"

"Nora needs you."

"I'll be right there."

He pulled his phone out of his pocket and punched in Burke's number.

Ellie frowned at him. "What about today's—"

"There's not going to be any— Burke, it's me. Get the car and meet me in front of the Harrison's house. *Now*."

He slid the phone into a back pocket and glanced at the second floor. "They can't film without Nora and me, and we're calling in sick."

"I'm going with you. With Jenna."

"What about Jody?"

Surprise flickered across her features. "What about her?"

"Doesn't she need—" He hesitated, suddenly feeling off-kilter with all this responsibility. "I don't know...adult supervision or...something?"

"She's old enough to fend for herself in her own place."

He glared at the smile twitching at the corners of her mouth. "How fast can you get dressed?"

"Fast."

"Good." He shoved her toward the stairs. "Go do it."

CHAPTER NINE

AT NOON, ELLIE SLUMPED in a plastic chair near the second-floor nurses' station, eavesdropping on yet another of Burke's phone conversations. The news filtering down the hall from Nora's private room was still inconclusive. Until the actress's assistant arrived, Ellie wouldn't be able to pry Jenna from her bedside.

She hadn't seen Fitz since they'd arrived. He was hovering protectively over his leading lady.

She had to give him points for quick thinking and quicker action. He'd rounded up all the right people, given everyone the right tasks in the right order and kept the lines of communication open.

Burke stopped his pacing and offered her the phone. "Fitz said you might want to call Jody and check in with her."

"I checked in with her an hour ago."

"You did give her this number, didn't you?" He didn't bother to disguise his amusement at his employer's fussing. "I'm supposed to mention—in a casual way, so that I won't cause you any undue anxiety—that a lot can happen in an hour."

"She's fine." Ellie grinned at Burke, enjoying his soft, precise British accent. Anyone who could deal with Fitz on a full-time basis while managing to retain not only his sanity but a dry and dignified sense of humor was a mighty impressive and fascinating human being.

She pointed to the phone he still held extended in her direction. "You just want me to take that thing off your hands for a while. God, it's annoying."

"The phone?" He slipped it into his pants pocket. "Fitz is a busy man with a complicated life."

"And it's your job to run it for him?"

"No, not really." He adjusted his glasses. "Though he prefers that it appear that way."

"Quite the actor, isn't he?"

"Spoken like a woman who sees through most of his efforts."

She rolled her eyes, and Burke surprised her with a slyly devastating smile.

"Fitz handles his own affairs," he said. "But he does have a rather strong aversion to being continually interrupted by miniature electronic devices."

"Phone phobia?"

Burke's smile took on a wicked edge. "An interesting turn of phrase. May I borrow it?"

Ellie decided she liked Fitz's assistant. "Go ahead."

A stranger with a backpack sauntered toward the station and spoke with the matronly nurse seated there. She shook her head, and he shrugged away from the counter. He turned and smiled at Ellie. "Hello there."

Suspicion had the short hairs along the back of her neck dancing a tango, and she narrowed her eyes at him. "Hey."

"Busy day around here, hm?"

"Maybe." She shot a glance at Burke, but his phone was back at his ear as he turned to stare out the long, low window behind her. "Maybe not."

"Heard there's a film crew working near here."

A tabloid guy—he had to be. He wasn't one of the film crew, and he sure wasn't a local, not fitted out like he was in fake army surplus. Paparazzi, maybe. She'd overheard the security people on the set discussing them.

She lifted a shoulder. "Yeah. Heard the same thing."

"You seen any of the actors yet? In town?"

"Nope."

He nodded and smiled a fake surplus smile. "Must be something, knowing there are some famous folks working nearby."

"It's something, all right." Something she suddenly felt protective about. The people out at Granite Ridge worked long, hard hours creating something that gave other people pleasure. It didn't seem right to trade that pleasure for a loss of privacy.

"Heard there was some trouble out on the set today," he said.

She shrugged a disinterested shrug.

Burke settled next to her, placing the phone on the tiny plastic table between them. "Want to go get something to eat?" he asked.

"No, thank you."

He stared at the stranger, who took the seat across from them. "Would you like something to drink?" he asked her.

"I'm not thirsty."

"I am." He never took his eyes from the man with the backpack as he leaned to the side to pull his wallet from a back pocket.

"What would you like?" she asked.

"Whatever you bring will be fine."

Burke didn't want a drink. He meant to keep this man, and whatever was in his backpack, away from everyone connected with the film, including her.

She studied the stranger slouching in his chair and looking as if he could wait forever. Paparazzi did a lot of waiting. And when they got tired of waiting, she'd been told, they had methods of stirring things up—like offering people money to start fights with celebrities.

Burke's phone chirped. He switched it off without checking the call and slipped it into his pocket, and then he steepled his fingers beneath his chin and continued to stare at the man with the backpack. Ellie rose and headed down the hall to warn Fitz.

BY FOUR O'CLOCK in the afternoon, Fitz still hadn't had anything to eat but aspirin and anything to drink but lousy vending-machine coffee. He craved a shower and yearned for a comfortable chair, and he'd been sorely tempted to hitch a ride with Jenna and Ellie and head back to the ranch. But there was one last crisis to deal with.

He squared off with Van Gelder in the hallway outside Nora's room.

"I don't agree with your 'assessment of the situation,'" he whispered. "You're not going to replace Nora on this film because that's the wrong decision to make. You know it is, damn it. She's perfect for the part, and you said yourself the chemistry is singeing the celluloid."

"I can't take any more chances," Van Gelder whispered back. "We're not even a month in. I say we cut our losses, now, and reshoot what we need to. If we keep her, and we keep shooting with her, and she pulls another stunt like this, we'll lose so much time we'll never make it up. And if we don't make it up, what do we do about the little problem of her expanding waistline, hm?"

"Her doctor says she's going to be fine."

"For now."

Fitz threw up his hands and stalked down the corridor

toward the little seating area where Burke waited, tense and solemn. Van Gelder stormed down the hall behind him. And trailing Van Gelder came Bernie Kagan, the film's producer. Somehow Bernie had gotten wind of the day's shutdown and managed to arrive in time to add to everyone's problems.

At least the short-term news was good. Nora was staying the night for observation, and then she'd be free to go back to her hotel room or trailer, to put up her feet and take it easy for a couple of days. Anna had arrived, arms full of flowers, and the two women were now engrossed in a local rodeo playing on the television.

"Damn it, Kelleran," said Van Gelder. "You know I'm right."

"I know nothing of the sort."

"We can't afford any more delays."

"The studio's concerned," said Bernie in his nasal drone. That was the usual extent of Bernie's contribution to any conversation: the bottom line. He was a walking, whining spreadsheet.

"Don't talk to me about delays," growled Fitz. He shoved his nose to within an inch of Van Gelder's and drilled a finger into the director's chest. "You know damn well why we're behind schedule."

"Fitz." Burke came out of his chair, one hand raised.

A series of metallic clicks whirred behind them, and Fitz spun to see a figure in fatigues duck into the elevator. He raced to snag the doors, but all he caught was a slice of an unshaven face and a gloating smile as they slid shut. "*Damn*."

"Great shot that guy got, Kelleran," said Van Gelder with a sneer. "I can see the trade headlines now. Trouble on the Set. Leading Lady Hospitalized, Leading Man Attacks Director. And let's not forget the tabloids—Is Fitz the Father?"

All the frustrations and anxieties and torments of the day

streamed through Fitz to focus like a laser beam on one convenient target. He grabbed Van Gelder by the collar and shoved him against the wall. "'Leading Man Attacks Director,' huh? Might as well give the trash slingers their money's worth."

"When you're finished there," said Burke softly, "I'd like a go."

Fitz snatched his hands away from Van Gelder and stared at his assistant in surprise.

"She doesn't deserve that," said Burke in that same calm and deadly voice. "She's done nothing to deserve any of this."

"Fitz." Anna stood near the nurse's station, wide-eyed, taking in the scene. "Nora's asking for you."

Fitz glared at the producer. "You don't have to say it, Bernie—the studio's concerned. Well, so the hell am I. Stick that up your assets column and figure out the balance."

ELLIE HUMMED A SENSELESS TUNE to Noodle that evening as she tethered him to one of the knobby barn support posts. She grabbed a pitchfork and entered his stall to tease and sift clumps of manure from the shavings spread over the floor boards. The quick pick through would keep Noodle's stall livable until she got the chance to shovel it out.

A shadow fell across the shavings and Ellie whirled around, the pitchfork raking a dangerous path through the air between her and the stall door.

Fitz slanted across the opening, one shoulder against the jamb. He glanced down at the sharp fork tines and then back at her with an eyebrow quirked in amusement. Although he'd obviously found a chance to shower and shave, he looked tired and a touch haggard.

Ellie didn't have to ask after Nora. If Fitz were here, she must be out of danger. He'd never leave her side otherwise.

She angled past him to toss the fork into the muck in the handcart and then swiped a loose strand of hair from her forehead with the back of a wrist. "What are you doing here?"

He shrugged away from the doorway and ambled toward her, twisting his mouth to the side in one of his cocky grins. "Thinking."

She led Noodle into his stall, stepped out and rammed the catch home.

"Don't you want to know what I'm thinking?" he asked.

"Sure," she said, wondering why he was taking so much time to get to the point, or at least to the conversation. He usually didn't need much of a reason—or much of that thinking he was so proud of at the moment—to start spouting off about something or other.

She lifted the cart by its worn wooden handles, and he followed her to the muck pile behind the barn. "So," she said as she scraped out the load. "What is it you're thinking?"

"That it's time I followed through on that kiss that got interrupted the other day."

She straightened with a sigh. She was ankle deep in filth and sweating with exertion. "You can't be serious."

He took the cart and led the way back into the barn, toward the spare stall heaped high with soft, spicy curls of wood shavings. "On the contrary," he said, "I take kissing very seriously."

She responded with an unladylike snort and began to pitch loose, fluffy forkfuls of shavings into the empty cart. "Well, you can just forget about it."

"I don't think so."

"What do you mean, you don't—"

He waded through the shavings and snatched the fork from her hands. She flung an arm out to grab it back and nearly lost her balance in the uneven wads of fluff. "What are you doing?"

"This." He tossed the fork into a corner.

"And this." He grabbed her by her forearms and hauled her up against his chest. Shavings scraps and hay flecks rose up and scattered around them, coasting on the scents of raw sap and overheated human bodies. Pete shifted and snuffled in the stall next door.

"I *am* going to kiss you," he said. "Right now."

"No. You're not." She tried to tug away, but her efforts were useless. Her pulse kicked into overtime. "No, Fitz," she repeated, her words spilling out in a quick and shallow rush.

He bent down until his lips hovered inches above hers. "Ask me," he whispered.

He didn't look quite so haggard now. He looked a little wild and a little dangerous, with a hell of a lot of compelling added to the mix. This wasn't the laid-back, easygoing charmer she thought she'd figured out. This was the take-charge, take-no-prisoners, steely-eyed warrior who'd been lurking beneath the surface.

And she was about to be served up as the spoils for all the battles he'd fought that day.

She knew she should make at least a token effort to fight him off, and she knew he'd let her go if she got serious about it, but her head fell back as he moved closer, and her eyelids fluttered beneath the moist sweep of his breath over her face. She swallowed and tried to force words out of a throat grown tight with—God help her—anticipation. "No."

"Come on, Ellie, just one kiss."

He let her wiggle away, and she climbed through the small mountain of shavings in the corner and bent to reach for the fork. "You're out of your mind."

"You may be right."

His hands settled on her hips, and in the next moment he'd flipped her off balance to toss her on her back. Before she could scramble for leverage, his big body sprawled over hers, pressing her into the spongy, aromatic pile.

Oh. My. God.

He circled her wrists in one hand and pinned them above her head. "I don't usually have to expend this much effort to get a girl to let me kiss her."

The realization that he was willing to expend it on her shivered through her, leaving her reckless and wild in its wake.

She spat a shaving from the corner of her mouth and glared up at him in feigned ferocity, preparing for round two. "So why don't you go kiss one of those other girls?"

"Because you're the one I want to kiss right now." He darted in close and brushed the tip of his nose against hers. "Come on, Ellie. Let me kiss you."

She thought of all the ways she could play this game with him, dark and intensely thrilling ways, and she stilled. "Go ahead," she dared them both.

One corner of his mouth quirked up. "Something tells me that might be a little risky."

She lifted an eyebrow. "I've had all my shots."

"Good to know." He settled more comfortably over her. "You wouldn't bite me, would you?"

She managed to convert a smile into a stubborn grimace.

"Promise you won't bite," he said as his body, long and hard, pressed against hers.

"I won't promise any such thing." She bucked against him, but he rode her as effortlessly as he rode her stock. "Get...off...me!"

"After you agree to let me kiss you without biting me," he said in his reasonable, agreeable voice. "Without hurting me in any way. Including, but not limited to, the five minutes immediately after I kiss you."

She thought the deal through, and then sighed in surrender and settled back into the shavings. "Just hurry up and get it over with, and then get off me."

"Sweetheart," he murmured with one of his brilliant smiles, "that's never been my style."

Oh. My. God.

Another thrill streaked through her, leaving her dazzled and delighted, and hot and wet, and oh, so ready for what was coming. But she'd die before she let him know it.

She rolled her eyes, and his grin showed her he'd seen through her act—and was enjoying every minute of their game.

"Okay," he said as he stroked a finger down her throat, "let's negotiate. I want you to promise not to bite or hurt me in any way. What do you want? Besides not getting kissed by me."

"I don't want to negotiate anything," she said with a feeble attempt to pull her wrists from his grasp. "I want you to let me go."

"Hm. Let me think about that," he said. "Nope. Try again."

"Oh!" She twisted and strained and arched with all her might, trying to dislodge him, but all she ended up doing was rubbing herself up against him like a cat in heat—which was just about how she was beginning to feel.

"Oh, honey," he said, "I love the way you negotiate."

"All right." She was panting from her efforts. "All right, I'll make a deal. I want you to promise to make it fast. I have work to do."

"Anything else?"

She narrowed her eyes. "Just one kiss."

"Just one?"

"One."

"How about starting with some warm-up nibbles?"

She groaned and shut her eyes. "I can't believe I'm lying here discussing this with you."

"Is that a *yes*?"

"All right," she said. *"Yes."*

"Now we're getting somewhere."

He shifted over her, and she nearly groaned again at the sensations all that friction was kicking up inside her.

"How about something a little more creative than one simple kiss?" he asked.

She opened her eyes. "Nothing wet and sloppy."

He tilted his head and stared down his nose at her. "I beg your pardon?"

"You know what I mean."

"Believe me, I don't." His gaze drifted to her mouth. "But open mouth. It has to be open mouth. For both of us."

"All right."

"And I get to hold you. I mean, not like I'm holding you now. Something a little more...romantic. And you can't try to get away."

"All right."

He released her wrists and slid his hands down to gently frame her face. His thumbs stroked her hair back from her temples.

Oh, my. She melted into the shavings.

"Much better," he whispered. Obviously pleased with himself, he began to lower his mouth toward hers.

It was the smug satisfaction on his face that set off an entire police convoy of warning sirens in her head. They were both a little too tired and a little too giddy, and not thinking too straight at the moment. Maybe this…this thing between them had ignited on its own, but that didn't mean they had to fan the fire.

She quickly pressed her palm against his chest. "*And*," she added, "this is it. No more kissing after this."

"What?"

"You heard me. I'll cooperate this time, but this is the last time."

He leaned back on one elbow and frowned down at her. "I can't agree to that. What if you want me to kiss you again?"

She probably would, but acting on it would be a huge mistake. One wild and wicked moment with a real live movie star would be memory enough. Anything more was far too reckless to consider. "Fat chance," she said.

"But still a chance. Come on, Ellie." He ran his fingertips through her hair. "If you make me promise, then I can never kiss you again, even if you want me to. Even if you beg me to."

God, she hoped it wouldn't come to that. "When hell freezes over."

"Famous last words." He skimmed a finger along the edge of her cheek. "I'll agree to one week."

"You'll leave me alone for a whole week?"

He narrowed his eyes. "That's wide open to interpretation. What exactly do you mean by leaving you alone?"

"No flirting, no teasing." God, she'd miss it. But they had to stop this before it got out of control. Again. "No bothering."

"Nope. I can't promise not to bother you. Not when you get to decide what 'bothering' is. Especially when just about everything I do and say seems to bother you."

"There's no 'seems to' about it."

He smiled and shifted again, moving one of his legs along one of hers, and she felt that smooth slide down to her core. He could bother her all he wanted, if it felt like this.

"Two weeks." She knew she was pushing it, but bargaining was so much fun. "Two weeks, since you'll get to bother me all you want."

"One week, and I'll try my best not to bother you at all."

She bit her lip and considered his offer. "All right. One week."

"One week, then. I can live with that." He sighed a sorrowful sigh, and then moved his body more intimately over hers. "It's not like it's a life sentence. Difficult, but an acceptable penalty to pay, especially when I think how much you're going to suffer waiting for the week to end."

"Hey, I'm doing you a favor. I should have started screaming fifteen minutes ago."

He slipped an arm beneath her and fanned his fingers across the back of her waist. "Let's save the screaming for about five minutes from now."

She rolled her eyes again. "What an ego."

"It's one of an actor's most valuable tools."

"Spare me the theatrical education, Kelleran. I've got two more stalls to muck out and a case of conjunctivitis to tend to."

"Be still, my heart. I'm surprised I don't have to use a club to beat my way through scores of rivals when you use seduction lines like that."

He wedged his leg between hers in another suggestive caress. "Okay. One kiss, a package deal. You don't injure me, and I don't try this again for another week."

"Got it." She shoved her chin up in a sacrificial pose. "Now get it over with."

"Okay." His mouth quirked in a wry grin. "As soon as I get my cue."

She took a deep breath and waited, watching his blue eyes roam over her face and throat, his long gold lashes framing every motion. Her body tensed and vibrated in an ecstasy of expectation. But after several long, agonizing seconds, he still hadn't made his move.

She huffed a little sigh of impatience.

"And there it is," he said and lowered his lips to hers.

She'd thought—after the weeks of thrust and parry, after the days of teasing and willful challenges, after the never-ending minutes of negotiation and discussion—she'd thought she'd be ready for this. But she was incredibly, wonderfully wrong. Nothing could have prepared her for this.

Fitz followed his game plan, raising her temperature with a series of tantalizing, torturing nibbles. He brushed and sipped each inch of her face, his fingers caressing her cheeks and his breath washing over her features as his warm body pressed hers deeper into the shavings. He teased and toyed at the edges of a kiss until she thought she would float away with the dust motes or explode with anticipation.

Or scream with frustration.

To her great mortification, a whimper escaped her. And in the next moment, while she still had time for rational thought, she realized she should have whimpered sooner, because his control snapped and the world erupted in flames.

CHAPTER TEN

HIS MOUTH CLAMPED DOWN, hard, over hers, and his tongue delved deep inside, and she groaned and wrapped her arms around his shoulders, arching up into him with the desperate need to meet his urgency with her own. He shoved a knee higher between her legs and she tossed a leg over his hips, and they wrestled and rolled once, twice, again through the shavings.

Now she was on top of him, tugging at his shirt and grasping at his hair, crushing her lips against his and trying to get close, closer, wanting more, so much more. Now he was over her, shoving one hand beneath the back of her waistband to knead her and draw her against his grinding hips, while his other hand cupped the back of her head to hold her trapped beneath his clever, ravaging mouth.

And oh, as glorious as it all was, it wasn't going to be anywhere near enough.

She twisted against him and sucked in the scents of shavings, manure, sweat and seduction. Her boot bumped the side of the stall, and she heard Pete stomp and nicker. Fitz dragged her to her knees, never losing contact with her mouth, and reached behind him to fling the fork through the door, where it clanged against the wood floor. His hands streaked, rough and frenzied, over her hips, her back, her belly, up the front of her shirt to her breasts, where his thumbs flicked across her nipples straining against the cotton shirt. She groaned and arched back, and they fell, sprawling in a greedy, breathless tangle of legs and lips.

On and on it went, heat and madness and the occasional choked and muffled laugh, until one of his smiles broke the suction and they fell away from each other, gasping for air.

He raised up on one elbow, pressed against her side, and stared down at her. "Well," he said. "That ought to hold you until the next one."

She dragged in a deep breath. "In your dreams, Kelleran."

He grinned and gently ran a fingertip down the slope of her nose. "I'm thinking that's just where you'll be, Ellie Harrison."

Oh, my. She hadn't been expecting that. Not that she'd been expecting anything, really, but if she had been expecting something from this man, it wouldn't have been anything quite so gentle or sweet. Not after that whirlwind they'd kicked up between them.

He'd kissed her brainless, driven her right to the edge of restraint, and now, while her body and mind were still reeling with passion, he'd sneaked in under her defenses and taken her down with soft affection and quiet, honeyed talk. She drew another shaky breath and tried to shove all of it back into the proper perspective.

The only problem was, finding the proper perspective on Fitz Kelleran was getting to be more and more of a puzzle. And she detested uncertainty.

She set her chin and lifted a knee toward a sensitive spot. "Off, Kelleran."

He rolled to the side as she scrambled through the fluff to find her footing. She slapped at the shavings clinging to her clothes and pointed at him. "Remember, a deal's a deal."

"Of course."

"A week."

"Tuesday. Got it." He stretched back on the pile in a lazy pose, his head cradled in his hands, and gave her an arrogant smile. "Think you can manage?"

"Oh, I think so."

She was mortified to find that her legs were still shaking as she staggered out of the stall.

TWO DAYS LATER, ELLIE STEPPED into the stirrup and swung up on Tansy to wait for the cue from Van Gelder's assistant. Behind her, the cattle in the temporary pen shuffled and shoved for another chance to be the first to charge out the gate when Brady swung it wide.

It had been a long morning. Four times now they'd set the cattle loose to drive them over the short rise heading away from the river, only to round them up and turn them back into the tiny corral while everyone waited for the director and crew to check the shot in the monitor. Each time the mock cattle drive was set in motion, it got harder to convince the herd to reverse direction and crowd back through the narrow opening into the pen. And with every minute lost on retrieving them, it was harder to convince the director things were going as well as they could under the circumstances.

She hoped they'd get this shot by lunchtime. The changes in the shooting schedule to accommodate Nora's absence were affecting normal ranch business. Cutting this bunch of heifers from a high pasture herd had stolen some of the ranch crew from their work on the new alfalfa field at a critical time.

Will loped up from behind the cameras and reined in beside her. "This had better be the last go-round for a while," he said. "I don't think those critters are going to let us pen them up again, especially that ring-eyed heifer with the kink in her tail. She's getting real spooky, and too many of the others are following her lead."

"I noticed." Ellie shifted in her saddle and glanced back at the pen. "They're thirsty, and the river's too close to ignore."

Will spun Ghost around and squinted up at the sun. "The camera crew are talking about switching over to the other side if we can't get this right. Something about lighting and angles and trampled-down grass. Danged if I can make out what all the fuss is about."

There was the signal. Brady swung the gate wide, and Jody whooped and waved her hat from the other side. Ellie tapped her heels to Tansy's ribs and loped down toward the river to head off any strays who might cut from the herd in search of water, careful to keep her head down and out of camera range.

A series of shouts alerted her to problems on the rise above, and the thundering ground beneath her warned that a whole lot of trouble was headed her way.

She wheeled her mount around and galloped along the rocky river's edge, heading for the break in the steep undercut along the bank, figuring the cattle would take the easy way down. A few yards ahead of her, Will, hunched over Ghost's withers, cleared the edge of the bank in a leap down to the belly-deep water and fought the current to bring his horse around in the slippery riverbed.

Seconds later, the ring-eyed white face swung into view above them and swerved along the sharp bank shoulder, but the heifer behind her was following too close and running too fast. She rammed into the ring-eye from behind, and both animals slid and scrambled down the slope, straight toward Will. Ghost reared up, and Will waved his hat to head them off, but the cows stumbled into the water, lost their footing and knocked the horse back. Will went flying.

"Will!" Ellie twisted Tansy out of the way, giving her space to bunch up and make a leap to safety, but the ring-eye shot out a leg out and tripped up the little mare. Tansy slewed sideways, and Ellie came out of the saddle and slammed into the water. In the next moment, another dozen white faces tumbled over the bank and scrambled into the riverbed, sending water flying as they headed her way.

Ellie staggered to her feet and lunged toward the far side, clawing at the water. Her drenched clothing sucked and pulled at her as she struggled to escape the big bodies and trampling hooves of the mob-crazed animals bearing down on her.

Someone grabbed her shirt from behind, and she was half lifted, half dragged out of their path. She recognized Hannibal's legs beside her, and Fitz yelled, "Step up!"

She shoved a foot onto the stirrup and grabbed for Hannibal's mane as Fitz hauled her against his chest. Beneath them, the big horse slipped and sought for purchase on the rocky bed, shuddering with every impact of the cattle churning the water around them.

"Hold on!" Fitz kicked and sawed at the reins, urging Hannibal into gaps between the shifting bodies of the heifers. They plunged into deeper water, floating free of the melee, and finally climbed the opposite bank of the river.

"God." Fitz crushed her to him in a breath-robbing embrace. *"Thank God,"* he murmured in her ear.

"Mom!"

"I'm okay," Ellie called as she kicked free and slid down to the ground. Jody barreled into her, and she gave her daughter a reassuring squeeze. "Where's Will?"

"Over here!" yelled one of the stunt riders.

Ellie stumbled along the bank, battling back the fear constricting her throat. "How bad is it?"

"He's okay." The rider knelt in the sandy river bar beside the foreman. "Just got his wind knocked out."

She fell to her knees beside him, dragging in air, willing him to do the same. A grimace twisted his face, and then he groaned.

"Will," she said. "Where are you hurt?"

"Kinda hard...to pinpoint...just one spot...right at the moment."

She looked up as Jody wrapped her arms around Fitz and buried her face against his side. He rubbed a hand over her shoulder in a casual, natural gesture of comfort, his gaze fixed on Will. "He can't be hurt too bad if he can't be more specific about it."

A sob escaped with Ellie's shaky laugh, and she rubbed the back of her hand under her nose. "Guess not."

Brady reined up beside the little knot of onlookers and jumped down to the sand to gingerly run his hands over Will's body. "Anything feel like it's broken?"

Will started to shake his head and winced. "Not broken, I don't think. Just kinda shook up...where I must've hit first. My shoulder. My head."

"Think we can help get you up on your feet?" asked Brady.

"Think I'd appreciate the assistance," said Will, "if you don't mind."

"Hey!"

Across the water, above the ruined bank, a couple of crew members waved at them. "We got the shot," one of them called. "Lunch break."

"They got the shot," said Fitz, his voice tight and cold. He gently removed Jody's grip on his soaked and filthy costume shirt and stooped to collect Will's hat from the ground. His expression was lethal as he glanced up at the retreating film crew. "Good to hear they managed to keep things in focus this time around."

THE FOLLOWING EVENING, Fitz rolled his shoulders to shake off the nervous twitch between them and raised the horseshoe knocker on the Harrison's front door. He hadn't crashed a party for years—and fast-talking his way past the Miramax security at the Biltmore might have been easier than getting himself invited to Jody's twelfth birthday party.

He was as nervous as he'd been all those years ago, and he'd spent nearly as much time getting duded up. He'd showered and shaved, dressed carefully but casually and slapped on a little cologne—just a little. He even carried a bribe wrapped in rainbow paper and a giant pink bow.

Maybe the reason his stomach back-flipped with every clunk of the knocker on the big oak door was that his motives for being here weren't exactly clear. He could easily slip the package to Jody on the sly, but for some unnatural reason he was drawn to be a legitimate part of this event.

Mostly, though, he wanted to make a point—or score a point—with Jody's mom. Just what that point was, and whether anyone was keeping score, he hadn't figured out yet.

The door swung wide, and a striking, leggy blonde with Jenna's soft blue eyes and Ellie's cool demeanor leaned a shapely shoulder against the jamb. Her linen outfit and beaded sandals were city chic. "You must be the actor," she said.

"And you must be the aunt." He waited for an invitation to enter, but she held down the fort with the formidable quirk of one brow.

Damn. Why did half the Harrison females have to be so prickly?

"Who is it, Magg—oh, Fitz!" Jenna shot her daughter an exasperated look and waved him into the foyer. "What a nice surprise."

"Hello, Jenna." He bent to brush a kiss against her cheek. "I understand someone's celebrating a birthday here tonight."

"Is that why you're here? Jody will be so pleased." She closed the door behind him. "Have you met Maggie?"

Maggie's smile dared him to tattle on her poor manners. "Yes, just now," he said diplomatically.

"I'll go spread the word about our surprise guest," Maggie said. "See you later, Fitz."

"Is that for Jody?" Jenna took the package from him. "You didn't have to do this."

"Yes, I did." He shoved his hands into his pockets. "I know better than to forget a lady friend on her birthday."

"I'm sure she'll love it. I hope you can stay for dinner."

"I don't want to impose." He glanced over her shoulder at balloons and streamers strung about the entrance to the next room, and that twitch between his shoulder blades started up again. "Especially on a family occasion."

"Family is a pretty loose term around here." She led the way through a wallpapered sitting room dotted with photos and ferns. "And there's always room for one more."

He smiled and tried to loosen up. "All right, then. Thank you, Jenna. Don't mind if I do."

She hesitated a moment before settling a hand on his arm. "I heard about what happened yesterday. With Ellie, down at the river. Thank you."

"There's nothing to thank me for. I didn't exactly stop to think about what I was doing." He wasn't the kind of man to make heroic gestures, because he never took heroic chances. The fact that he'd been consumed by an overpowering urge to act when he'd seen Ellie in trouble was something he preferred to shove deep into his subconscious.

She dropped her hand. "All the same. I thank you."

He followed her into a bright and airy kitchen where a few ranch hands lounged against glossy tiled counters, and she made the necessary introductions and handed him a beer before ducking outside with the gift. The aromas of barbecued chicken and grilled corn drifted in through yellow checked curtains at an open window, accompanied by laughter and the whine of a country tune. Across the room, a wide table held a speckled enamel pitcher stuffed with sunflowers. A long, low slab of hand-decorated birthday cake awaited the main event, its candles listing like drunken soldiers in untidy lines.

The film's set designer couldn't have duplicated the perfection of the homey scene if he'd tried.

He frowned at his beer. Had he been reduced to this—to viewing every homespun scene in normal life as if through a camera lens? Maybe it was time to back out and back off this friendship with Jody and this...whatever it was he had going with her mother.

"Fitz?" asked a familiar female voice in a familiar, suspicious tone. "What are you doing here?"

Damn. He'd missed his exit cue and was stuck onstage. He turned to face Ellie—and his doubts drained through the soles of his Gucci loafers.

She stood, arms akimbo, at the foot of a narrow service stairway, wrapped in a soft gauzy top that draped over her jeans, with sparkly drops at her ears and a delicate, glittery chain around her throat. Her hair was a thick, reddish cloud waving around her frowning face.

Feminine was an intriguing new look on her, but she didn't have the right attitude to pull it off. Funny how all that ambivalence about the issue just added to her allure.

"*Eleanor Louise,*" said Jenna as she swept back into the room. "Fitz was kind enough to take the time from his busy schedule to stop by with a present for Jody, and I've asked him to stay."

Ellie's cheeks flooded with pink, and Fitz almost felt sorry for her.

"Thank you for coming," she said, self-consciously twisting the lace-edged hem of her top.

"You're welcome," he said with a wicked grin. "*Eleanor.*"

"Fitz!" Jody dashed past her mother and skidded to a stop in front of him. "Are you here for my birthday party?"

"That's the rumor."

"All right!" She raced back toward the stairs. "Wait'll I tell my friends."

"Friends?" he asked.

"Five preteen girls." Ellie's lips spread in a wicked grin of her own. "Big fans of yours, I'm sure."

"Sounds like fun," he said and took a fortifying gulp of beer.

ELLIE WONDERED, for the hundredth time that night, what Fitz Kelleran was up to. There had to be some agenda behind those dazzlingly innocent smiles he cast her way every so often.

So far she couldn't fault his behavior. He deflected the focus from his presence and tried to blend in—as much as it was possible for a Hollywood superstar to fit seamlessly into a Montana preteen's birthday party. And what he couldn't accomplish with those smooth social skills he pulled off with that famous charm. He traded barbs with Maggie and winked at Jody and her friends. He even took a turn at the ice cream churn.

Slices of pie and cake were dolloped with Jenna's homemade peach ice cream, and Jake helped Brady pile a bushel of presents in front of the birthday girl. The guests oohed and aahed over each card and gift, and through the little ritual, Ellie sneaked glimpses at Fitz, wondering what he made of it all. He seemed to think it was terribly fascinating and plenty of fun.

"This one's from Fitz," Jody announced, and the partygoers stilled. He shifted on the picnic bench, looking slightly uncomfortable with the sudden attention.

"Well, go ahead," said Maggie. "Open it."

"The card first," Ellie insisted.

Jody read the generic greeting card rhyme to the crowd and finished with an equally generic, "To Jody, from Fitz and Burke."

"Burke's in town tonight," said Fitz. "He sends his good wishes."

"Thank you," said Jody. She stared at the package, looking as if there were a few nerves mixed in with her anticipation.

Ellie swallowed, as anxious as her daughter. There could be anything under that wrapping. Something appropriate for a twelve-year-old girl or some extravagant Hollywood bauble she couldn't possibly accept. Or the kind of odd, awkward item two childless bachelors might choose. "Let's see what you got there."

Jody set the big bow aside, carefully unwrapped the pretty paper and gasped. "Oh, *Fitz*."

"What is it?" asked Chico, as breathless as Jody.

"It's a camera." Jody looked up at Fitz with amazement and joy and her heart in her eyes. "A digital camera."

The smile he returned was so shy and tender it pierced clear through Ellie, too. How could her daughter deal with a grown man who could wrap a woman around his finger like this? He'd crush her young heart and leave it flattened in the dust before this film shoot was over.

Jody pulled the tiny camera out of the box and held it up for everyone to see, and Ellie slumped back against her chair. Her ancient office computer probably wouldn't be able to handle the digital chores, and her printer didn't work in color. Well, hell. It looked like this present of Fitz's might prove to be a whole lot of trouble and expense.

"There's something else in the box," said Maggie. She passed an envelope to Jody.

Jody took it and smiled at Fitz. Her smile dissolved when she saw what was inside. "Oh, *Fitz*," she whispered.

"What have you got there?" asked Jenna.

"It's a gift certificate." Jody glanced at Ellie. It was obvious from her expression that Fitz and Burke had exceeded the legal gift-giving limit, even one that might be extended slightly for millionaires. "To Ellison's Office Supplies," she added.

Ellison's Office Supplies—and computer-related necessities. Leave it to Burke to be thorough, thought Ellie.

"Thank you, Fitz," said Jody with a brave smile. She might not have shared his acting talents, but she managed to come up with a line of dialogue that hit all the right marks. "You knew just what I wanted."

CHAPTER ELEVEN

WHEN MOST OF THE PARTY GUESTS had departed and the cleanup operations were under control, Jenna crossed the side yard and slipped down a narrow gravel path to the tiny foreman's cabin. She rapped a quiet knock on the front door and then stepped over the threshold into the darkened living space.

Shadows shrouded familiar forms. There, lining the long wall beneath the peeled-log ceiling beams were the oversize shelves she remembered, crammed with books of every size and description. Will often explained that he was never really alone, not when he had all those characters in all those stories to keep him company.

A massive chair hunkered down in a dim corner, one arm draped with the night-faded stripes of an old Navajo blanket. And there were his photos, dark rectangles rimmed in dull silver, ranged along a fir mantel planted in the river-rock chimney. Pictures of the Harrisons—Ben and herself, Ellie and Tom, and Jody, proud and straight on her first pony. Only one of Will, posed with Tom as they held aloft their team roping silver belt buckles. Nothing else, nothing of the people he came from.

"Will?"

"In here." A triangle of light streamed from his open bedroom door to slant across the rough-sawed plank floor like a beacon.

She didn't move from her spot near the front door. "I brought you some birthday cake and ice cream."

"Come on back, Jenna."

She moved through the gloom of the front room to pause in the nimbus of his wide doorway, filled with sudden doubt about all her neighborly intentions. She reminded herself that this was merely a sick call on an injured hand. Just cake and ice cream and Will.

Oh, but look at him, sighed the girlish voice in her head. Look at all that smooth, dark skin, at the stark and exotic contrast against the plain white sheet folded at his waist. Look at his wide chest and long arms, so curved and roped with muscles and tendons.

She looked at the man who'd scrambled her thoughts and set her pulse to pounding with a tender, searing kiss a handful of days ago, and she wanted more of the same.

"Is that your peach ice cream?" He smiled at her. "And Jody's favorite chocolate cake with buttercream frosting?"

"Yes."

He set the book he'd been reading on a nightstand with the precise movements of a man avoiding pain, and then he eased back to the pillows stacked against the simple iron bed frame. "Will you bring it to me?"

She walked to the edge of his bed as his smile spread in a straight white slash across his dark, lined face. He'd always had a slow, rare treat of a smile.

"How are you feeling?" she asked.

"Right now, I'm feeling mighty fine." He reached for the plate in her hand and set it beside the book, never taking his eyes from hers, and circled her wrist with his fingers. "In fact, now that you're here, I'm edging close to perfect."

He tugged, gently, and pulled her nearer. "There's only one thing that could make me feel like I'd reached that point."

"Will, I—"

"Jenna," he whispered. "Kiss me."

He drew her down to nestle beside him on the old quilt. She told herself she didn't want to hurt him by pulling away— that's why she didn't resist.

She let him lift his hand to stroke through her hair, let him spread his fingers like a fan across her scalp, let him guide her mouth to his, and she had no excuses for what she was allowing, for what was happening.

"Kiss me," he breathed against her lips. He paused, waiting, and with her next breath she pressed her mouth to his.

She flowed into the kiss, buoyed up on a current of soft, warm sensations, spinning in a torrent of sharp, hot emotions. The cabin, the cake, her purpose for being here, the reasons why she shouldn't be doing this—everything dissolved with the reality of Will's lips moving over hers and the mingling of their breath. She dissolved, too, and reformed, becoming the woman hidden beneath her skin, the woman who remembered what it was like to be desired, what it was like to coax a man's arms to come around her.

She leaned slowly, carefully against him and reveled in the tension of his arm as it circled her waist. She was young, and vibrant, and more herself than she'd been in years, and she poured it all into this one kiss. She became the Jenna she was inside, in the deepest corner of her heart, in her secret self. The Jenna she saw in his eyes.

He moaned and shifted beneath her, but she knew he was past pain, past care, and that she was the one who had taken him to that place. She sank deeper into the kiss and joined him there.

FITZ HUNG AROUND AFTER Jody's party broke up, watching and waiting for an opportunity to catch Ellie alone. He grabbed his chance as she cleared the last of the party leftovers. "Ellie. Got a minute?"

"Mmm-hmm." She lowered an oversize tin tray near one end of a folding table and began to pile on condiment containers, cups and the odd piece of silverware. "I was hoping to catch you before you left, anyway."

"I'm in no hurry." He added plastic salt and pepper shakers to the tray.

"You don't have to do this," she said.

"I don't mind."

They worked in silence for a few minutes, ferrying dinner items to the kitchen. She gathered and loosely folded the checked tablecloths as he dumped the salty slush from the ice cream bucket over a gravel path.

"What's on your mind?" she asked.

He slipped his hands into his pockets. "I just wanted to make sure Burke and I didn't offend you with Jody's gift."

"Burke?" She dropped the cloths on one of the tables and took a seat on the bench. "I'm still trying to figure out who played what part in this."

"The camera was my idea."

"And it was a good one, as you saw for yourself. Jody said you knew just what she wanted."

"Yeah, well…" He shrugged. "I came up with the idea, but Burke took care of everything else. The card, and the paper and the bow, and…everything."

"Everything." Ellie smoothed her top where it draped over her thighs. "Like the gift certificate?"

"Okay, maybe that was my idea, too. I asked him to

make sure she had everything she needed. You know, like batteries."

"Batteries."

"Lots of things need batteries." He shifted from one foot to the other, needing to find his balance. "And...some other things."

"Things like a spare memory chip for the camera, and a printer to make the photos, and the special photo paper. And a computer to run the software, and—" Ellie waved her hand in a circle in the air. "All kinds of things. Expensive things."

Fitz knew his smile would be a weak and pitiful thing, but he pasted it on anyway. "Funny how things add up."

"Ha, ha," said Ellie.

"Are you going to make her give it back?"

She rose from the bench and collected the pile of cloth. "I haven't decided yet."

"Ellie, wait." He caught her arm. "I didn't mean—"

"To offend me." She stared down at the linens in her hands. "I know."

"I only wanted—I wanted to give her something nice. Something I thought she'd enjoy." He released his hold on her. "I don't have a lot of practice at this. I guess things got a little out of control."

She bit her lip and shifted her gaze toward the house, where amber evening light filtered through lace curtains. A song about cheating women poured from an upstairs window, and the murmur of voices drifted through the back porch door.

"Ellie." He reached for her hand, but then he remembered their crazy agreement and let his arm fall to his side. "It's different for me. I think you and Jody understand that."

"Oh, I understand it all too well."

She sighed and set her bundle back on the table. "It

hurts a little, you know, not to be able to give her every-thing I'd like to. I tell myself it's good for both of us, that it keeps me working hard and keeps her from taking things for granted, but every so often something happens that pokes at the sore spot. It makes me sore," she added with a tiny shrug.

"I'm not competing with you."

Her chin came up at that. "You couldn't if you tried."

"I know." He searched for a way to maneuver past her de-fensiveness. "I may have more money than most people, but I've tried not to let it set me apart. Deep down, I'm still a simple man with simple tastes."

"Like a beachfront home in Malibu."

"I have to live somewhere, and it's a good investment."

"And your pick of models and actresses to date."

"Those are the women I meet at work."

"And a garage full of classic sports cars."

"An adolescent fantasy played out when I was ten years younger," he said. "The last car I bought was a truck."

She tilted her head to one side. "Leather upholstery? Fancy sound system?"

He tossed out his arms in frustration. "Okay, you've got me. I'm spoiled rotten, clear through to my worm-eaten core."

She gazed beyond him, into the dusk. "You've worked hard for what you've earned. What you choose to do with it is none of my business."

She turned to the side and fingered the tablecloths. "We're worlds apart, Fitz. I don't know if you can understand what that camera and all the trimmings represent to me, in terms of how many head of cattle sold, how many man hours squeezed out or scrimped on to squirrel away the funds. How we have to prioritize our lists of nonessentials. Or how sometimes, in the bad times, we have to prioritize the essentials, too."

He opened his mouth to speak but realized he didn't have anything to say.

"I'm not being critical when I say you can't understand my life here," she said. "That's just the way it is."

One of the ranch dogs darted by, barking at an invisible intruder in the bushes. From the other side of the house, someone called a farewell, and a car door thumped shut.

She rubbed her hands over her arms. "You and Jody have gotten pretty close lately."

He shifted and leaned to look her straight in the eye. "I'd never do anything to hurt her. You've got to know that much about me."

"There are all kinds of ways to hurt a person, Fitz."

"It's just a camera," he said, floundering.

"It's a lot of time and attention from an attractive, exciting man. The kind of man a young girl might spin a few fantasies about."

"It's not like that. I don't—"

I don't what? He'd stumbled into something a little like quicksand here. Burke had tried to warn him, but he'd gone ahead and stepped right into it.

He raised his hands, grasping at straws. "I don't know what to do. What to say."

"To me? Or to Jody?"

He curled his fingers into fists and crammed them into his pockets. He didn't have the right words to express what he was feeling for either of them, because he wasn't sure exactly what his feelings were. Friendship? Attraction? A strange kind of affection? How could he define these things when the edges and boundaries kept blurring and shifting?

How could he justify taking the time to purchase a camera

and crash a party, to linger over cleanup chores when he had a dozen more important, more essential things to do with his time—things like making business calls and studying lines? He'd told himself a dozen times to avoid getting involved with a complicated woman, and this kind of complication was exactly the wrong thing to get involved in right now.

He stared at Ellie, at her dark eyes glinting with gold in the twilight and her shadowy hair waving around that delicate, foxy face. Had he thought he was sinking in quicksand? Hell, he'd already sunk in up to his neck. He was mired so deep he might never get unstuck and uninvolved. How and why it had happened didn't matter anymore. All he had to do now was find a way to survive.

"I don't know what to say," he said again.

She shifted closer and looked up at him, and she seemed to peer straight through him and out the other side. "What do you *want* to say?"

"That I care about your daughter. Very much. If that's all right," he added.

"She deserves to have people care about her."

"Yes, she does." He quirked one corner of his mouth up in his get-out-of-jail-free grin. "She also deserves a digital camera with all the trimmings."

"Yes, I believe she does."

He chuffed out the breath he'd been holding. "Okay."

They smiled at each other, and he was ridiculously relieved and grateful for this one small, special thing they shared in the midst of all the things they didn't.

Gradually their smiles faded, and the comfort seeped out of the space between them as something else flowed in to take its place. Something intense, something male and female.

Above them, the window closed and the music dulled to a

pulse. The charcoal-scented breeze ruffled the neckline of her soft, filmy top and rearranged her hair along her collarbone.

Slowly, cautiously, he teased a knuckle beneath the strand of hair at the base of her throat, taking great care not to touch her, and slipped it over her shoulder. He slanted his face toward hers, close enough to inhale the faint trace of shampoo. She tipped her head, slightly, to one side, exposing her slim, graceful neck to his lips, so tempting, agonizingly close, and her eyes lowered in a sultry crescent of dark lashes.

He tortured himself by shifting closer, until his leg nearly brushed hers, another step in their erotic dance. He imagined she'd taste of peaches and buttercream frosting, as sweet as summer and as hot as a tumble in the hayloft—or the shavings—at noon.

"Eleanor," he whispered.

Her eyes flickered open in surprise, but then she fluttered her lashes, teasing him back without missing a beat. "Yes, John Fitzgerald?"

He backed away with a grin. "I'd better go."

"And I'd better go check on the girls."

She swept up the tablecloths, and he stepped back to let her pass, wanting her more at that moment than he'd ever wanted another woman. He was sure of it. "Good night, Ellie."

"Good night, Fitz."

"Say good night to Jody for me, will you?"

She turned and shot him a witchy smile over her shoulder. "Yes," she said, "I will."

I GUESS THINGS GOT A LITTLE out of control.

Ellie tossed her pencil down on her office desk the next morning and buried her face in her hands as Fitz's voice echoed in her mind, taunting her. Things were a little out of control, all right. Her daughter's welfare, her ranch business, her personal life...

She glanced up at the rasp of a boot heel on the wood floor and was surprised to see Will standing in the doorway. "What are you doing out of bed?"

"Looking for my paycheck."

"I would have brought it over."

"Maybe I wanted to be dressed and standing when I took it from you."

She studied him closely, checking for signs of concussion.

"Stop looking at my eyes like that," he said. "They match up just fine, right on either side of my nose."

"Okay." She lifted a stack of envelopes and pulled his from the bottom. "Here it is. Better hope I can wrangle another payment from Kagan or this might be the last one for a while."

Will carefully lowered himself into one of the scarred leather chairs facing the desk. She decided to ignore his slight wince.

"What's the holdup?" he asked.

"Some song and dance about the rescheduling." She rubbed at the tension headache behind her brow and tried not to wince herself. "I explained that the rescheduling affected us, too. It's added thousands to what we budgeted for—hell, at this point, I'm not sure the contract's worth the paper it's written on. And in the meantime, he's not answering his phone or his messages, and he's got all his assistants and secretaries giving me the runaround."

"They were running late with the last payment." Will looked down at his hands. "Have they made it yet?"

She sighed and closed her eyes. "No."

"And it would cost more to sue than to wait."

"Can't wait much longer." Ellie fingered the little stack of envelopes. "I got another extension on the line of credit to cover payroll this week. God knows when the bank's going to reach its limit with my begging."

"I s'pose the interest is whittling away at the profits."

"What profits?" She slumped in her chair. "I wonder what Tom would have done. I wonder if he would have taken this whole thing on in the first place."

She smiled and glanced at Will. "It would have been just like him, don't you think? Sometimes I wonder if that's why I did it. For Tom, in a way."

"Tom isn't here." Will's words hung suspended between them in a long, tense silence. "You did it. If it's a failure, it's your failure. And if it's a success, then that's yours, too."

"You're right," she said, straightening in her chair. "It's mine. Every bit of it."

She picked up the paychecks. "If you're up to it, you can distribute these and set the men to work today. I have a few phone calls to make, and I'm not going anywhere until I get through to someone with answers."

FITZ RAISED HIS HEAD from the dusty set road, squinting at film villain Nick Berluzzi as he swiped at the fake blood trickling from the corner of his mouth. "Bet you're thinkin' you got me beat, Danner." He spat and started to rise, staggering a bit off balance as he favored one knee. "But if I was you, I wouldn't be puttin' any money on it just yet."

Van Gelder watched the feed on the monitor and nodded his approval. "Okay, that's it for now. Set up for the next scene."

Burke threaded a path through the crew, holding his cell phone aloft.

Fitz plucked the phone from his hand. "Kelleran."

"Fitz! Jim Barton here. I hear you've been busy up there."

"Not too busy to read your script, Jim." Fitz headed for a bit of dappled shade and relative privacy across the road. "It's a good one."

"I didn't call to press you for an answer on that project. I figure Myron's been doing enough of that for both of us."

Fitz joined the director in a friendly chuckle over Greenberg's methods of persuasion. "He knows how to earn his keep."

"Just wanted to touch base with you myself," said Barton. "Let you know how much I'd like to work with you again. It's been a while."

"When did we wrap on *Knight Errant*?" asked Fitz about the forgettable costume drama. "Eight years ago?"

"Nine."

"Time flies." And both of them had moved on to bigger and better things, thank God.

Barton paused, probably hoping a little sentiment would sift into the silence and soften Fitz up for whatever pitch might be coming. "I hear you've been shopping for a producer."

The Virginian. What had Barton heard? What did he want? "Rumor has it," said Fitz.

"I hear Lila at Warner likes what she's seen."

Interest. That was definite interest in his voice. God, if Barton wanted a chance at it….

The two gold statues on Jim Barton's mantel proved few people could tell a story better on film. He'd made a career of taking quiet, intimate tales and turning them into blockbusters. And, at its core, *The Virginian* was an intimate story of love and betrayal. If Barton took it on, he might choose to narrow the scope or restructure the narrative…and he'd tell the story his way.

His way, not Fitz's.

"It's got potential," Fitz said.

"I'd like to take a look," said the director, "if that's all right."

Fitz struggled against an illogical wave of possessiveness. "I'll have Burke send you a copy."

Even before he flipped the phone closed, his thoughts were racing ahead of the talk, the maneuvers and the deals, running through all the what-ifs. Bigger risks, bigger results.

Elephants over the Alps.

He closed his eyes and tried to refocus on the work at hand before he turned to walk back to the set.

ELLIE LOOKED UP FROM HER LABOR on a new fence line late that afternoon to see Fitz, on Hannibal, loping her way. She pulled off her hat to fan her face and neck as she waited for him to rein to a stop before her.

"Howdy." He flashed one of his famous grins. "I get a kick out of saying that."

She grinned back. "And you do it so well."

"Be still, my heart." He clapped a hand over his chest. "I do believe I just received a compliment from the queen of the butt busters."

She tossed her braid over her shoulder. "I don't know what you're talking about."

"You've been on my case since the first moment you laid eyes on me." He crossed his hands on the saddle horn and leaned over them. "You know, most people try to be nice and make a good first impression when they meet someone."

"I tried to be nice when I first met you." She set her hat back on her head. "But then you got obnoxious, and I gave up."

"Butt buster," he muttered.

"Ass kisser," she mumbled.

They glared at each other for a few moments in mock disgust but couldn't keep the grins from sliding back in.

Trading this kind of teasing with Fitz was the most fun she'd had in longer than she could remember. Whacking away at him and trying to poke holes in that charm was a little like punching at a piñata—a few satisfying thumps, a little harmless damage and plenty of sweet stuff spilling out in the end.

"Putting in a new section of fence?" He slid down and dropped Hannibal's reins on the ground.

"That's the plan."

He hefted Brady's heavy post-pounding contraption and frowned. "Don't you have anyone to help?"

"When I headed out this way, I was in the mood to pound something into the ground." She took a deep breath and let it out on a tired sigh. "I'm just about recovered now."

"Mind if I give it a try?"

She waved at the pile of stakes on the ground near their feet. "Be my guest."

He pulled off Hannibal's saddle, and they settled into a routine that suited the job and each other. She drifted into the pleasure of a daydream or two, but reality kept crowding back in as she remembered, while he pounded posts and pulled wire, that he got paid millions for doing not much more than sitting around and looking pretty. He sure wasn't a hardship on the eyes, not with his long, lean build and the muscles rippling beneath his sweat-soaked shirt.

And God, could the man could work. She hadn't planned on being the first to quit, but her mouth felt as if it were stuffed with fresh cotton. "Thirsty?"

He shoved his hat back and scraped his sleeve over his forehead. "Yeah."

"I've got water." She pulled off her gloves and headed for

the thermos on the ground near Tansy's saddle. "But I've only got one cup."

She offered him a drink, but he smiled and shook his head. "Ladies first."

She shrugged and gulped it down, and then refilled the cup for him.

"How much is in there?" he asked, pointing to the thermos.

"It's nearly full."

"Good," he said, and then he pulled off his hat and dumped his cup of water over his head.

She laughed and dodged with a shriek when he flicked some of the wet her way. "Don't be starting something you can't finish, Kelleran."

His eyes snapped to hers, and they grew hot and dark. She clamped down on a little lick of lust, sorry she'd started something she couldn't finish, either.

CHAPTER TWELVE

FITZ CONCENTRATED ON THE COOL WATER dripping down the back of his neck instead of the arousal pounding through his system. Damn that stupid agreement not to touch her for a week. Well, he only had a couple more days to hold out.

He handed her the cup and watched her refill it, and he tried not to imagine—in too much detail, anyway—dragging her down to the ground, tugging the waist of her shabby jeans down around her boots and sinking into her.

They stacked the tools and resaddled the horses. And then he fell in beside her in an easy jog, swishing through the silver-edged grass and startling the occasional hopper into a whirring leap to safety. The land rolled like ocean swells toward mountains hunkered down behind a rippling haze.

Wide open spaces beneath that famous big sky, balm for a soul like his. This place made his ranch look like a patch of scrub on a studio back lot—worn out, arranged for effect, and false by association. Lately he'd found himself lusting after the land the same way he lusted after its owner.

"Ever think of selling this place?"

She tossed him a knowing look over her shoulder. "Ever think of buying it?"

"All the time." But he didn't usually have so much trouble figuring out a way to get what he wanted. "I'm just not sure I could afford it."

"I'm not sure anyone could," she said after a long pause. "It's not just a place. It's my life. My daughter's life, my mother-in-law's. I couldn't—wouldn't put a price tag on that."

They rode in silence for a mile. Above them, a buzzard glided in its spiral search pattern, looking for an easy meal.

"What did you want to do with your life?" he asked. "Before you ended up doing this?"

"What makes you think I ever wanted anything but what I've got?"

"Doesn't everyone?"

She slowed Tansy to a walk and sent one of her slitty-eyed looks his way. "You have to promise you won't laugh at me."

"I can promise to try."

She studied him for several long, considering moments before shifting in her saddle. "When I was a little girl..." She gnawed on her lip a bit and started again. "The first thing I ever wanted to be was...Miss Longhorn."

"Miss Longhorn?"

"My daddy took me to a rodeo, when I was...oh, I must have been about four or five. There was a parade, at first, with a bunch of cowboys and clowns, and then along came a big, white convertible. And in the back of that car were some of the most beautiful ladies I'd ever seen. One of them had long, blond hair. She was holding about a hundred pink roses, and she wore a crown."

She turned her little mare toward a clump of cottonwoods crowding a wide elbow in the stream ahead, and he followed.

"That crown sparkled like nothing I'd ever seen before," she said. "It caught the lights over the arena and sent them shooting right into my eyes, nearly blinding me with its glory."

He smiled. "Some crown."

"It was something akin to a miracle," she said with a sigh.

"And her gown——her gown was a pale, pale yellow, kind of ivory, I guess, and it floated all around her, and out behind her, trailing back over the car like a cloud. I thought she was a princess, maybe even the Rapunzel who let down her golden hair. I asked my daddy who she was, and he told me she was Miss Longhorn."

The horses stepped into the filtered light beneath the trees, and cool air flowed like liquid over his skin. The cloying perfume of sap and ragweed hung in the shadows.

"I thought if I could be Miss Longhorn," she continued, "and have dozens of pink roses to hold and wear a sparkling crown and a pale cloud dress, my life would be perfect, forever and ever, like my very own fairy tale."

She lifted a shoulder in an embarrassed shrug. "Not a very realistic career choice."

"At least you had high standards." He smiled at her and ducked beneath a low-hanging limb. "You still do, you know."

They followed a nearly invisible elk trail to a slow-moving pool below a fallen tree. The horses bent their heads and sipped while water bugs skated across the marbled green surface and dragonflies darted on opalescent wings around their legs.

"How did you end up here?" he asked.

"My daddy came here for work and stayed all of six months. When he left, I stayed behind. And now I have Jody, and new reasons to stay and hold on to this place. For her."

She gazed at him with her chin in the air and determination in her eyes. "I spent the early part of my life wishing for a home, for a place and a purpose of my own. I never want my daughter to feel like she doesn't have those things."

Fitz studied her features——the slope of her freckled nose, the sweep of her gold-tipped lashes, the curve of her cheeks and the strong line of her jaw—and he decided she was beautiful, too, in her own way. As beautiful as any Miss Longhorn.

As beautiful as any woman he'd ever known. He hadn't been paying the right kind of attention to the right kind of details—the kind of details that shaped the skin from the inside out.

His saddle creaked as he leaned toward her. "And what do you want for yourself, Ellie Harrison?"

"For myself?"

The genuine confusion on her face tugged at him, hard. He admired her, and at the same time, he felt…sad for her. And a little sad for himself, as if he were missing out on something he'd never get the chance to know. "That's right," he said. "For you."

"I don't want—I don't need anything. Nothing at all."

"Wanting and needing aren't the same things."

She gave him a steady, shuttered look, and he knew she'd pulled back, just beyond his reach. He wondered how far he'd be willing to stretch to close the gap. The moment hovered between them, thick with questions and possibilities, and then it trickled away like the water beneath the horses' bellies.

"Your turn," she said. "Tell me what you wanted to be when you were young."

He stared down into the water. "I wanted to be a fish."

"A what?"

"A fish."

Hannibal raised his head, and Fitz pulled in the slack on the reins. "Remember that scene in the cartoon version of the King Arthur story, when Merlin helps Arthur use his imagination to become different animals? One of the animals was a fish. Well, I wanted to do that, too. I wanted to be a fish."

Her laugh was a little rusty, a little throaty, kind of sexy.

She didn't laugh often—or enough, he thought, and he was glad he'd tricked her into it.

"You are a fish," she said. "You're just like Arthur—the Arthur in the movie. You use your imagination and your talent to become other people. As an actor."

"Well, I'll be damned." He stared at her, amazed at her insight and a little rattled at the fact that she'd aimed it in his direction. "I never thought of it that way."

"Well, then." She turned Tansy away and started back through the trees. "Now you have."

"Wait a minute." He guided Hannibal to her side, trying to hold on to the connection between them. "Don't stop just when it's getting interesting."

"You mean, now that we're talking about you?"

Ellie touched her heels to Tansy's sides and shot off in a canter. Hannibal's longer stride caught up to Ellie's mount in no time, and they rode together over the next rise, and the one after that, at a steady pace. He recognized a landmark snag a mile or two from base camp, and he wished he could figure out a way to extend the visit.

Ellie reined to a stop. "Down there, on the right," she said, "along that line of willows. See them?"

He leaned close to follow the line of her pointing arm, and saw what she wanted him to see—a half-dozen female elk. "Will they run off, now that they've seen us?" he asked.

"Not unless you do something stupid."

He shook his head. "I just can't catch a break with you, can I?"

"Is that what you want from me, Kelleran?"

An interesting question with a dangerous answer. He let his gaze drift over her again as she sat, straight and still in her saddle. Desire was easy to recognize, but it was only one ingredient in the mix of emotions roiling through him. "I think we both know what I want."

"Me."

"That's right."

"And my place."

"Name your price, Ellie."

"It must be nice to have enough money to snap up every little thing your heart desires. But my home—Jody's home—isn't for sale. And as for that other item on your shopping list…"

She pressed a knee against Tansy's side and spun the mare in a tight half circle so she could face him down with a challenging stare. "You were right," she said. "You can't afford it."

BURKE'S CELL PHONE CHIRPED from the dinette table as Fitz entered his trailer that evening. He checked caller ID and thought about ignoring the call, but since he'd just spent a couple of hours relaxing in the fresh air with a fresh-mouthed woman, he figured even Greenberg couldn't put too big a dent in his good mood. "Hello, Myron."

A long, hot stream of expletives spewed into his ear, followed by some unpleasant attempts at manipulation. To make matters worse, he didn't have the satisfaction of hanging up on his out of control agent—Greenberg beat him to the punch.

He'd been wrong about the dent in his mood.

Burke stepped into the room from the direction of the bathroom as Fitz dropped the phone on the narrow kitchen counter.

"Sorry about that," said Burke. "What did I miss?"

"Nothing. Greenberg. The usual rant."

"He wants you to do Barton's film and forget about *The Virginian*. Preferably permanently."

"Like I said—you didn't miss a thing."

Fitz pulled a beer from the refrigerator, flipped off the cap and took a deep drag. "Barton's script is a sure bet. Probable Oscar bait. And the deal would mean millions more, up front, on signing. More for the next project."

Burke glanced at him in surprise. "You're going to sign?"

"If I do, it'll be my decision." He set the bottle on the counter with a snap. "Mine. Not Greenberg's."

"What are you going to do?"

"I don't know yet. But there is one option that just occurred to me." Fitz smiled with grim determination. "I could shut Greenberg up. Permanently."

A STRANGE, STACCATO PINGING pulled Ellie out of a dream, up through layers of sleep to wake in her shadowed room. Moonlight traced lace patterns through the curtains, and Jenna's peonies on the nightstand beside her filled the room with their honeyed scent. She rolled to her side, too tired to investigate, and her eyes drifted shut.

There it was again—the clicking of gravel tossed against glass.

"Give me a break." She climbed from the warmth of her bed and stalked to the window in time to see another tiny rock ricochet off the lowest pane and clatter down the porch roof shakes to land in the rain gutter.

She flicked the catch, yanked up the window and twisted through opening. "Cut it out!"

"Shh!"

Temper shoved her farther out the window. "What do you mean, 'shh'?"

"Stop yelling." Fitz stepped from behind a lilac bush. He

held a finger to his lips and said in a stage whisper, "Someone will hear you."

She shoved sleep-tousled hair out of her eyes. "What in the hell do you think you're doing?"

He slipped his hands into his pockets and rocked back on his heels. "It's Tuesday."

"What?"

"It's about three minutes past midnight." His smile flashed like white neon in the dark. "It's Tuesday."

"Thank you so very much for letting me know. I'll be sure and verify that fact on my calendar when I get up in the morning." She yawned and raised her hand to the window catch. "Now go away."

"The week's up, Ellie."

A week. One week since his kiss—and open season on the next one. Exhilaration and lust pumped through her system. "Don't move," she said. "I'll be right down."

She tossed a jacket over her cotton gown, tugged on a pair of boots and raced on skidding toes through the silent house. She moved through a waking dream now, her mind filled with thoughts of sweet embraces and heated caresses, and her heart overflowed with the romance of a midnight summons at her bedroom window and a handsome man waiting for her in the moonlight.

Out into the night she ran, her white gown billowing behind her on jasmine-perfumed air, her feet sinking silently into summer-long grass, her entire being concentrating on Fitz's outstretched arms and welcoming grin. Time and motion were distilled in a moment of exquisite anticipation, and then he hauled her against him, his hard body wrapping around hers, his soft hair tickling her nose, his breath exploding in her ear. He swung her in a wide, stomach-tickling circle, and then his hot, impatient mouth found hers, drenching her in liquid heat and unspoken promises.

He ended the kiss with a groan and rested his forehead against hers. "I want you, you know."

"I know." She wrapped her arms around his neck and held tight to the miracle. "But I have no idea why."

"That makes two of us."

She tossed her head back and laughed up at the sky. "Just this once, I'm not going to bust your butt for saying something like that."

"Thank you." He traced a path of kisses along her jaw, the warmth of his lips leaving a moist trail to cool in the night air. She shivered from the contrast of sensations, and he hugged her close and nuzzled the sensitive spot below her earlobe.

"The next time I promise not to kiss you for a week..." he said.

"Is there going to be a next time?"

"*No.*"

His hand dove beneath her jacket and closed over her breast, kneading, the calluses on his palms scraping her nipple through the thin fabric of her gown. She arched against him, twisting, filling his hand, straining closer.

He groaned again. "But hypothetically, if I *were* to promise something insane like that?"

"Hm?"

"Shoot me." He moved in for another deep and drugging kiss. "Put me out of my misery before the misery part, okay?"

"But you won't make another promise like that."

"You do know the meaning of hypothetical, right? When I say that I—"

She reached up and took his face in her hands. "Fitz?"

"Yeah?"

"Shut up and kiss me."

"Yes, ma'am."

And he did kiss her, as only he could, thrilling her down to her toes and back up again, hitting all the sweet spots along the way.

"I did mention that I want you," he whispered against the side of her neck. "Right?"

"Yes."

He nipped at her earlobe. "So…can I have you?"

She exhaled a sigh full of wishes and frustrations as her dream dissolved into reality. "It's not that simple."

"Lady, nothing about you is simple."

She tucked her forehead below his chin. "It's not just me, it's the situation. We're coworkers. I have an impressionable young daughter. We have no privacy. You—"

"Ellie."

"Yes?"

"Shut up and kiss me."

"Yes, sir."

ELLIE HIKED DOWN THE DUSTY track toward the *Wolfe's Range* town set with Will a week later. Too many early morning shots, too many late-night chores, too many production details, too little sleep in between it all. She was close to exhaustion, and yet she was buoyed up on an invisible raft of…joy. That's what it was—impossible, incredible joy.

So many times during the long days she'd look at Fitz, and he'd glance her way, and a special smile would light his face—a secret smile, just for her. Or he'd manage to pass by, conveniently close, and run a fingertip down her arm in that soft and gentle way of his, or he'd whisper something risqué that made her laugh. Or he'd corner her, in some semiprivate setting, to catch her up in an embrace that curled her toes and weakened her knees.

She sighed and tingled over the memory of his most recent kiss and smiled a special, secret smile of her own. She'd been doing a lot of that during the past week, too.

"Maybe you'd better see a doctor," said Will, squinting at her. "Lately you sound like you're coming down with a case of asthma."

"I don't have asthma."

"Too bad," he said, shaking his head. "Might be nice to have a medical cure for what you've got."

"I don't need a cure." She sighed again, an unhappy sound as she remembered how quickly the shoot would end. "What I've got is going to clear up on its own in a couple of weeks."

"Can't come soon enough for me," Will muttered.

"Has Trish been pestering you again?" She tilted her head and batted her eyelashes, eager to turn the tables on him. "A big, strong, brave cowboy like you?"

"Mom!"

Jody darted through a cluster of grips as they drew near the camera boom on its cumbersome dolly. "Mom! Will! Guess what?"

"Jody!" Ellie braced herself as her daughter plowed into her, nearly knocking her off her feet with an excited hug. She stepped back to take Jody by the arms and turn her around. "Where did you get those clothes?"

"It's a costume!" Jody tugged up the suspenders of an oversize pair of old-fashioned work pants. "Sasha gave it to me to try on for size. She's going to shorten these things here, and roll up these pants, and fix the shirt and stuff, and then I'm going to be an extra! I get to walk along the board-walk and look in a shop window."

"What are you talking about?" asked Ellie.

"I'm going to be in the movie, Mom!"

Ellie looked down into her daughter's ecstatic face and battled back a hot spike of anger. "That's...that's great, sweetie."

"Can you believe it?"

"No, I can't." *Yes, I can—and I'm going to kill him.*

"They're even gonna pay me!"

"Imagine that," said Will.

Of course, Ellie thought. In the end, it always came down to money. Some people scrapped and scraped to get their share. And certain others had plenty to dole out on a whim.

Jody's glow faded a bit at the edges. "It's okay with you, right?"

Ellie brightened her smile. "How could it not be?"

"Ellie." Trish jogged over with her clipboard. "We need your signature on this release."

Trish handed over the paperwork and shoved her hands into her back pockets, which thrust out her breasts for better viewing. Will muttered something about a sick calf and stalked off.

"This is a wonderful thing you're doing for Jody," Ellie said as she scanned the brief contract. "Was it your idea?"

"No." Trish lifted a hand to her headset and argued with an invisible crew member.

Jody bounced on her toes, stretching to read over Ellie's shoulder. "See?" she whispered. "See how much they're gonna pay me?"

"It's a fortune," Ellie whispered back. "Very generous."

"It's scale," Trish told them both. "Nothing out of the ordinary. You can sign right here," she said, pointing to a blank line near the bottom of the page.

"It's a lot of money for a twelve-year-old to make for walking up and down a bunch of wooden planks all afternoon," said Ellie. She scrawled her name and handed the clipboard back to Trish. "Who set this up?"

"Fitz said he'd talk to the casting director," said Jody. "And then a couple of hours later Trish took me to see Gran, to see if it would be okay, because we couldn't find you."

"I'll have to thank Fitz myself," said Ellie. "Where is he?"

"He's not in this shot," said Trish. She waved a hand toward the trailers. "I saw him head that way."

"I'd better get back to wardrobe." Jody tossed off the term like an old pro.

Ellie nodded and started up the road, working up a champion fit of temper.

"Mom!" Jody called after her. "Don't you want to come and watch the rest of the costume fitting?"

"Of course, hon. I'll be back in a couple of minutes."

"All right!" Jody dashed back toward the set.

Ellie watched her go, reminding herself to take a moment to be grateful, for Jody's sake, instead of angry, for her own.

But only that one moment. Because, in the next, her anger was too damned big to shove aside.

CHAPTER THIRTEEN

ELLIE STALKED THROUGH THE ROWS of trailers parked in base camp, hunting for the one with Fitz's name on the door. His was one of the larger models, though no fancier than the rest, and displayed the same simple identifying card, hand-lettered in wide black ink and taped to a metal door.

Feeling like a trespasser, she hunched her shoulders and glanced to either side. No one seemed to be in the neighborhood this afternoon.

She stepped on the lowest metal step and knocked, and then backed down to the ground and waited. No sounds came from inside. She hesitated a few moments more before rapping against the curtained door window again. "Kelleran!"

Fitz, feet bare and shirt hanging unbuttoned, opened the door and grinned down at her. "This is a nice surprise."

She glared up at him. "Are you alone in there?"

His smile faltered, just a bit, and then spread, slow and seductive, across his face. "Why do you want to know?"

"I don't want any witnesses to your murder."

He stepped to one side and waved her in with a sigh. "Now what's wrong?"

"What's wrong?" She squeezed past him into the tiny living space and whirled to face him. "What's wrong? What I'd like to know is what in the hell made you think it was all *right* to arrange for my daughter to appear in this movie without my permission."

He shut the door behind him and leaned back against it, his face pokering up in that relentlessly neutral expression she recognized as his personal take on stubborn.

"The opportunity came up," he said, "and we had to move fast if we were going to make it work out for her." He slid his hands into his pockets. "She's real excited about this, Ellie."

"I know she is." Resentment and guilt ricocheted through her and stoked her temper. "I got the full force of it blasted in my face not five minutes ago."

"Sorry you found out that way."

"Me, too." She edged up against him to give him a blast of her own. "Real sorry."

He had the sense to step aside, out of range. "Look, I was just trying to do something nice for her. Something special. What's so wrong with that?"

"You went too far this time, Kelleran." She trapped him in a kitchen corner and aimed a finger at his breastbone. "I decide what's right for my daughter, not you."

He moved her hand aside. "And she has no say in this?"

"She's a minor. I had to sign a paper that says so."

"She's a person."

"A person who has pushed the limits of this situation to the point of disobedience."

"That's between you and her."

She threw her arms wide. "That's my point, exactly."

He edged past her and headed back to the living area, where he lifted a costume hat off the uncomfortable-looking sofa and offered her a seat. She refused with a shake of her head.

"Okay," he said, "I guess we should have waited, and I owe you an apology for that. But I told you—we didn't have time." He relaxed his stance and stuck his thumbs in his front pockets. "I just don't see the harm."

"Why am I not surprised?"

"What's really going on here, Ellie?" He cocked his head to one side. "Afraid I'm going to tempt your daughter away from the life you've programmed for her? A life that has to be lived on a certain patch of ground in Montana, so she'll never stray more than a few yards out of your sight?"

She didn't like the detour the argument had taken. "Don't be ridiculous."

"I'm trying to be reasonable."

"Then stay out of it." She headed toward the door. "Just stay the hell out of our lives."

He moved to block her way. "Is that what you really want? For Jody? For you?"

Yes. No.

She was trembling—from hunger and exhaustion, from an adrenaline overdose and emotional overload.

And oh, God, she was afraid. It wasn't like her to turn away from a fight, but suddenly every motive that had driven her in here turned deserter and fled.

Why did this man have to make everything so difficult?

She didn't need this kind of trouble in her life. She didn't need the charming words and the suggestive glances, or that teasing manner and those melting kisses. She didn't need him; she didn't want him. She didn't, not really.

Oh, but she did.

She wanted to curl up and find solace in a snug, secure place—in Fitz's strong, warm arms, damn it. Why did he have to be the one she wanted to run to, when he was the one she was so upset with? Why did he have to be so good at getting her so riled up, and in a dozen different directions at once?

He shook his head and gently wrapped his fingers around her arms. "*Ellie*."

His sweetness undid her, again. Strength and resolve leached out of her at his touch, and her weakness frightened her more than anything else. She battled her way out of her dark and doubting place and twisted out of his grip.

"I get to decide what I want for myself," she said. "And what I want is for you to stay away from me."

"We have to work together."

"Fine. We'll work. We'll have a working relationship. Nothing more."

She stepped aside and waited for him to move from the door.

He frowned at her. "I don't want you to leave while you're still upset."

"It's too late for that."

"Obviously." He sighed and scrubbed at the back of his neck. "I knew you had a temper, but I didn't realize it could get out of control like this."

His words hit her like kerosene on a campfire. She struggled for control, to prove she still had it. "Are you finished?"

"No, not yet." He headed toward the kitchen and opened the door of the miniature refrigerator. "Want something to drink?"

"No. Thank you."

"You know I would never hurt her," he said. He selected a bottle of beer and closed the door with his hip. "Jody is—she means a lot to me. You know that. I just wanted her to have a part in this, something special to remember. I just wanted her to have a chance."

"A chance?"

"A chance to do something else in her life."

A fresh wave of anger and hurt rushed through her. She told herself she was overreacting and swallowed to ease the tightness in her throat. "Before she ends up trapped on this ranch?"

"I didn't say that."

"You didn't have to. It is ironic, though, considering how much time you spend poking your nose into every nook and cranny on this place."

He pried off the bottle cap and tossed it on the counter. "I didn't realize I was being such a nuisance."

"I didn't expect you would."

That was a nasty little jab, and she knew it. But the pain inside her continued to well up and spew out in hurtful words. "You haven't had much experience not being the center of attention. Makes for an incredibly self-centered person, I imagine."

"A person doesn't have to live life in the spotlight to be self-centered," he said softly and then took a sip of his beer. "It's entirely possible for a person to get so wrapped up in her own prejudices and insecurities that she stops seeing or caring about the wishes of other people."

"You have no right. You have no right to say something like that to me."

"You're right. I don't have that right." He set the bottle down and rested his hands on either side of it. "But I wish I did, Ellie. I wish I had the right to talk to you, about your life, about anything. I wish you wanted to share. I wish...I want us to be friends. To remain *friends*."

She closed her eyes and tried to muster up enough goodwill to meet him halfway and accept his apologies. But she was feeling too raw, and it was too easy to fall back on her standard escape clause. "I've got work to do."

"Yeah, I've noticed. That's some high and mighty work ethic you've got going there."

He shoved away from the counter and shot her a glare that told her a world of hurt was headed her way. "Maybe if you weren't so damned busy setting an example for your daughter, you'd have the time to see what she wants for herself."

"I think I know my own daughter better than you do." She angled her chin up in a defensive move. "She loves this ranch."

"Yes, she does. She loves it more than you realize." He moved out of the kitchen to stand before her. "Because for her, it isn't a burden. It isn't a penance."

She gasped, slashed to the bone, clean and neat. The blood would gush and ooze later, she was sure of it. "That's a terrible thing to say," she whispered.

"Yes, it is, and I'm sorry for having to say it." The muscles along the edge of his jaw rippled with tension. "It must be even more terrible having to live with it. I'm sorry for that, too."

He jammed his hands into his pockets and brushed past her on his way out the trailer door.

FITZ HIKED DOWN TO THE SHADE of the cottonwood trees beyond the stable corral. Where was he supposed to go, damn it? He should have kicked Ellie out. The trailer was his space. She owned practically every other spot outside of it.

Damn the woman. Damn the way she made him care and then shut him out. And damn the fact that he did care—about her, about her daughter, about her oversize shackle of a ranch and all the people on it.

What in the hell was he doing, wasting his time on a miniature harpy with a shitload of obsessions and insecurities? Damn him, too.

He lashed out viciously at a low-hanging branch and nearly stumbled over an exposed root snaking toward the creek. Breaking his neck might solve some of his problems. Or drowning. Or being trampled in a cattle stampede, or getting eaten by a grizzly. Montana seemed to offer so many more options for ending it all.

"Fitz." Burke jogged after him, phone in hand. "Fitz!"

Fitz waved him away. "I'm not in the mood to deal with that thing."

"It's Shelley Speelman."

Shelley Speelman, agent. A tiger lady with a lot of class and a string of A-list clients to match anyone's.

Burke caught up, breathing hard. "If I were on my deathbed," he said, "and my dying wish were that you'd keep a cell phone, and actually leave it on, would you do it for me?"

"Your deathbed?"

Burke handed him the phone. "If you don't agree to use one of these occasionally, it might come to that."

Fitz took the phone and pinched the bridge of his nose with his other hand. "Shelley? Fitz Kelleran. Sorry to keep you waiting... No rumor, it's a fact."

He listened to her sympathy over his supposed rift with Greenberg and her smooth segue into a smoother pitch. Burke moved off a discreet distance, not bothering to hide his disapproval.

Fitz snapped the phone closed and tossed it at his frowning assistant. "What's wrong with you?"

"Are you going to sign with her?"

"Probably won't have to. Once Greenberg hears we've been talking—and I think that'll happen at the speed of sound—he'll come crawling."

Burke hunched his shoulders and scowled.

"What?" asked Fitz.

"This isn't like you."

"What isn't like me?"

"This—" Burke waved a hand toward Fitz with disgust. "This underhanded wheeling and dealing. This isn't your style."

"You're the one who wanted me to exec produce. This is what it would take—wheeling and dealing."

"Not like this." Burke shook his head. "You have the reputation of an up-front guy, Fitz. Don't lose it over this film. Don't let it turn you into a Greenberg clone. It's not worth it."

"If you don't like how I'm handling this, you don't have to listen in."

It was a low blow, and Fitz knew it.

Damn. He was hurting, sliced and diced and neatly double teamed in one afternoon, but that didn't excuse the way he'd lashed out at two people he cared about.

Cursing, he twisted away to kick at a stone and sent it scudding into the creek.

"Maybe I should head back to L.A. for a while," said Burke. "I could use some time to check up on the house and a couple of other things, make sure everything's okay back home."

Fitz stared at the ripples on the surface of the creek. The water dodged and tumbled, but it still managed to stay on course and get where it was going. "Yeah, okay. Good idea. If you think that's the way to handle this."

"I don't know how to handle this," said Burke, and he turned and walked away.

CHAPTER FOURTEEN

THREE DAYS AFTER HER ARGUMENT with Fitz, Ellie shifted from one sore foot to the other. The forced inactivity of waiting around on the set was making her back ache and her eyes cross.

Jody wasn't faring much better, from the looks of it. She scuffed her costume boot against one of the dusty boards on the town set and spun in a half circle, a bored little jig set to some internal rhythm. Around her, adult extras chatted quietly, waiting for the assistant director to give them the order to take their places and run through the shot.

For the fourth time.

"How much longer do you think this is going to take?" asked Jenna. She visored a hand against her eyes and watched Jody hop over a crack on the walk. "I want to get dinner started."

"It could be another minute. It could be another hour. Hard to tell, sometimes," said Ellie. She took a sip from the water bottle she'd brought from the catering truck. "I haven't been able to figure it out, and I've been watching this routine since it started."

"How can they stand it?" asked Maggie.

"I have no idea." Ellie shook her head. "It's my idea of a personal hell. I swear, this kind of thing wears me out more than a shift pulling calves in a January blizzard."

"I can't imagine what it must have been like for Fitz when he was a boy," said Jenna. "Day after day like this, stuck on a movie set when other boys his age were out with their friends."

Ellie didn't want to imagine a younger Fitz feeling as dejected—day after day—as Jody looked at that moment. He had too much energy, too much vitality, too much of the devil in him to keep it bottled up like that indefinitely.

No, she didn't want to think about it at all. It hurt too much. But she looked for him in the crowd of actors and crew members, knowing it would hurt even more when she found him.

They'd hardly spoken since the scene in his trailer. He'd been pleasant enough whenever their work required them to speak to each other, but now she'd seen the differences between Fitz the actor and Fitz the person. And she realized he'd been completely honest, and completely himself, with her from the beginning. Every moment, every conversation— every kiss—had been the real deal.

The Fitz she'd worked with since their argument was a surface Fitz, a three-dimensional version of someone who belonged on a movie screen. Even his voice was different, somehow. It was his voice, his inflection, yet missing...his personality.

The Fitz she'd known had disappeared.

And she missed him, more than she thought it would be possible. She missed her friend.

Because she was watching him, she caught him casting another of his protective glances Jody's way. He'd been checking on her all afternoon, hovering without seeming to hover. He'd beamed like a proud daddy the first time he'd watched her on the monitor, and his delighted grin had pushed and pulled so hard at Ellie's heart she'd thought it would pop right out of her chest.

Damn Fitz Kelleran. Damn him for caring for her daughter nearly as much as she did herself. And damn him for forcing her to examine her life at Granite Ridge.

It had been a rough and raw three days.

"I think we should invite Fitz for dinner," said Jenna, checking her watch. "To thank him for doing this for Jody."

"She doesn't look all that grateful at the moment," said Maggie.

"No, she doesn't." Ellie smiled. "I'll bet her chores are going to seem a lot less burdensome over the next few days, even if they aren't quite as glamorous as all this."

"Just the way our place will seem blessedly boring after this circus packs up and leaves," said Jenna. "Don't you think?"

Jenna was right. Life would sift back into its regular pattern, and they'd all go on from here, just as they were meant to. No glamour, no excitement. It's what she'd been wanting, what she'd been waiting for, from the first moment of the first hassle.

So why was she already wallowing in regrets?

"Yes," said Ellie. "Go ahead and have Jody invite Fitz for dinner. Might as well enjoy Hollywood while it's sitting on our front doorstep."

And she'd have the chance to say some things that needed saying.

FITZ KNOCKED ON THE FRONT DOOR of the big white ranch house. He was hosed down and slicked up again, and his stomach was flipping through the cartwheel routine. Just once he'd like to reach for that knocker without feeling like a salesman peddling a Hoover that couldn't suck up the small stuff.

As much as he hated groveling, he was prepared to do his share tonight—but only his share, and only if Ellie did some of her own.

God, he hoped she'd give him a chance. He missed her, much more than he'd expected he would. So much more than he cared to miss any woman—and that was a problem.

Maggie opened the door, and he stifled a groan.

"It's the guest of honor," she said with a smirk.

"And the family butler," he responded, wiping it off her face.

"Too bad I can't stay." She moved past him, slinging the strap of a stylish bag over the sleeve of a designer top.

"Yeah, too bad."

He turned to see Ellie framed in the doorway. A floaty floral dress coasted over her curves and ended above slender ankles and bare feet.

He stared at her long, pale toes, forgetting why he was there, forgetting for a moment why he had to keep his distance as a wave of heat washed through him.

When had he developed a foot fetish?

"Hey, Fitz," she said in a soft voice.

His head snapped up. "Jody invited me."

"Yes, I know." She flushed prettily and stepped back. "Come in."

He stepped across the threshold and they both paused, staring at each other, for an awkward moment. He braced himself for a scowl or a scold, but her mouth twitched at the corners in a tentative smile.

He stood there, transfixed by that subtle upward tilt of her lips and her scent, as sweet as a flower garden after a spring shower. He inhaled it like a diver coming up for air.

Jody bounded down the stairs and into the entry, her damp hair combed back from her shiny, scrubbed face. "Hey, Fitz."

"Hey, Jody." He held out his hand and she gave it an enthusiastic shake. "How's it going?"

"I'm a little tired."

"Me, too. And hungry."

"Gran'll be glad to hear it."

"Better not keep her waiting," said Ellie.

He followed them into the dining room, where Jenna was lighting slim tapers. A bowl of fat roses was centered on a lacy cloth.

Jody pulled a chair from one of the long sides of the table. "You can sit here, Fitz, across from me."

"This is just a simple family dinner, nothing fancy," said Jenna as she took her own seat and passed him a platter of thick pot roast slices and glistening vegetables.

He decided the best way to play the simple-family-dinner scene was to enjoy the meal and ignore the soft and barefoot woman on his right. Keeping his mouth full would give him a good excuse to keep it shut.

AN HOUR LATER, ELLIE WATCHED Fitz tip back in his chair and rub a hand over his belly as he grinned at one of Jody's remarks. After slowly unwinding during a long and meandering dinner conversation, he looked at ease for the first time in days. More like himself.

It seemed he couldn't hold a grudge any longer than she could hold on to her temper. What a pair they made. She was so giddy over their flaws she wanted to crawl into his lap and lick him up for dessert.

When he followed them into the kitchen with his own

stack of plates, Jenna tried to shoo him away. "This is just a simple family dinner, nothing fancy," he reminded her. Soon he had water splashed across his slacks and a dish towel slung over his shoulder.

Ellie leaned against the island with her mug of coffee and enjoyed the show, watching the tendons and ropy muscles of his forearms ripple above soapy water as he washed and Jody dried. His manner was easy and routine, reminding her of a comment Burke had made about Fitz's passion for cooking. Obviously, the man was more at home in a kitchen than she was.

The man was simply…at home.

It was unfair, she supposed, to continue to find that a surprise. A face and a talent like his should never seem ordinary, and yet their sum was simply…Fitz.

The four of them lingered around the tiny kitchen table, talking and laughing over mugs of coffee and cocoa until Jody yawned, hugely, for the third time. She dragged herself to her feet to go through her nightly routine of wishes and kisses, and wrapped her arms around Fitz's waist in a sleepy, sloppy hug. "Night, Fitz."

The stunned pleasure on his face made Ellie's throat cramp up in a warm knot. He slipped an arm around her daughter's neck and kissed the top of her head. "Night, Jody."

Jenna moved from the table to dump her leftover coffee into the sink. "I think I'm going to turn in, too. Night, Fitz."

"Night, Jenna." He tugged on her hand to bring her close enough for a kiss on her cheek. "Thank you."

Ellie sipped her cool coffee and listened to the frogs chirping in the hydrangeas beneath the kitchen window, waiting for Fitz to say something more, but the tension they'd dammed up during dinner flooded back into the room.

"Thank you, too," he said at last.

"There's nothing to thank me for." She took a deep breath and stood. "Can you stay for a bit? A bit longer?"

His assessing gaze roamed over her features. "Yes."

"Will you step out on the back porch with me?" She set her mug on the table. "There's something I need to say to you."

She led the way through the mudroom and flicked the switch for the light fixture over the back porch door. Fitz stepped outside and strolled to the edge of the porch to rest his elbows on the railing. A dusting of sugar-crystal stars outlined his profile against the indigo sky.

"Did you bring me out here to strip another layer off my hide?" he asked.

"No." She twisted her fingers together and squeezed. "I want to apologize for overreacting the other day."

"You've got nothing to apologize for."

"Don't make this any harder for me than it already is."

He turned to face her, and his grin was a brief slash of white in the long shadow beneath the eaves. "Lady, I don't think you know how to do things any way but the hard way."

She tightened her grip on her fingers and her patience. "Are you going to let me apologize or not?"

"All right." He quirked an eyebrow. "You were about to say…"

"That I'm sorry. Sorry for stripping a layer off your hide." She looked down at her hands and eased her fingers apart. "And I want to thank you for giving Jody the chance to be a part of the film. She was thrilled to death."

"Yeah. I could tell." Another smile spread across his face, scoring his cheeks with deep, dark grooves. "I got a kick out of it, too," he said. "She's a great kid."

"Yes, she is. She deserves to have a thrill come her way every once in a while."

She willed away the tension that crept in by habit whenever she discussed her daughter with him. There was no reason for her reaction—there never had been, not really. "You've become an important part of her life this summer. I appreciate the time and attention you've given her."

He turned back to the porch rail. "I don't need your thanks for that. I told you—I enjoy her company."

"I believe you do."

She moved toward him and edged her hip against the handrail. "How could you stand it—when you were younger, I mean. Acting. The work, the tedium."

He frowned and shrugged, and she bit off her questions. "Sorry," she said. "I didn't mean to pry."

"Friends are entitled to pry a little, aren't they?"

"Is that what we are?" She tipped toward him slightly, drawn by hope and longing. "Friends?"

He stared at her in an odd, searching way. "I don't know what we are. I've never had a relationship like this with a woman before."

He reached out, slowly, and took her hand, and she curled her fingers through his.

"I don't know what term I'd use to describe what we're dealing with here," he said. "I don't make it a habit to kiss a woman I'm in an adversarial relationship with."

"Adversarial relationship?"

"Yeah, that pretty much sums it up."

"Hm," she murmured. "I kind of like the sound of that."

"Why am I not surprised?"

He released her hand and moved to the deeper shadows in the corner. He nudged the wide porch swing hanging there, and the metal chains protested with a low, rusty squawk.

"I spent a rough night last night, worrying about Jody,"

he said. "Sure, I wanted to do something nice for her, but I wanted to do it for me, too. God, the look on her face when I told her—"

A wistful smile flickered across his features and quickly faded. "It was a completely selfish thing I did, when you get right down to it. All I gave her was a chance to experience the work and the tedium. And I should have known better."

"Because of what your parents did?"

He grabbed a chain and lowered himself to one side of the hanging bench. "What I began to understand last night— while I was stripping off the bits of hide you missed—is why my parents did what they did. And I realized my motives were exactly the same."

Had she thought, just an hour ago, that he was an ordinary man? She continued to underestimate him. "But they're not the same. And at least you're trying to figure things out."

He huffed out a cynical wreck of a laugh. "I told myself— I tell everyone—that my parents dragged me from one acting job to another because they wanted it more than I did. The truth is I'm a fraud, not a victim. I could have quit any time."

CHAPTER FIFTEEN

FITZ LEANED FORWARD, with his elbows on his knees, and rubbed his hands together. He hadn't planned on spilling his guts, but it was looking more and more like a night for the hara-kiri routine. Pity, too, because the stars were out and Ellie was in a friendly mood. He should have been making his big move on her instead of reaching for a short sword.

"The truth is, I didn't quit because I like acting. Maybe I didn't like it so much at first, or maybe I liked it for different reasons back then, but—damn," he whispered, "I *love* it."

He fisted his hands. "I've got something big stored up inside me, Ellie, just waiting for me to pull it out and dazzle you all."

"What are you waiting for?"

He glanced up, surprised by her question. Not many of the women he'd spent time with cared enough to dig that deep. "I'm waiting for the right role, I guess."

"Will you find it, do you think?"

"I think I already have."

She slipped into the empty spot beside him. "Tell me about it."

So he told her about *The Virginian*, about the story and the film he thought it could become, about his plans and the deals and the difficulties in bringing it all together. She listened carefully, and asked insightful questions, and her enthusiasm for his vision rekindled his own.

"So, this director who called," she said, "this Barton. Do you want him to direct it?"

"I should. He's good."

She hummed, a throaty and sexy hum, while she thought that through. He waited for the next question or observation, surprised by how much he wanted to share.

"Right now," she said, "it's your movie. If Barton directed it, it would be his."

She'd summed up his dilemma more neatly than he'd managed on his own.

"I can't direct it," he said. "It's too much work, and it would take a lifetime of charm to get through it in one piece."

She shot him one of her slitty glances from beneath her lashes. "You're not nearly as lazy as you pretend to be. And you're not nearly as charming as you think you are, either."

He laughed and stretched back against the squeaky swing. "So, you think I should direct *The Virginian*?"

"I think you could do anything you set your mind to. You just have to figure out what that's going to be."

God, she was incredible—and she made him feel that way, too. She made him feel he could do anything, be anything.

And then she shifted back against him and leaned her head against his shoulder, and his thoughts scattered into the night. He wrapped his arm around her, settled them both more comfortably against the back of the bench and launched them in motion with a shove of his foot.

The swing groaned and squeaked its complaining rhythm, a counterpoint to the croaking frogs. Fat white moths kamikazed the yellow porch light, and the shreds of a breeze sent papery rose petals whirling across the floorboards. Down the road, one of the skulking ranch dogs yapped at a rustle in the dark, and a late-night cluster of film crew laughed over some unknown remark.

He pressed his mouth to her hair and moved his lips over the cool, silky strands. The sound of her sigh floated up to him, and he felt himself slipping into an affection for this woman that grew sweeter and deeper with each moment.

"I should go in," she said.

"Don't. Not yet."

"It's getting late."

He caught her by the hand as she rose, holding her in place. "There's one more thing I've got to say."

He stood and pulled her closer. "It's about that adversarial relationship thing."

"What about it?"

He traced a fingertip down the side of her face. "It's kind of a mouthful."

"I suppose it is." She smiled and wrapped her arms around his waist. "What do you suggest instead?"

"Friendship."

"Hm." She angled her head. "I guess that would work."

"It has to. The way I see it, we're a couple of seriously messed-up people." He kissed her forehead. "You with that temper of yours, and me with my overdeveloped conscience." He dipped and caught her earlobe in a soft nip. "Who else would want us?"

"I have no idea."

He smiled and lowered his mouth toward hers, but she pulled back. "Why *do* you want me?" she asked.

"Maybe I'd better find out."

He tickled his fingers up her spine and slipped the tiny button through the catch at the back of her dress. She shivered and tipped her head back. "What are you doing?"

"Something I've had in mind ever since I saw you at the door in that dress." He trailed his hands down her sides and back up again, skimming his knuckles along the deliciously heavy swells at the undersides of her breasts, torturing them both. "I'm curious about what certain parts of you feel like through this thing. Or under this thing—I'm not picky."

"Fitz." She went up on her toes to brush her mouth against his ear. "Wrong time, wrong place."

"Damn." He refastened the little button and sagged away from her. "You'd think I'd wise up and choose a better setting for my big move."

"You've got a move?"

He straightened and stared down his nose at her. "I've got a few. More than a few. Dozens—no, hundreds."

"Impressive."

"They are."

He flexed his fingers and fought back the urge to seduce her out of her reasonable mode. "I don't suppose you'd care for a demonstration, say…tomorrow night?"

She stiffened. "The Cattlemen's Association Barbecue is tomorrow night."

"Are you going?"

"Yes. I never miss it. But I don't know—"

"If I'd like to go with you?" He flashed his most dazzling smile. "I thought you'd never ask."

FITZ CONGRATULATED HIMSELF on the evening's midsize move as he hiked down the hill to base camp. Making a move on a female friend was something he'd never tried before, but then he'd never had a female friend like Ellie. Besides, tricking her into a date was almost as much fun as some of the other tricks he'd been planning to pull on her.

His good mood dimmed a bit when he saw Burke's rental car parked near his trailer. He was glad they'd smoothed things over during the mutual cooling-off period, but his assistant's return meant it was time to get back to business.

"Welcome back," he said as he let himself into his living quarters. "That was a quick trip."

"Spoken like a man who didn't spend the greater part of the day shuttling from one long line and cramped seat to the next." Burke was wedged into the dinette, hunched over a copy of the script for *The Virginian*.

"I can't believe I'm about to admit this," said Fitz as he swung into the kitchen to grab a bottle of water, "but I actually missed you."

"Only because you forgot to keep your phone with you, or forgot to turn it on when you did." Burke sank back as far as the cramped space would allow. "Six times. Not that I'm counting how often I had to call Trish and ask her to track you down."

"That often?" Fitz dropped down on the sofa and kicked off his shoes. "Well, now that you're back, you can track me down yourself."

"Ah, yes, the one aspect of my employment I most enjoy."

"I just came from dinner with the Harrisons." Fitz fingered the bottle's plastic cap. "Ask me how it went."

"All right." Burke closed the script. "And then you can ask me about my dinner with Barton."

"Barton took you to dinner?"

"He asked me to deliver this." Burke closed the script and shoved it across the table. "He's made several notations in the margins. He'd like to discuss it with you in greater detail, whenever you've an opening. He even offered to take a meeting out here."

Fitz hesitated a moment before pulling the script from the table. "What do you think of Barton?"

"As a director?" Burke removed his glasses and scrubbed at a smudge. "He's in a class by himself. Possibly the best there is, for this kind of material, anyway."

"And that's what I said I wanted. The best."

Fitz stood and walked to the kitchen. "I've been thinking I can do more with this project," he said. "With my career. With my life. That maybe it's time I tried something…more."

Burke shoved his glasses up his nose. "Don't tell me you're having a midlife crisis ahead of schedule."

"Do you think I could do it?"

"I've been the one after you for months to give it a try." Burke eased out of the booth and headed to the door. "Just answer one question. Why would you want to?"

"You mean, why would I want to work that hard?"

Burke's smile was slow and knowing. "That's an even better question."

"You remember a couple of minutes ago," said Fitz, "when I said I'd missed you?"

"Yes."

"I lied."

"FITZ? ARE YOU AS DECENT as you're going to get?"

He opened the trailer door and waved Nora in. "Make yourself comfortable," he said as he backed toward the bedroom, tucking a clean cotton shirt into a new pair of jeans. "We can talk while I'm finishing up here."

"My, my," she said, sniffing at him. "Hot date?"

"Maybe."

She cocked her head to the side and studied him. "Is it that cute little sound tech? The blonde with the sunflower tattooed around her navel?"

"No." He ducked into his room to tug on his boots and checked his shave in the tiny mirror before sauntering out to join her. "Water?"

"If I drink another drop, I'm going to float away, I swear." She sighed and stretched out across his sofa. "I miss coffee. I miss my bladder."

He laughed and bent to drop a kiss on her head as he made his way to the kitchen. "Soon you'll be missing your waistline."

"I can't wait." She spread her hands across her flat stomach. "So, who's your maybe date?"

"Ellie Harrison."

"No."

"Yes." He twisted the top off a fresh water bottle and chugged half.

"Fitz. What are you doing?"

"What do you mean, what am I doing? I've been invited to attend the local Cattlemen's Association dinner with our location hostess."

"She's a widow. And a mother."

He stepped back into the living area and shot a hip against the edge of the table. "I've been warned. More than once."

She narrowed her eyes. "You're wearing Acqua di Gio."

"Yeah. So?"

"That's your seduction cologne."

He aimed the bottle at her. "You know, there's such a thing as knowing too much about another person."

"But I do know you, and that's why I wonder why you're dating Ellie Harrison. She seems like such a nice woman."

He inclined his head in a mocking nod. "Thank you."

"You know what I mean."

"Actually, I don't." He set the bottle aside. "How about filling me in?"

"I just think you should give this situation a little more thought. For both your sakes."

"Because she seems like such a nice woman?"

"Because I know you, hon." She closed her eyes. "I've been so preoccupied, with the baby, and the shoot, and trying to make it through the day without spending most of my time wrapped around the nearest toilet. I should have realized what was going on."

"Nothing's been going on."

"Now that I think about it," she said, ignoring his interruption, "the puzzle pieces are falling into place. I'm beginning to see what I've been missing." She swung her feet to the floor and sat up to face him. "I think you may be more serious about Ellie Harrison than you realize. And if she's serious at all about you, you could both be in for a lot of trouble."

"I know." He smiled halfheartedly. "Believe me, I know."

"Do you?" She hauled herself up and stepped toward him. "If you *are* serious about her, you're going to want to set up housekeeping, like you always do. But I can't picture you holed up out here indefinitely. And Ellie doesn't seem the type to sit on the beach all day—not to mention dealing with the Hollywood snob system and the tabloid press."

He winced as he imagined Ellie and Jody in the tabloids.

"And what about her daughter?" she continued. "I can tell you from personal experience that teenagers can manufacture a living hell for anyone who separates them from their friends for any stretch of time. And I haven't even mentioned the complications of marriage yet."

"Don't stop now, darlin'." He grinned weakly. "You're on a roll."

"The Harrisons aren't the housekeeping kind of people, Fitz. They're the marrying kind. And what if you finally decide that's what you want, too, and Ellie wants more children? You'd make a wonderful father, hon, but are you ready for that kind of commitment?"

He twisted one corner of his mouth in an ironic half smile. "And here I thought I was just going out for a little dinner and dancing."

She crossed her arms and gave him a level look. "I'm only telling you these things because I'm your friend."

He considered passing a personal law against having women as friends.

"I appreciate your concern." He flipped his wrist over and glanced at his watch. "But I don't have time to deal with it right now."

"I didn't mean to preach. But I've seen the two of you together. At first I thought you were just—I don't know, teasing her, like you always do, and she was just teasing back, the way you like. But now that I think about it…"

She narrowed her eyes, studying him again, and he tried not to squirm.

"There's something more there. It's the way the two of you look at each other…." She took his hand in hers and gave it a little squeeze. "It would break my heart as much as it would break yours if you got in over your head."

"Thanks." He squeezed back. "I mean it."

"I know you do, hon."

She leaned in and kissed his cheek. And sniffed at him again, damn her interfering ways.

She stepped back, and he tugged at her hand. "Wait," he said. "Why did you stop by?"

"Oh!" A smile spread, wide and brilliant, across her

gorgeous face. "You remember that nice doctor, the one in town? He agreed to see me today—on a weekend, bless his heart."

She paused for dramatic effect. "I heard the baby's heartbeat."

"God. *Nora.*" He took her in his arms and hugged her, gently. "Let's have a toast. I've got time for a toast."

"A toast?"

"I'll open a bottle of my finest water."

CHAPTER SIXTEEN

ELLIE STABBED THE MASCARA WAND into its tube and swallowed another batch of Saturday night jitters. Why had Wayne waited until the last minute to ask her to the dance? He would have been spared the misery of being turned down, and she could have avoided this date with Fitz.

"You're going to look great, Mom." Jody lounged in the bedroom doorway.

"Thanks," she said, trying to scrape up more black gunk. "Once or twice a year, I like to see if I remember how to do this."

"Wait'll Fitz sees you."

Ellie stared at her reflection in the tiny mirror over her dresser and wondered for the hundredth time what a man like Fitz saw in a woman like her. She chalked it up—again—to his perverse sense of humor.

Jody strolled into the room. "Is this what you're wearing?"

"Why?" Ellie turned and checked the long-sleeved chambray blouse and ankle-length denim skirt draped over her bed. "You don't think I should?"

Jody fingered the blouse. "What about that red sweater Gran got for you last Christmas?"

"It won't stay up on both my shoulders at the same time."

"*Mom*." Jody rolled her eyes. "It's not supposed to."

"Well, I can't relax with that thing slipping and sliding around."

"What about your other skirt? The straight black one?"

"That short one with the slit up the back?" Ellie snorted and turned back to the mirror. "I worry what I'm putting on display every time I bend over in that thing."

Jody flopped on the bed and settled back on her elbows. Ellie could see her daughter watching as she stroked on a little blush. "I thought Gran was taking you out to dinner in town tonight."

"She is. But we're waiting to see Fitz pick you up," said Jody. "I want to watch him do it. I think he likes you."

"I think so, too." Ellie ignored her clenching stomach and smiled at her daughter's reflection. "We've become good friends."

"No, Mom." Jody shook her head. "I mean he *likes* you."

"Well, I like him, too. He's fun to work with."

"*Mom.* Don't be obtuse."

"Where'd you learn a word like that?" Ellie decided the blush made her look like she was coming down with a rash. She grabbed for a tissue and swiped it off.

"On MTV. It's very educational."

Ellie rolled her eyes and turned to face Jody. She swiveled her head from side to side. "Well? What do you think?"

"I think you need more blush."

"Why would I want to look like I've coated myself with a bunch of junk?"

"To let the man in your life know you're making an effort to look fabulous for him."

"Is that what it says in those magazines of yours?"

Jody slanted her a superior look. "At least one of us is trying to be informed about these things."

Ellie brushed on more powder. "Fitz is *not* the man in my life."

"He could be."

"No, he couldn't." She needed to remind herself of that fact as much as Jody needed to hear it. "The only thing we have in common is our work on this film, and that's going to end in another week."

"What about lipstick?" Jody asked. "Got anything red?"

"Nope." Ellie held up two cases. "Pink and orangey-pink."

"The orangey-pink would go great with that red sweater."

"I am *not* wearing the red sweater."

Ellie twisted the bottom of a lipstick case and watched the pinkish cone rise from its little chrome missile silo.

"He could, you know," said Jody. "He could be the man in your life."

Ellie shook her head. "Now who's being obtuse?"

"Not me." Jody straightened. "I've seen the way he looks at you."

"No you don't." Ellie dropped the lipstick and faced her daughter. "Not this again."

"Mr. Hammond looks at you, too. He's stayed for dinner twice now. And he calls you all the time. Gran says he's interested. Just because you're not interested back doesn't mean I wasn't right about him in the first place."

"Well, you're not right about Fitz."

"Oh, I'm right about it, all right." Jody's grin was evil. "He's got the hots for you, big time."

"He does not." Ellie's cheeks were getting warm.

"And you've got the hots for him, right back."

Ellie gasped. "Jody!"

"You do Mom, admit it."

"I'll admit no such thing." Ellie bit her lipstick-free lower lip. There was likely a special corner of hell for mothers who lied to their daughters about the very things they didn't want their daughters lying to them about.

"It's okay," said Jody. "I'm old enough to have this kind of talk." She patted the bed next to her. "Come on, Mom. I think it's time we discussed sex."

Ellie choked on a laugh. "I don't know whether to tan your hide or—well, hell, I can't send you to your room, because you'll probably just pick up another outrageous idea from one of those magazines you've got stashed under your bed."

"They're not outrageous. They're normal, human ideas. You told me yourself sex was a normal, human activity."

"And not something you should be thinking about for a long, long time."

Ellie turned back to the mirror and wondered how she could herd this conversation off in another direction.

"I'm not thinking about it for me," said Jody. "I'm thinking about it for you. And Fitz."

Ellie's cheeks flared like twin stoplights—now she really didn't need that blush. How in the world was she supposed to respond to that last remark, when she'd been sneaking and sniffing around the same thoughts herself?

She grabbed another tissue and started scrubbing. "Jody Lynn Harrison, I swear, I—"

"Ellie!" Jenna's voice drifted up the stairs. "Fitz is here."

"Mom." Jody rose from the bed and stepped in close. "Wear the red sweater. And the tightest pair of jeans you own. And the orangey-pink lipstick. *Please.*"

Ellie closed her eyes and sucked in a deep breath. "How do you feel about all of this—about this date tonight?"

Jody slung her arms around Ellie's waist and gave her a quick, tight hug. "Hopeful."

"It's not real, you know," Ellie said. She slowly swept her meager makeup supplies into her top drawer. "None of it is. A date with Fitz Kelleran is just a kind of fantasy, like something in the movies. You shouldn't be hopeful about things like that."

"Mom." Jody shook her head. "There you go again, being obtuse. Fantasies are the best things to be hopeful about. Everything else just happens, whether you wish for it or not."

Jody walked to the door and paused at the threshold. "Don't worry about a curfew or anything. I won't wait up." And then, with a parting grin, she was gone.

Ellie stared at herself in the mirror, fantasies and realities tumbling around in her mind, making her heart race and her blood heat. She should take the time to deal with her daughter's mixed-up notions, but there was a handsome, charming man waiting downstairs.

I want you, you know.

Well, she wanted him, too, in the worst way. And in the best way, and in all other possible ways, and—well, hell.

Speaking of hell, that was probably right where she was headed for what she was thinking. Straight to her own special corner. Because she was thinking maybe it was time. Time to stop postponing what had been building between them and act on it, if for no other reason than their time together was growing short.

If she wanted to make a fantasy real, first she had to reach out and close her fist around it. It was as simple as that. Everything else—all the complicated things like the morning after, or the one after that, or every morning to come for the rest of her life—well, she wasn't going to think about those things right now. If they wanted each other tonight, they could have each other.

She dropped to her knees, pulled open the bottom drawer and tugged out her red sweater.

THE CATTLEMEN'S ASSOCIATION Barbecue was a smoke-scented, ear-splitting, toe-crunching, elbow-poking crush. The buffet dinner line snaking through the fairgrounds exposition hall didn't appear to be moving, which bothered Fitz no end after he got a whiff of tangy sauce drizzling over spit-turned beef and mesquite chips. He bent down to yell in Ellie's ear. "Shouldn't we go get in line?"

"Don't worry," she said. "There's always plenty for everyone."

She waved at someone across the cavernous room, and the curve of her hip brushed against his thigh. He'd been intensely attuned to her every movement and hypersensitive to her every touch for days now. A good bout of sex would take the edge off this unnatural state of awareness. Too bad that was out of the question now that Nora had dumped that load of crap in the general vicinity of his conscience.

Talk about hitting below the belt. She'd almost crippled his libido.

"Guess they can always go shoot some more food," he said.

"Watch out for the buckshot. It's murder on your teeth."

Her mossy-brown eyes crinkled at the corners and laughed up at him through lashes thickened and sooty with mascara. Her sweater dipped over her left shoulder, and he sneaked another glance at her breasts. It was his expert opinion that she was braless under that nubby red knit. He slipped an arm around her waist and tickled a thumb up high just to make sure.

A tall, darkly tanned man in a checked shirt and a string tie narrowed his eyes at Fitz from across the room. Ellie stiffened and eased herself out of his grasp.

"I've got some people I should say hey to," she said. "Do you mind?"

"Not at all." He stared at the man and tried to place him. The face was familiar. "I'll catch up with you when I can."

She nodded and headed toward the overstuffed shirt.

He fixed on her location and made slow but steady progress in her wake, smiling through dozens of introductions and pumping hands like a politician. And keeping one eye on the man who was leaning in too close to his date, poaching on his territory.

Wayne Hammond. The guy with that white ten-gallon hat. It had to be. Jody's description was right on the money, and nothing else made sense.

Fitz posed for a few pictures and ignored the paparazzi who were fighting for footing just like everyone else. He hoped the novelty of his celebrity would fade soon so he and Ellie could steal some time for themselves.

Something pillowy bumped into his arm and his beer sloshed over his sleeve. "Well, hello there, handsome."

He glanced down through lacquered platinum layers into Tammy Faye Bakker's face. No, not Tammy Faye—her cosmetician.

"Charlene." Ellie reappeared at his side, her smile frozen in a grimace. "This is Fitz Kelleran."

"Well, I know who it is, honey." Charlene batted her eyes at him, and he could almost feel the draft.

He glanced down when one of Charlene's pillows scratched his arm. Sheriff's stars were pinned to the pointy tips of her front pockets. He wondered if they were pinned to the pointy tips underneath and winced. They could be. Charlene looked as if she were feeling no pain.

Ellie slipped a hand through his elbow. "Fitz, this is Charlene Miller. She's married to our local sheriff."

Charlene thrust her stars out for viewing with the naked eye. "Gotta support the law, right, honey?"

She threw her head back and laughed, and nearly lost her balance. Ellie reached out and steadied her. "Where's Howie?"

"He got a call and took off." Charlene leaned in against Fitz's chest. He leaned forward in a defensive move and tipped her back on her heels.

"He's always taking off," Charlene said with a pout, "just when things get interesting, if you know what I mean."

"Yeah." Fitz glanced at Ellie. "Interesting."

She craned her neck around, searching the crowd. "Maybe Dusty can take you home, Charlene."

"Don't wanna go home," she said, sipping what looked like whiskey from her plastic beer cup. "Just got here."

"Have you eaten yet?" Ellie motioned at someone behind them. "Maybe you should have something to eat. Have some coffee."

"Don't want coffee." Charlene threw an arm around Fitz's neck. He could feel her drink splash and seep across the front of his shirt. "Wanna dance. You wanna dance with me, handsome?"

"I don't know how," he said.

Another flash blinded him as he tried to peel her off, and he hoped it wasn't a paparazzi. "These country moves are a little confusing for a city boy," he said.

"Charlene." Ellie pried her loose, although the big blonde outweighed her by several pillows. "Let me find Dusty. He'll call Howie and get you some coffee."

"Don't want coffee." Charlene staggered a bit. "Wanna dance."

Charlene swung out and clipped Ellie on the chin, and then

she teetered like a chainsawed tree waiting for someone to yell *timber*. Ellie gave her a shove and down she went.

Fitz stared at Ellie as she stood over Charlene with her fists curled at her sides and fire in her eyes, and his heart tumbled over in his chest like a lottery bin with the winning ticket stub spinning inside.

Flashbulbs lit the place up like Rockefeller Center at Christmastime. One of the good ol' boys yelled, "Catfight!"

"Let's get out of here," Fitz said as he grabbed Ellie's arm. "I just lost my appetite."

AN HOUR LATER, ELLIE SWALLOWED the last of her cheeseburger and wiped her hands on a paper napkin printed with Walt's logo. She rubbed her bare feet against the prickly wool of an impromptu picnic blanket and sighed with regret for the missed chance of a dance with Fitz. She'd wanted that one memory to dream over after he was gone.

He grabbed the wine bottle he'd nipped near the exit of the Association dinner and swung it in her direction. "Refill?"

She nodded and lifted her paper cup. "Just a little."

He splashed more wine into her cup and tilted the bottle against her truck's hubcap. Slanting back on one elbow, he gazed at the swirl of stars in the wide, black Montana sky. "Sure is a nice night."

She snorted. "Sure is. A drive-through dinner on a horse blanket spread in a pasture. Pure heaven."

"You're not going to start apologizing again, are you?"

"Nope." Her shoulders lifted on another deep and disappointed sigh. "No point to it, anyway."

"This isn't so bad." He reached over and ran a finger down her instep. "It all depends on the company."

She wriggled her toes. "You trying to flatter me, Kelleran?"

"Nope. No point to it, anyway."

He turned his face back toward the stars, and one of those long, comfortable silences slipped into the private space between them. She enjoyed trading secrets and barbs with him, but it was times like these she'd miss the most when he was gone.

"I'm sorry we never got to have that dance," he said.

"Me, too."

"You like to dance?"

She wriggled her toes. "It all depends on the partner."

He rose and extended his hand. "I'm sure you'll find me the best you've ever had."

She let him haul her to her feet, and she wobbled a bit as the earth rocked beneath her. "Guess that wine's got me feeling a little light-headed."

"Maybe it's not the wine." He ducked into the truck cab and fiddled with the radio dial. "Maybe it's the company."

"You know that actor's ego you're always bragging about?" Mournful lyrics about lost love spun into the night air, and she closed her eyes and swayed to the tune. "It's amazing. It's like there's another person with us, wherever we go. It's like this—"

He tugged her into his arms. "Ellie?"

"Yeah?"

"Shut up and dance."

She looped her arms around his neck and tucked her head below his chin, where it fit so well. His heart beat strong and sure beneath her cheek, and his warm breath washed over her hair.

"You seem different tonight," he said as he skimmed his fingertips up her spine. "As much as I enjoy the old Ellie— the one who knocked Charlene Miller on her ass—I sure do appreciate this new version, the one who wears lipstick and sexy sweaters."

"The sweater was Jody's idea."

He stilled. "Now that's a scary thought. For several reasons. None of which I care to examine at the moment."

He set them moving again in a soft, shuffling circle. When the music dissolved into an advertisement for Pete's Hardware, their steps continued in a private rhythm.

A guitar segue to a lazy, romantic tune slowed their pace. A spook owl called from a ghostly stand of fir trees, and the scent of crushed grass wafted around them. Fitz slipped his big, warm hands around to fan across her back, and she rested her forehead against the base of his throat. He smelled of stale cigarette smoke and French fries, with a subtle layer of some smooth and fabulous cologne. And underneath it all was the scent she recognized as Fitz himself.

They moved together, and fit together, like they'd been designed for this moment. And she let herself drift, for a while, on a dream of *what if.*

What if he stayed, and she stayed with him, just like this. What if he kept wanting her, the way he said he did, and she kept wanting him the way she did right now. She knew her dream could never be the forever kind, but maybe tonight she could steal one small piece and keep the memory as long as she wanted.

She sighed and arched back for the pleasure of looking at him. And when she added a little more sway to her step, just to add a little more interest to the dance, she felt him respond.

That light-headed feeling rushed back through her, scalding and potent. If tonight was the only time she'd be with him like this, she wanted to experience everything he could make her feel. It wasn't wise, it wasn't *her*, but she wanted, just this once, to be helpless with desire, to feel...

To feel something dark and reckless and intensely, wickedly thrilling.

He lowered his hands to her waist and moved her a few inches away from him. "You're not one of those women who can't hold her wine, are you?"

She wrapped her arms tighter around his neck, delighted with her effect on him. "Nope."

"Let me rephrase that last question. No, you can't hold your wine, or no, you're not that kind of woman?"

"Neither." She ran her fingers through the thick hair edging over his collar. "Do you like the new Ellie better than the old one?" she asked.

"There's no safe answer to a trick question like that."

She slid one of her legs against his with the next dance step.

"That felt like another trick question." The music kicked up in tempo, and he turned away to switch off the radio.

She stepped to the edge of the blanket. "It's not the wine, Fitz, and it's no trick. I know what I'm doing."

"I'm sure you think you do." He turned to face her, adorably stern and noble. "But I have to warn you, Ellie— I'm only human, and a weak and miserable excuse for a human at that. If you keep doing..."

He motioned awkwardly at her, and she caught his hand to pull him closer. She raised his fingers to her lips and nipped at his knuckles.

"...Whatever it is that you're doing," he said, "I don't know if I..."

She stroked her hands up his chest and over his shoulders, and she felt him tremble in the instant before he lowered his mouth to hers for a breath-robbing, pulse-thudding kiss.

"I can't seem to help myself when it comes to you." He rested his forehead against hers. "All bets are off tonight, Ellie. Anything can happen."

"I'm glad to hear that." She lifted a hand to caress his face, and she watched him struggle against his desire before he turned his head to press a hot, moist kiss into her palm. "Because I want you to make love to me."

CHAPTER SEVENTEEN

FITZ TRIED TO MAINTAIN the outward appearance of a cool and calm consideration of Ellie's announcement, but he figured the full body spasm had blown his cover.

Why was he hesitating at all? Isn't this what he'd wanted for days—no, weeks—okay, since about five seconds after she'd hit him right between the eyes with her first shot of sass?

Well, there were those excerpts from Nora's lecture that were still circulating in his brain. Some of her phrases were starting to fuse with his own doubts and take on a life of their own. And there was the fact that having sex with Ellie would be like having sex with his best friend—in a completely non-Burke sense of the term, of course. Sex could change their relationship, and he didn't want that to happen.

The change, not the sex. He'd just have to figure out a way to keep that change from happening, and fast, because in spite of all the reasons not to have sex with Ellie Harrison, he sure as hell wasn't going to be the one to say *no* right now. Not when she looked the way she did, and felt the way she did, and wanted him the way she did. And not when he wanted her the way he did—beyond any reason at all.

But maybe he should give that *no* thing one quick, tiny try, just to make sure his conscience didn't mug him in the morning. "Is this one of those examples of my bringing out the worst in you?"

She tipped her head back to look up at him through the shadowed crescent of her lashes. "Is making love with you the worst thing I could do?"

Her arching back brought her hips into even closer contact with his, and her next step dragged her belt buckle across his bulging fly. She had to know one part of his anatomy was ready and willing. Now if he could just get his circulatory system to redirect a little more of his blood supply back north, maybe he could get his brain in sync. Maybe he could even come up with a coherent response to her question.

He had to come up with something—other than the something that had come up below his own belt buckle—even if it was a cop out. "I don't know. Could it be?"

"Maybe." She sighed and closed her eyes. "Maybe it's just tonight. Maybe I just got caught up in that 'all bets are off, anything can happen' stuff. You're right. I'm not feeling like my usual self tonight."

She sure didn't feel like her usual self to him, either. Liquid and flame, she was magic beneath his hands. Her hair waved about her face, softening the angles and deepening the curves. Her eyes were dark, reflecting the night sky with flashes of starlit glints he knew were jade and gold. Her scent, her voice, her movements, her essence enveloped him in a sensual haze.

"How are you feeling?" he asked.

She laughed her rusty laugh and tipped up on her toes. "*Free*," she whispered.

A world of smothered wishes and chained-up dreams seemed to brush across his face with her breath. Her sorrows and fancies seeped and swirled through him, winding around his heart and squeezing it tight. He knew in that moment he would grant any request she made tonight.

All bets were off. Anything could happen.

He lifted his hands to frame her face. "I've always thought that's a good way to feel. I want to help you keep feeling that way."

"You do." She opened her eyes and gazed at him with a somber smile. "I don't always like it, but you do."

"Ah, Ellie." He lowered his forehead to hers. "I don't mean to make things difficult for you."

"You've just got a natural talent for it, I guess."

"One of many."

She pulled back and narrowed her eyes at him, one of his favorite expressions. He dipped his head and skimmed his lips over hers once, twice, before sinking into a soft, slow, sampler of a kiss.

A tremor passed through her, and then she relaxed against him in surrender. He fought an almost overpowering urge to wrap his arms around her and hold her. Just to hold her, and support her, and keep her safe.

But that wasn't his place. And it sure wasn't his style, or hers. She didn't need him to prop her up or protect her, and he wasn't the man to do it, in any case. What she wanted and needed right now—what she'd asked for—was a lover, and that was a role he could play with professional skill.

That's all it would be tonight: a role. That's all he would be tonight: an actor. He knew from experience that he could separate the acting, and the actions, from his own drugging desire. And he silently promised them both that he'd stick to the script and remember all the reasons to maintain a clear distinction between the professional and the personal.

There were no reasons to tangle their emotions with sex.

She hadn't offered any, and neither had he. No strings attached—fine. An offer, not an agenda—good. Mutual agreement about motives—even better.

So why did this tidy arrangement coat his gut with an oil slick of resentment and regret? Something bigger, and deeper, and darker was clouding his conscience tonight, but he sure as hell wasn't in the mood to wrestle with the consequences.

Her fingers eased around his neck to twine through his hair, and his pulse surged with each bass beat of his heart, heavy and hot. He wanted her, as he always did, but tonight the anticipation had reached a plateau of pleasure with an intensity all its own. The satin slide of her mouth against his, the silken touch of her hair on his face, the press of her breasts against his ribs, the tickle of her fingertips at his nape were an intoxication rediscovered and deeply savored. He thought he could spin this yearning out forever, if forever felt like this. But then one of them shifted, and her belly brushed against his erection, and his patience imploded on a groan.

He grabbed the hem of her sweater and pulled it over her head to suckle, deep and hard, as she writhed against him. He tugged at the snap on her jeans, and she pushed his hand away in an impatient struggle to undo the catch herself. He fumbled the first couple of shirt buttons through the first couple of holes, but when her busy hands pulled the tails from his pants and attacked his jeans fly, he popped the rest of the buttons in his haste to catch up with her.

They tripped and staggered down to the rumpled blanket, and she wrapped herself over and around him, and he scrambled for sanity, trying to slow the pace, eager to treat her to a little of the famous Fitz finesse. Then she stuck her tongue in his ear, and he almost lost what was left of his mind.

He rolled over her, kicking the bag of hamburger wrappers

out of their way, and struggled to find his professional focus. Their ragged breathing drowned out the sounds of the night, and the scents of fir trees and pasture grass mingled with spilled wine and fast food and body-warmed cologne.

He hovered over the scene, and yet within it somehow. He watched his hands, edged in moonlight, glide over the sexy subtlety of her curves. He listened to the purr of her sigh and smelled the salty tang of her arousal. He was intensely aware of the rigid pucker of her nipples beneath his fingertips and the lazy slide of her thigh along his own, and yet he fought the urge to sink below the surface sensations. He refused to drown in the sea of murmurs and scents and contours and textures, the presses and caresses of skin and muscle and movement.

Instead, he pleasured her, with all his skill. She whispered to him, and he answered. She arched against him, and he wrapped himself around her. She spread her body for him, and he slipped inside. They smiled together, and moved together, and grew taught and insistent and demanding in their mutual passion, together. Everything, every touch and stroke, was as perfect as he could make it. Everything, every stimulus and response, was as intense as he had imagined it could be.

But somehow, in spite of his rigid control, everything was slipping out of focus. This was Ellie moving beneath him in the moonlight. This was Ellie's voice laughing in his ear. So in sync was he with her every mood, so intent was he on her clenching, shuddering pleasure, so lost was he in the glorious, thrusting violence of his own, that his hovering, watching self joined with his sweat-streaked, emotion-charged self. And when she gazed up at him, with hope and trust and a sweeter affection than he'd ever seen in a woman's eyes, he found he had no defenses to keep her from looking deep inside him and seeing whatever she wished—and everything he felt for her.

And in those dangerous moments before control collapsed in climax, he slipped out of his role and into the reality of making love with Ellie Harrison.

ELLIE CLASPED HER HANDBAG to her heart and tiptoed a two-step toward her room shortly before dawn. Everything here was the same—Great Grandma's painting of the mountains still hung in its barn siding frame, and the scent of furniture polish hovered in the corners as it always did. Only the person dancing through the shadows was different. Wild and wanton, and wickedly, ridiculously pleased with the fact. Her body shivered with sensual memories and ached in places that had craved a man's touch for far too long.

She felt like a woman.

For this one thin slice of time winding around the familiar things in her ordinary life, she wasn't just a mother, or a daughter, or a ranch hand. She'd been transformed by a talented man's touch into something new and extraordinary. A lover.

Loving Tom had been comfortable. Logical, inevitable. She hadn't fallen in love with her husband, she'd slipped into it without a ripple in her routine. Loving Fitz could never be any of those things. The man demanded her attention and challenged her mind, he battered at her values and laid siege to her resistance. It seemed at times he might seduce her very soul.

She already craved the next nerve-tingling free fall, the frenzied, delicious abandon of tangling her body with his. And yes, she adored the heart-tripping emotions that tumbled and twined around and through it all. She had tried—oh, how she had tried, from the very beginning, to deny what was happening to her as she fought every slippery step from cautious friendship to reckless lovemaking. But now it seemed senseless to dam it all up and deny herself this drenching joy.

"Late night, hm?"

Ellie shut her eyes at Maggie's question and waited for the embarrassment and resentment to run its course before she turned to face her.

Her sister-in-law stood with one shoulder propped against her old bedroom door, her cover-model frame draped in some fabulous concoction of lace and silk from her perfectly toned shoulders to her pedicured toes. Even with her face unpainted and her hair sleep rumpled, she made Ellie feel frumpy by comparison.

"Don't tell me you waited up."

"Okay, I won't. And please, don't think you have to share the details." Maggie held up what looked like one of Jody's tabloids, folded to an article inside. "I could probably read a more interesting version next week, anyway."

Ellie snatched the thin magazine from her outstretched hand and stared at the grainy photo on the page. There was the grassy expanse of her own side yard, framed by the crooked willow tree and Jenna's lilacs, and a couple standing in seeming intimacy—a man in casual clothes and a woman in jeans and a gauzy wrap top. The caption below asked how deeply superstar Fitz Kelleran might be involved with the little widow on the big ranch.

"Bastards," said Maggie.

Ellie's hand trembled as she handed back the tabloid. Panic snaked down her spine and punched into her gut, stripping her naked and leaving her exposed and violated—and available for public purchase. And in the next moment, when that first wave of fear and grief had subsided, the one emotion remaining was a cold, clean, towering rage.

FITZ SCRUBBED A HAND over his face and tried without success to recall his lines for the morning's first shot. With a half-hearted curse he dragged the *Wolfe's Range* script back into his lap. Outside his trailer, the hustle of another day on location raced the sun to the starting gate. Filming didn't stop for Sundays when the schedule was this tight.

His thoughts wandered again to the glint of sheer devilry in Ellie's eyes when she'd climbed into his lap in the truck the night before. The woman was an energetic lover. He was going to have a hard time—and a hell of a lot of fun—keeping up with her.

Burke's four-beat tap on the door was a handy excuse to toss the script aside. "Come in."

Burke entered the trailer after a quick, discreet check for lingering company. "Did you have a good time in town last night?"

"Define *good*."

"Was the food good?"

"I don't know."

"You didn't eat?"

"I didn't stay for the barbecue."

"What *did* you stay for?"

"Approximately forty-five minutes."

Burke slipped his hands into his pockets. "What happened?"

"Nothing, at first. Met a few people, posed for a few photos, the usual."

"And then?"

"And then the sheriff's wife came on to me," Fitz said with a grin, "and Ellie knocked her on her ass."

"God."

"We didn't pose for those photos, but I wouldn't mind seeing some of them myself."

Burke frowned. "Speaking of photos…"

Fitz waved the problem away. "I'm sure you'll find some way to handle the flak."

"That's what you pay me for." Burke pulled a folded magazine page from his pocket and passed it to Fitz. "How do you want me to handle this?"

Fitz stared at the tabloid photo of Jody's birthday party, his anger white hot. He crumpled the page in a tightly knuckled fist. "I'll handle this."

ELLIE TRAILERED HANNIBAL and Noodle, the gelding assigned to the film's villain, out to the set along Skunkback Creek shortly after eight o'clock Sunday morning. Thoughts of love-making and tabloid photos tumbled and chased each other through her mind. The images and the memories bled together, until she had trouble separating one from the other.

And since her fury had yet to lock on a logical target, too much of it was turning back in on herself.

She wondered if her friends and neighbors had read the fictional account of her relationship with Fitz, and then she told herself they knew her well enough to dismiss the innuendos. She imagined the worst, and she reasoned it away, and she tied herself up in knots that she yanked loose again in frustration.

Too bad she wasn't paying much attention to her lectures.

She longed to talk to Fitz, the one person who would understand, more than anyone, how she felt. But she needed to put enough distance between the two of them to prevent her family's private lives from becoming public entertainment.

She parked the van in the open spot Trish indicated and waited through the routine of another morning on the set. Stand-ins posed while techs took readings; assistants scrambled from spot to spot. Van Gelder argued with the cinematographer, and the actors stepped out of the makeup trailer and strolled toward the dusty set.

Ellie sucked in her breath with a helpless, visceral reaction to her first sight of Fitz and blew it out again with a shaky, disgusted huff. What a fool she was, letting him get to her like this, letting him worm his way into her life. Still, she couldn't take her eyes off him. She watched him consult, rehearse, pace. She cringed from the murderous intent behind his recited lines and grinned when he tossed a joke to the crew.

And because she couldn't look away, she was staring at him, suspended somewhere between yearning and despair, when his eyes first met hers. His hot, electric gaze snapped and sizzled right through her, trapping her in its raw, possessive grip. Every cell in her body responded to what she saw on his face. It was all too much, she realized. Too powerful to ignore, too destructive to handle—and too late to do anything about it.

Well, hell. She'd fallen in love with him, fool that she was.

When she led the horses to their place in the next shot, he found a moment alone with her. "We need to talk, Ellie. Tonight, when we're finished. Come to my trailer."

The worry and pain in his eyes told her he'd seen the tabloid. She shook her head. "There's nothing to say."

The muscles in his jaw rippled as his gaze swept over her. "Then you can sit and listen," he told her before turning away.

When they broke for lunch, she hiked up the hill to the house, looking for Jody and Jenna, but there was no one home. No sign of trouble, no note of explanation for their absence.

She sat on Jody's pink and ruffled bed and bit back tears of frustration and fear. She had no idea how this would affect her daughter, and no idea how to manage it.

She choked down a couple of aspirin tablets for lunch and let off some steam with a bout of useless, helpless cursing as she slammed out the back porch door.

Fitz was watering the horses when she returned to the set. "Talk to me," he said. "I figure you saw that article, and I know how upset you are."

"You couldn't possibly know how upset I am." She twisted the knob on the hose from the trailer tank. "Not unless you have a child whose twelfth birthday party makes for interesting reading in supermarkets across the country."

He shoved his hands into his costume pockets. "Come to my trailer tonight. We need to discuss this, and we can have some privacy there."

"No," she said. "I'm not sure there is such a thing as privacy around here. Not anymore."

He muttered a curse and stalked away.

The afternoon wore on, oven-hot and desert-dry. The actors sweat through their costumes and makeup, and the crew's tempers grew short. Fitz was everywhere her eyes settled, and his glance sought hers repeatedly, concerned and reassuring.

Surely it was some kind of damnation to feel the way she did, to be so tempted, beyond reason. She didn't want to become another item of gossip on the set. She didn't want to disappoint or embarrass Jody, or Jenna, or Will. She didn't want her secrets exposed on the shelves at North Town Market. She feared she wasn't strong enough to resist him, and her weakness unnerved her.

She spread feed for the horses where they were haltered at the trailer, and he passed by as she worked. He reached out and stroked a finger down her spine, and she shivered at his touch. "I want you," he said.

"I know," she whispered when he was gone. "I want you, too."

The crew worked through dinner, racing the softening light of dusk to finish the day's scheduled shots. Exhaustion settled over her like a blanket. She realized she hadn't eaten or slept since the day before.

When it was over, Fitz helped her trailer the horses. He came to the stables after he'd changed his costume and worked beside her as she groomed the horses and turned them into their stalls. His stubborn silence itched along her skin, and his steady presence chipped away at her resolve. And then, when the last bolt was shoved home and the last tool was in its place, he turned her into his arms, scrambling her thoughts and destroying her intentions with an impatient, searing, tender, kiss.

"Talk to me," he said.

"I don't know how to talk about this."

"I do." He wrapped his arms tightly around her, and he felt so good, so strong and solid and safe.

"I want to make love with you," he said.

"We shouldn't."

"Say yes, anyway."

"This is crazy. This is—"

"I know." His lips hovered over hers. "Say yes."

"Yes," she whispered.

Fool.

CHAPTER EIGHTEEN

THOUGH THE DAY WAS FADING to the muted colors and sounds of a summer evening, Will felt something sharp and bright stirring in the air. Maybe it was the raw scent of the aftershave still cooling on his cheeks, or the crinkle of a clean shirt against his skin. Maybe it was the novelty of new boots peeking out from beneath his freshly pressed jeans. Or maybe it was this unexpected break in his routine—and the none-too-subtle way Fitz had waved him away from Ellie and the horse trailer—that sent possibilities streaking through him like lightning bolts.

Normally he took a bit of a detour to avoid the base camp of vans and trailers crowded together like oversize aluminum cans on a grocery-store shelf. But he knew the swing gang was dismantling the town set tonight, and he figured just this once he could cut through the area without disturbing anyone.

He rounded the corner of one of the biggest vans and barely avoided tripping over a large box. Trish popped up from behind it. "Hey, Will."

The shower-damp hairs on the back of his neck prickled, standing at alert. "Hey, Trish."

He watched her shove at the box and bend to slip her fingers underneath the upended corner, while his conscience fought a skirmish between good manners and good sense.

"Here," he said, taking her by the shoulder to gently angle her back before she hurt something. "Let me help you with that."

"Thanks." She straightened and stepped into his path. "Maybe I should track down a dolly."

"Okay. I'll take this wherever you want it to go."

She tilted her head and gave him an overly friendly smile. Up close like this, that look of hers was setting off alarm bells loud enough to wake the dead in the next county.

"That's a very generous offer." Her tongue flicked out to touch her upper lip. "I just might have to take you up on it."

Before he had a chance to step out of range, she snugged her lithe body up against his and caught him around the back of the neck. "Would you like me to take you up on it, Will?"

She nipped at his lower lip and then settled her mouth over his for the rest of the meal.

His lips compressed to a tight grimace beneath hers, and he reached up to drag her fingers from where they'd locked behind his neck. "I wouldn't want you to be getting the wrong idea here," he said when he'd managed to pull back a couple of inches from her suction-cup mouth.

"Don't worry," she said, bouncing back up on her toes to have at him again. "I won't."

He stiffened like a block wall against her soft insistence, and she finally settled back on her feet. And then he heard the spank of a light metal screen against a doorjamb and caught a glimpse of pale blue linen over Trish's shoulder. He glanced up to see Jenna standing on the steps of a nearby trailer, staring at them, her eyes wide with shock.

"Excuse me, Trish," he said as Jenna stumbled down the steps and fled toward her house. "There's something I need to do right now."

He marched up the road and took the front porch steps two at a time. Without pausing to knock, he let himself in through the massive main door and swept his hat from his head as he made his way toward the kitchen.

He found her at the sink, viciously scrubbing a potato for the roasting pan beside her. "Jenna."

"Did you wipe your feet?"

He sighed. "No."

"Too late now."

"Yep, I s'pose it is." He sighed and hung his hat over a chair. "Guess what's done can't be undone."

She tossed the potato aside and took up another, and he winced at the fury in her jerky motions.

"Jenna." He took one step toward her, and then thought better of taking another when her shoulders hunched in defense. "Maybe you're thinkin' I should have backed away from that woman when she first came at me. Looking back on the whole scene, I can see where I might have done just that, if I'd have known what she had in mind."

"I don't need you to explain what happened back there."

"No, I don't s'pose you do. Maybe it's me who needs to do the explaining, so I can be sure you have something to think about besides what you saw."

She stopped her scrubbing and collapsed against the counter, her shoulders sagging and her head dropped low. "I don't want to do this."

He took another step toward her. "Jenna," he said in his gentling voice.

She whirled to confront him. Pink spots of temper rode high on her cheeks. "Don't you use that tone with me."

He stopped and spread his hands. "All right."

"I know you didn't start that kiss. I know you didn't give that woman any reason to think you'd kiss her back."

"Then why do I feel like I've got a problem here?"

"I don't know." She tossed the potato behind her and it thumped around in the sink. "Why should you have a guilty conscience when you weren't at fault?"

Damn woman. He'd been trying to get her riled up for years, and now that she was finally showing some spit, she'd turned the heat on him. "I don't."

"Then where's the problem?" She turned back to the sink and grabbed the bruised potato.

"Are you angry with me?"

She grasped the edge of the sink and squeezed. "Yes. I know it isn't fair, but yes, I am."

"Then let me apologize."

"For what?" She spun on him again. "For a kiss you didn't want? You didn't want it, did you?"

He swallowed, miserable in spite of his clear conscience. "No."

"A beautiful young woman throws herself into your arms, and you're horrified."

"That's it, exactly." He smiled, even though his insides were twisting and flapping around like cottonwood leaves in a thunderstorm. "You do understand."

"I understand a man would have to be dead not to enjoy attention like that."

"Can't say I'm dead, so I guess I can't say I didn't enjoy the general idea, no. Just didn't enjoy the kiss." He swallowed again. "And I don't like the fact it got you upset. For that reason alone, I wish you hadn't seen what you did."

"But I did see it." Her chin trembled a bit. "And I'm glad I did."

She moved to the table and slumped into a chair. "Seeing you like that, with a younger woman's arms around you...it's what I needed to see. Before I—before I let myself make a mistake about the two of us."

Despair rolled over him in familiar waves, thicker and blacker this time than he'd ever known it. "You know I would never do anything to hurt you. You said you understood."

"I do." She smoothed her hand over the yellow-checkered tablecloth. "You're not that kind of man."

He strode to the table and rested his hands on the other side, bending toward her. "Then let me say I'm sorry for what you saw, and let me make it up to you somehow." He wanted to reach out to her, but he didn't dare. He ground his fingers into the linen. "Please, Jenna."

"Don't beg." Her voice was a whisper. "I can't stand it."

"You don't leave me with much of anything else to do."

She spread her fingers carefully in front of her and stared down at them. "You're an attractive man, Will Winterhawk. Attractive enough for a woman like Trish to take it in her mind to throw herself at you."

He sighed. "That's one compliment that doesn't feel too good going down right now, but I thank you for noticing."

She went on as if he hadn't spoken. "You're still a fairly young man. In your prime, as modern standards go. You'll be wanting children when you find a woman to settle down with."

"Not every man needs a child of his own blood."

"No, but every man should have the opportunity."

She gazed right through him with wintry eyes. "I'm twelve years older than you, Will, and past the age of having children. You've told me, time and again, that my being older doesn't matter to you. But it matters to me. It matters to me that my hair is turning gray, and that the wrinkles are coming on faster than I ever thought they would, and that I'm going to be frail and elderly long before you."

"Jenna—"

"No, Will." She pushed away from the table and walked to the service stairs. She placed her hand over the newel post, and her knuckles whitened as she squeezed it. "*No*."

ELLIE WALKED WITH FITZ to his trailer, and when he shut the door behind them they both lost what was left of their minds.

That's how it seemed as clothes flew, as fingers slipped and feet grappled for a hold, as curses and moans filled the tiny, stuffy space. He shoved her up against the wall, and she dragged him down to the bed. Over and over they tumbled, racing toward oblivion.

She knew what was coming, what he could do to her, and her body thrilled to his every touch, wild with need, urging him on. He responded to her every move, her every gasp, driving her faster, higher, on and on. Their mingled breath grew harsh and ragged, and their heat-slicked skin slapped and slid, and their eyes met and held, sharing the shock and the pleasure, the wonder and the panic and the longing. She wrapped her legs around him to pull him close, and he closed his mouth over her breast to draw her in, and then she was pumping against him, and he was stroking into her, hot, slick, deep, touching the core of her, taking her to the edge, holding her prisoner there.

He kissed her, oh, so tenderly, and then he buried his face in her hair. "*Ellie, Ellie,*" he whispered, over and over, with each thrust of his body, until she gasped and arched up and took him with her into insanity.

They collapsed, their limbs tangled on the thin, stiff mattress, coated in exhaustion and sweat. He rolled to her side with a groan.

"Give me a moment—" he said between deep breaths, "well, maybe a couple of moments…and then I think we should…do that again. We're going to have to…keep at it until we get it right."

She punched weakly at his shoulder. "What did we do wrong?"

"I forgot to do that—" he raised a hand and made a limp circle in the air, "—that thing with my thumb that you like."

"What thing?"

"You'll see. I made a note of it last night." He grinned at her and leaned in close to rub his nose over hers. "I was paying attention. Weren't you?"

She frowned. "Did I do anything wrong?"

"You didn't bite my ear."

"You like it when I bite your ear?"

"Yes."

"Anything else?"

"Why don't you bite me all over, and I'll let you know." His teasing smile faded. "I'm sorry, Ellie. About the pictures."

"Fitz—"

"Especially the one of Jody." That little muscle in his jaw began to tick. "I know it's not enough, but I—"

She lifted her hand to his lips. "It's not your fault."

He kissed her palm and moved her hand aside. "I know it isn't, but I can't help feeling this way. It's like a disease. And I'm the carrier."

She sat up and snatched for his sheet to cover herself.

"There isn't a cure for this, Ellie."

"Yes," she said, "there is."

Her words strung between them like tension wire.

Suddenly she was crushed beneath him and pinned by his possessive kiss. "No," he said against her throat as he settled between her legs. "No cure. Not for this."

Someone knocked at the door, four short raps. He growled and rolled away, to the edge of the bed. "Not now, Burke!" he roared. "Go away."

She struggled and shoved at him so she could escape. "I have to go," she said.

"No," he said and trapped her body again below his. "Not yet."

"I need to talk to Jody."

"So do I."

She opened her mouth to argue, but he clamped his hand over it. "I need to talk to her, just as much as you do."

He waited for her nod, and then he lifted his hand.

"It's late," she said. "I'm sweaty."

"I have a shower here."

"I'm hungry."

"I'll feed you. And Jody and Jenna too, if they'd like."

She bit her lip. "No, I don't—"

He lunged across her to snag a cell phone from beneath the shirt tossed over his bedside table. "Call them and say you're going to be late," he said, "and that I'm taking you out to dinner."

"Fitz, I—"

"Here's what's going to happen," he said in a patient and reasoning tone. "First we're going to take a shower—I know it'll be a tight squeeze, these trailer showers aren't designed for two—but we can be creative."

He pulled the sheet aside and trailed the phone between her breasts, down to circle her navel.

"Then we'll go get Jody—Jenna, too, if she wants to join us—and I'll treat everyone to something at Walt's. We'll have that discussion about this tabloid business, and then we'll drop Jody and Jenna back here." He shoved the phone into her hand. "And then you and I can head out to some back pasture to see if we can improve on our truck technique. Now make the call."

"Our truck technique?"

"There's a certain position I think we should try. Call."

She stared at him, looking for a reason to do what her sensible self told her she should do—eat a quiet dinner at home with her family and get a good night's sleep. But what she saw made her want to stay. Forever, if he asked, and that was the biggest reason to leave, now, before it was too late.

Because what she read in his features was affection, and warmth and humor, and a gentle desire sweetened with longing and tempered with uncertainty. And all of it was focused on her.

Ellie, Ellie...

"Call," he said.

"Yes," she said. "All right."

FITZ SPRAWLED ACROSS his trailer sofa Monday morning, a bedroom pillow scrunched behind his head and his feet propped on the arm at the other end, staring at Barton's notes for *The Virginian.* Interesting ideas. Creative camera angles and intriguing narrative strategies. None of it was what Fitz had envisioned, but it was full of possibilities.

This morning, the world was bursting at the seams with possibilities.

His thoughts detoured to last night's dinner conversation. He'd reached an understanding of sorts with Ellie and Jody over Walt's burgers, and though he suspected Mom was still a little shaky about the tabloid situation, her daughter was taking it all in stride. Hell, the little minx-in-training wrangled a private cell phone out of the deal before Ellie put the brakes on the guilt trip.

Jenna had declined his dinner invitation, claiming a headache. She'd seemed drawn and distracted—he hoped she wasn't getting sick. He'd jog up the hill later today and beg for a cookie at her back door so he could check up on her.

He watched Burke approach the trailer steps and waited for the knocks. One, two, three, four. Then...nothing.

"Come in."

The door swung open in a slow and cautious arc, and Burke's head and shoulders finally made an appearance. He made a show of checking the trailer's interior, including the open doorway to the bedroom in the back.

"I'm alone," said Fitz.

Burke opened his mouth, probably to make some smart remark, but then wised up and pointed to the script spread across Fitz's knees. "What do you think of Barton's ideas?"

Fitz shrugged.

"You've had it for days. What have you been doing?"

Fitz tossed the script on the dinette table. "I've been thinking."

"About Barton's ideas?"

"About Disneyland."

Burke raised one eyebrow. "Disneyland."

"Yeah. Haven't been there in a few years." Fitz scratched at his chin and stared out the window. "I think twelve is the perfect age for a visit. Don't you?"

"Twelve." Burke's lips thinned in a grim line. "Jody."

"And Ellie. I'm thinking they'd both like to see it. And the beach. Maybe a whole day at the beach, with a picnic or something." His mouth kicked up in a grin. "I'm a big fan of picnics."

"Fitz." Burke shook his head. "What are you doing?"

"I'm trying to do something nice for a couple of very nice people."

"Both of them? Or does one just happen to come packaged with the other in a miniature bonus size?"

"Watch it," Fitz said quietly.

"I'll be damned if I'll stand on the sidelines and watch you pull a stunt like this right now." Burke stalked to the kitchen alcove and grabbed the coffee supplies. "I've just spent the past week keeping your script on half a dozen front burners, not to mention dousing a couple of career brush fires."

"And you've done a hell of a job, for which I'm giving you a substantial raise. Effective the beginning of last month."

Burke dropped the carafe on the counter and slapped his hands on either side of it. "It's not the money I care about, and you know it. Damn it, Fitz, when are you going to get your priorities straight on any of this? When is the big head going to stop letting the little head do its thinking for it?"

"I told you to watch it."

The murder Fitz felt must have shown on his face, because Burke's features smoothed to a perfect blank. "So, that's how it is," he said quietly.

"How do you know how it is?" Fitz jumped up from the sofa and paced to his bedroom doorway and back. "Hell, I don't even know how it is."

The two of them stared at each other in a long, taut silence.

"Damn you," said Burke.

"For what, exactly? I've lost track."

"For hurting her." Burke picked up the carafe and filled it with water. "You will, you know."

"No, I won't." He could deny it to Burke, but there was no denying the battles he'd been waging with his conscience since sometime before dawn. He rubbed at his chest, trying to ease the vague ache that seemed to have taken up permanent residence. "I don't want to hurt her."

"You never do."

"It's different this time."

"I know." Burke studied him with what looked suspiciously like pity. "This time it's going to hurt you, too."

"And why is that?"

"Because you've fallen in love with her."

CHAPTER NINETEEN

"NO." FITZ RAISED A HAND and shook his head. "No, I don't think so."

Burke did his Mr. Spock eyebrow trick and waited.

"Not all the way in love, anyway," Fitz mumbled.

Burke finished his preparations and flipped the switch on the coffeemaker.

"Look," said Fitz, "the end of the shoot's going to put a whole lot of distance between me and any complications that might be developing here."

"Not if you start inviting those complications for visits to California."

"I said *might* be developing." He tried to shove his hands into his pockets, but they slipped over the front of his sleep sweats. "Nothing I can't handle, anyway. I've got things under control."

"I can see exactly how much control you've got over things. All I need to do is look at your face."

"Damn." Fitz scrubbed his hands over the evidence and then laced his fingers around the back of his neck. "*Damn.* What am I going to do?"

"Can't you figure it out?"

"How the hell am I supposed to do that?" He threw his arms wide. "I've never been in this situation before."

"Me neither," said Burke. He settled on the sofa and

crossed his legs in that British way that drove Fitz nuts. "How does it feel?"

Fitz laughed a tired, ugly laugh. "Like every cliché in every B movie that's ever been made."

"That bad, huh?"

"Nope." Fitz dropped his hands and smiled. "That good."

Burke rolled his eyes.

"No, really." Fitz's smile spread. "You should try it."

"This is going to be really, really painful to watch."

"What is?"

"She's going to take you apart," said Burke as he examined his manicure, "piece by piece, and put you back together like Frankenstein's monster. She's going to make your life such a hell that Satan himself will be hiding behind your shoulder, taking notes. She's going to eat you for breakfast and spit out the hairy parts."

"Yeah." Fitz grinned with pride. "She's something, isn't she?"

"Yeah, she's something, all right." Burke sighed and shook his head. "I suppose, in some twisted version of fate, you two deserve each other."

"So." Fitz dropped on the sofa beside him and leaned forward, his elbows on his knees. "Do we have your blessing?"

"For what, exactly?"

Fitz tossed up his hands. "Who the hell knows?"

"Fitz." Burke reached for the script. "You've got to figure things out. And soon."

"I know. School will probably start up again soon. I can't see Ellie pulling Jody out of school to go to Disneyland."

"Fitz." Burke gave the script a little shake. "Pay attention here. Sundance's darling, Grant Robbins, wants to see this. And Malakoff at Paramount wants a meeting."

Fitz froze. His heart flipped and flapped around, trying to find a comfortable fit in his chest. "Holy shit. We've got a hot property."

"Looks that way," said Burke.

Fitz jumped up to pace and rammed a hand through his hair. He was about to take his first baby steps as a player in Hollywood, and he didn't want to fall flat on his face. "I've got some decisions to make."

"Preferably some decisions that don't involve standing in a long line for a nausea-inducing ride in a spinning teacup."

"Yeah." Fitz took the script from Burke's outstretched hand. "What was I thinking?"

That he could launch a new phase in his career and start a relationship with a single mother at the same time? He needed to prioritize. One thing at a time—and he was holding his first priority in his hands.

His fingers tightened around the pages. He knew it had to be this way. It was the only thing that made sense in his life right now. He shoved aside the nagging, gnawing suspicion that his enthusiasm for this project was diminishing with each encouraging development, and he told himself to focus. *Focus. Get it back. Get it going.*

Going, going... *Gone.* This was one act he wasn't sure he could carry off.

ELLIE BRACED HERSELF in the open doorway of Will's cabin Tuesday evening and watched him pile his books into a packing box. "So it's true," she said. "I don't think I believed it until now."

He shot her a neutral glance over his shoulder. "When have I ever told you I was going to do something, and then not gotten around to it sooner or later?"

She dropped down on the wide rolled arm of his oversize chair. "Guess I was hoping this was going to be a case of later. Much later."

"I'll stay until the filming's done, like I said. That's plenty late as it is."

So many men had left her behind—her father, Ben, Tom—but this parting seemed particularly painful. She swallowed past the swelling, burning knot in her throat. "Why are you doing this?"

"I told you. I've got no hope of changing my situation here. And it's not enough, not anymore."

"Have you been that unhappy here?"

He squinted at her in that way of his that made her want to squirm, the way that made her think she was supposed to answer her own question—and not necessarily the question she'd spoken out loud. "There's all kinds of unhappiness, little girl. Some of it isn't so bad, so you end up tolerating it longer than you mean to, at first. And some of it gets to be so bad you can't tolerate it a moment longer."

"We love you, you know. All of us," she added.

"I know." He layered in more of his books. "I love you, too. All of you."

"Then don't go."

The moments stretched out between them, silent and sorrowful, as he filled the box. She wallowed in her misery as another piece of what made him the special man he was got sealed up, labeled and set aside. It was like watching him fade away, bit by bit, right before her eyes. "What can I say to make you change your mind?"

"I don't think you can find the right words, or the right kind of power, to change this situation." He tapped the fat marker pen against the palm of his hand. "It's got nothing to do with you."

"If Tom were here, he'd know what to say."

Will whirled and flung the pen at the rock wall above the fireplace. *"Damn it!"*

Ellie jumped so hard at his violence she nearly fell off her perch.

"Damn it to hell and back," he said. "When are you going to get over your habit of invoking the name of Tom Harrison as if he were the answer to all your problems?"

"I don't do that."

"The hell you don't."

Will towered over her, fired up with an anger he rarely set a match to. "Or maybe you're so used to thinking that way you don't even realize when the words pop out of your mouth."

She shoved her chin up toward his. "I know very well what comes out of my mouth, just like I know what thoughts put the words there to begin with. And Tom isn't mixed up in all that much of it."

"He shouldn't be there at all." Will took her by the arms and lifted her to stand before him. "He's a memory, Ellie— that's all he is for any of us now. Let him be. Move on," he said in a voice so low and intense it made her ache to hear it.

He gave her a little shake. "You've got your whole life ahead of you, and you can't spend it second-guessing your every move with speculations on a dead man's wishes."

"I just…" She gasped in horror as one hot tear spilled down her cheek. "I just get so scared, sometimes. About the ranch, about Jody. Wondering about Tom like that makes me feel…"

He waited her out, ignoring the evidence of her distress, just the way she knew he would. Where would she ever find someone else like him, someone to stand up to her and offer her support at the same time? "It makes me feel like I'm not so alone," she whispered.

He shook his head. "What a sad and sorry substitute for a world full of flesh-and-blood possibilities."

He eased his grip and smoothed his hands down her arms before stepping back. "I've been so damned proud of you these last three years. I should have told you, and told you often. You've worked as hard as anyone I've ever known, and been braver than most. And you've made it easy for me. Comfortable, and…and right, between us. That's a big part of why I've stayed on as long as I have."

He picked up the marker. "And all those reasons make it truly difficult to say the next thing I have to say. Lately, I'm disappointed in you, Ellie Harrison. Truly and deeply disappointed."

She longed to flee from this room, to deal with her shame and grief in private. But she forced back the tears and stayed in place to hear him out.

"You've got more potential in you than Tom Harrison ever had, because you've got more common sense to go with it," he said. "But you squander a piece of that potential every time you stop to consider him in everything you do."

A different kind of pain lanced through her with his gentle reprimand. "I thought you were his friend."

"No one ever had a better one, on either side. But we both know Tom was a dreamer. Good dreams, most of them, but dreams all the same. Dreams that sometimes kept him from appreciating what he had right in front of him." His smile skewed to one side. "Guess I've made it a habit of loving people for their faults, instead of saving up those faults to use for spite."

A couple more tears made a break for it and raced down her cheeks. "Well, hell," she said and rubbed them away. "I hate it when I'm leaky."

"I know." He nodded. "Strong women usually do."

"I am strong." She snatched at the bandanna he handed her. "I know I am. And it's a bad habit to lean on Tom, even though he's not technically around to lean on. I know that, too. I've always known it. I think I do it to cast some of the blame his way if things don't work out."

Will's slow smile told her he'd arrived at that conclusion several steps ahead of her.

"You told me, a while back," she said, "that if I don't own up to the things I do, if I try to slough off the failures, then I can't take any credit for the successes, either. Well, okay. I'm taking charge now. No more second-guessing."

"That's the Ellie Harrison I used to know." He moved back to his boxes of books. "She can handle things here just fine after I'm gone."

"I sure wish I didn't have to, Will."

He stared down into an empty box on the floor beside him. "I know."

An hour after she'd sniffed up the last of her tears over Will, Ellie sought solace in the mindless, soothing routine of grooming Hannibal. He seemed more Fitz's boy than hers now, but the big red horse had never been too particular about who was on the other end of a handful of oats or a rubdown with his softest brush. Fickle—that was Hannibal.

Sometimes it seemed as if the whole world was a fickle place on some level or other. Death, desertion, betrayal—it all came down to changes no one could control, no matter how hard a body worked or fought. So what was the use of working and fighting? Might as well roll over and quit.

If only she knew how to do that and still live with herself. And Jody.

She had a daughter. Someone to care for, to feed and clothe, and to educate by example, if nothing else. And she had to do those things herself if she wanted Jody's respect along with her love.

So she'd muddle through, somehow. She'd train a new foreman and find a way to pay off the new debts along with the old, and claw her way through to surviving another winter. She'd deal with the courting Wayne seemed so determined to put them both through. Just jot it all down on her personal list of things to do, a short column of miracles to pull off. She'd done it before.

But oh, God, she didn't want Will to go. And she was sick to death of struggling with debt and burying her fears, and fighting off the temptation to let a man help shoulder the worst of her troubles. She leaned her head against Hannibal's big, warm rib cage and let the deep animal sounds drown out the dark, energy-sapping thoughts.

"I'm sure going to miss this big ol' boy."

She turned to face Fitz. There he stood, as he so often did—as she'd first seen him—with his hands crammed into his jeans pockets and one shoulder shoved against the handiest vertical structure. He grinned at her, sublimely confident and casual about his wealth and his success, full of charm and cheer and more than his fair share of good looks.

She'd resented him once for having all the things she couldn't seem to scrape together for herself. Now she smiled back at him and let herself delight in the small miracle that had brought him here to shed a little of his magic her way.

And because her love for him was a once-in-a-lifetime fantasy, she'd never tell him her secret and tarnish the memory. She wouldn't hand him words he'd heard from scores of other women or reduce what they'd shared to a cheap cliché. She'd take what he offered and share what she could, and then she'd let him go when the time came for them to part. And maybe her heart would only break a little, because she'd be prepared ahead of time with plenty of logical reasons to patch up the cracks.

She swung back toward Hannibal to sweep the brush over his flank. "He's kind of special," she said, "isn't he?"

"Yeah. He is."

"He sure has taken to you these past weeks."

"I like to think so." Fitz ambled over to stand beside her. "It's one of the reasons I want to buy him."

Her fingers tightened on the brush. "Buy him?"

"I want him, Ellie. I've got a place, a small ranch in California. I can keep him there."

"He's not for sale."

"He could be."

Sell Hannibal? It would be like breaking off another piece of her world. Too many changes, too many losses. Too many to deal with, today, or next week, or the week after that.

Damn Fitz Kelleran. Damn him for waltzing in here and stealing Hannibal's affections, for stealing hers, for turning everything inside out and upside down. Damn him for having the money to buy whatever he wanted, for having the ability to satisfy whatever whim struck his fancy before dashing after the next notion.

For leaving her behind when he did.

But wasn't that exactly what she'd expected all along? What she'd been waiting for since the moment he'd arrived? She should be glad to see him leave, and relieved to slap the last specks of filmmaking fairy dust from her world.

"He's not for sale," she said again.

"You said it yourself, that first night. He's stock. Good stock."

He shifted toward her with a stiffness strangely out of character for him. *Good*, she thought. *Let him feel a little awkward, a little guilty. Let him beg for what he wants for a change. Let him see what it feels like.*

The bitterness welled up inside and washed through her, soaking her in her own misery, leaving her feeling small, and mean, and far more guilty than Fitz could ever feel.

And why should he feel guilty at all? He'd been nothing but kind and patient. And loving—so very loving.

If she couldn't take the pain, and she couldn't hold on to the joy, then she'd settle for nothing. She willed herself to be numb to it all. Calm, cool, logical. She could do this one thing. And then she could move on to the next thing, and the next. She could say goodbye to Will, and goodbye to Fitz, and then she could dig in for the long, lonely haul ahead.

She made another pass with the brush. "I know he's come to mean a lot to you," she said. "And I s'pose we could use the money I'd charge you a lot more than we could use him."

"Going to make me pay, huh?"

"Through the nose, Kelleran." She shot him one of her snotty glances, but the tension at the edges of his smile told her he could see through her act. "I have a pretty good idea just how much you can afford to pay."

"Maybe."

He stepped in close and gently turned her to face him. His eyes, as they roamed over her features, were shadowed with something new and disturbing she couldn't fathom. "And maybe," he said as he pried the brush from her fingers and tossed it to the ground, "I'm about to figure out just how much I can afford to lose."

He lowered his hands to her waist and pressed his lips to her mouth, and kissed her in a way he'd never kissed her before. It was a shy and uncertain kiss, a wistful and longing kiss, a kiss that sought her permission, and asked her blessing, and begged her to give him more than she'd offered before. A cherishing kiss that melted the ice walled around her heart and filled it with warmth and the whisper of possibilities.

She kissed him back, in a way she never had before, risking everything, willing to give him anything, all that she had—to offer herself, if he wanted her, if only he could find the words to ask.

But he wouldn't ask, and she wouldn't offer. He hadn't made any promises, and she'd made plenty to herself. So she'd keep her promises, and settle for this momentary pleasure and another memory to treasure through the days and years ahead.

His expression was shuttered when he set her away from him. "Think about my offer," he said. "I'll pay any price you think is fair."

"All right." She searched his eyes for some clue to the unspoken meanings she heard in his words, but it seemed he'd found a way to block his thoughts from her. "I'll let you know," she said.

He reached out and softly traced a finger along Hannibal's neck. "Thank you."

She glanced down at the brush near her feet and knew there was no point in continuing the consolation grooming. There would be no consolation in anything connected with Hannibal, from this moment on. One more change, one more loss. How much more could she bear?

She looked up at Fitz, and he took a deep breath, as if he were about to say something. He stared at her for a long, empty span of time. And then he turned and walked away, and she realized she could bear that, too.

CHAPTER TWENTY

FITZ FUMBLED FOR THE CELL PHONE buzzing like a bumblebee trapped in his back pocket. He wasn't sure he'd ever get used to the damn thing, but if it kept Burke happy, he guessed it was worth risking a heart attack every time it went off.

He glanced at the little message screen and frowned. Five o'clock, Friday night, charity bash, blah, blah—Burke's electronic method of nagging at him. Yeah, he'd completely forgotten about tonight's party. Completely on purpose.

Welcome home. Less than a week back in California and he was already facing tuxedo duty.

Six days. One hundred and forty hours. He knew the amount of time down to the minute, because he'd ached with missing Ellie through nearly every one of them. He missed her sass and her teasing, missed her reluctant smiles and the stubborn tilt to her chin. He missed her soft, generous kisses and her fiery, no-holds-barred approach to lovemaking.

He sighed and stooped to haul one last armful of brush out of the bed of his pickup truck. He wasn't making much progress on the ranch cleanup he planned to finish before summer's end. It looked as though he'd have to hire some extra help in addition to the contractor he'd set to painting the house and the barn.

He pulled off his gloves and glanced at the outbuildings as he stalked around to the driver's cab door. What a sorry sight this place was. He could easily spare the money to bring it back to glory. But he refused, from willful pride and guilty sentiment, to let someone else take on his responsibilities. He owed it to Gramps. The man had found the time to take him in, had made the effort to raise him. The least Fitz could do was honor his memory with a little time and effort of his own.

Kruppman was still campaigning for a sale. His financial adviser managed to wedge a mention of an "interested buyer" into every conversation. But selling the ranch meant cutting the last tie to Gramps and turning his back on the one place that had held him safe during a childhood of insecurity. It hurt to think of placing a monetary value on something that was the closest thing to a family heirloom he was ever going to have in his lifetime. Gramps had poured his entire adult life into these dusty acres, and Fitz couldn't walk away from them.

And because he accepted those parts of himself, because he could acknowledge those feelings, he came closer than most people to understanding what Ellie felt about Granite Ridge—something so big and so deep he could only stand at the edge of it and try to imagine the heat and pressure at its core.

When he brought Ellie and Jody out here—and Jenna, too, if she wanted to come—his tiny ranch was the only place that would feel like home, and he wanted to make it beautiful for them. Colorful paint and flowers, for a start. They could shop for whatever they fancied and fix up the place to suit themselves. He thought they might enjoy that.

He smiled as he imagined Gramps's reaction to a bunch of women fussing over his place. Probably turning over in his grave, although the old man would have loved the idea of Fitz using his ranch to woo a woman.

Is that what he was contemplating? Wooing Ellie Harrison?

He rubbed the heel of his hand across the ache in his chest and faced the truth: *yes*. He wanted her, and he couldn't imagine ever not wanting her.

That was that, then. The biggest decision of his life had turned out to be one of the simplest.

He climbed into his truck, headed to the highway and turned south toward Malibu. Could he actually reinvent himself without a script? Without a director coaching his every move and a crew making him look good doing it? Could he chuck a lifetime career of self-absorption and self-indulgence and refocus on someone else?

If that someone else was Ellie Harrison, the one answer to all his questions was still *yes*.

TWO HOURS LATER FITZ'S SPIDER purred to a stop beneath the Beverly Hills Hotel's porte cochere. Press flashes popped like explosions in a fireworks factory as he flipped his keys to an eager valet.

"Fitz, darling!" Kay Thornton, Hollywood's best-preserved grand dame and tonight's charity hostess, dropped an air kiss in the vicinity of his right ear and steered him to her more photographic left side. "What a delight!"

"Just doing my part for the cause," he said. He slipped a hand around her bony back before he turned and tossed a smile at the photographers. "What is the cause tonight, anyway?"

"Oh, *Fitz*." Kay pressed in a bit so she could angle her chin up at him. Her borrowed designer diamond choker blazed in the flashbulb snowstorm. "You're such a tease."

He spun a few suitably bland lines for the reporters before moving into the lobby. The scene reminded him of the Cattlemen's Association shindig—minus the good food, the great music and the nice folks. He had a sudden craving for one of Walt's burgers.

He cut through the crowd and found Nora out by the pool. He twirled her into his arms, and her kiss was moist and right on target.

"Samantha's here," she whispered. "She's been looking for you."

Probably hoping to link up with him for a photo op—or something more—and boost her sagging celebrity status. "Thanks for the warning."

She wiped a fleck of her lipstick from the corner of Fitz's mouth. "Jenna sends her love. She also says you're in the doghouse with Ellie. Honestly, Fitz, how could you get into so much trouble long distance?"

"I made the mistake of mentioning a Disneyland trip to Jody without checking with Mom first, and she's busting my butt over it." He shrugged. "I figure I'll lie low for a while to let the worst of her temper blow over, and then play the groveling routine for all it's worth until I get what I want."

"I think groveling will suit you just fine," she said, studying him. "I'm happy for you, hon. For both of you."

"Thank you, darlin'." He studied her back. "How are you holding up?"

"Fine. And strangely calm, now that the paperwork's behind me." Nora had filed for divorce the moment she'd returned home. "I should have done it sooner," she said with a glittering smile. "It seems to have cured my morning sickness."

He gave her a gentle goodbye hug before wading into the crowd, aiming for the patio bar. He didn't want a drink, but he figured that was the best place to start in on film business.

He flashed his smile and nodded his head in the briefest of greetings, collecting air kisses and slapping backs while on the move, avoiding the trap of an actual conversation. He figured he could slip in, grab a neat shot of his favorite whiskey, check out the players and plan his strategy for the evening. He noticed a Paramount producer chatting up the latest indie-director sensation—a two-birds-with-one-stone setup.

God, he loved the irony of the situation. The biggest trademark of his acting career—the one talent the critics dismissed as personality rather than craft—might turn out to be his handiest business asset: his charm.

He saw an opening and slipped to the bar while the slipping was good. And in the next moment, he saw the reason for the sudden pathway and the heightened interest of the audience lining the gap. Sam was draped over one of the tall stools, her long legs exposed to perfection in a strategically slit gown.

"Damn," he muttered. He sucked up a sigh and prepared to deal with the inevitable, whatever the inevitable turned out to be this time. "Evenin', Samantha."

"Oh, *Fitz*," she said, with a little hitch in her delivery that was two parts faked surprise and one part false emotion. At least her acting had improved. "You look *wonderful*."

"It's the tux."

Her fingers manacled his sleeve. "Oh, Fitz, don't turn away from me. Please don't make a scene."

He glanced down at her hand. "I don't make scenes."

"That's right." Her pout had improved, too. "You never did."

"And I'm not going to start now." He tried to shrug her off, but she stuck. "So you'd better let go."

"Fitz, sweetheart. We need to talk."

She dragged her clutch purse against her cleavage and began to dig through the spangled bag. The movements tipped her off balance, and she wobbled on her perch. He stepped in closer, ready to catch her if she listed too far to one side. If Ellie had been here tonight, she might have found a way to semi-accidentally help Sam list into the pool.

"What are you doing?" he asked.

"Looking for my car keys."

The aroma of too much scotch wafted up to compete with a thick cloud of musky perfume. "You're in no shape to drive."

"Oh, sure I am. I'm a very good driver." She leaned forward, mashing a breast against his arm. "And I'm in very good shape. Ha!"

She lifted her valet ticket like a trophy. "Look what I found."

"Sam." He made a grab for the card, but she twisted away, nearly colliding with the studio exec behind her.

"Let's go," she said as she overcorrected and stumbled against his side. "Somewhere private, so we can talk."

There was no way he could get that card without creating a scene. Already the patio crowd had swelled, drawn to the drama.

He curled his fingers around her arm. "All right, you win. Where's your car?"

"It's—oh," she giggled. "I don't know. The nicest young man took it when I pulled up. He'll give it back, don't you think?"

"I'm sure he will." Fitz pulled her away from the bar and angled toward the big glass doors. "But we'll use mine."

"Oh, *Fitz*," she said, moaning his name like an orgasm. A couple of Japanese investors raised their glasses and bobbed their heads in smiling salutes. He scowled and plowed through the lobby.

"What's the hurry, Kelleran?" asked a grinning casting director as they brushed by. "Meter running?"

A nasty tide of predatory laughter lapped at his heels as he half dragged Sam toward the entry. A blast of sheet lightning blinded him for an instant, and he remembered the press crowded at the door. "Damn."

"Are we going to your place?" Sam asked as she tossed her hair back and smiled for the cameras. The popcorn flashes picked up speed as he barreled his way through the gauntlet.

"No," he said.

"My place?"

"Yes."

"Oh, *Fitz*," she said and looped her arms around his neck like a noose.

He pried her off, collected his keys from the valet and hoped he wouldn't have to explain this evening's fiasco from a doghouse crouch.

ELLIE SMELLED THE SMOKE long before it smeared the eastern horizon. She put in a call to the fire and aviation office, but she knew in her gut, before she got the official word, that the wildfire spreading above her summer pastures was moving toward Granite Ridge. She made arrangements to get Jody to town, left Jenna packing their most important belongings and set Jake to the task of preventive measures at the ranch buildings. Then she saddled Tansy and galloped out with Brady, Chico and Milo toward the mountains.

The grassland rolled out before them, mile after mile, as dry as powder beneath the bruised sky. They splashed through sloughs trickling with stingy flows and darted through stands of thirsty timber. The sharp thuds of shod hooves drummed loud and insistent on the hard, packed ground, and sweat flecked the horses' necks as they strained forward in the race.

Brady called for a stop when they spied the first tendrils of smoke ghosting, thin and blue, through the tall firs of the foothills. "I'll head south with Ellie, along Beavertail Gulch. Chico, you and Milo head up along the northern boundary." He told them to cut the fence line and let the livestock work its way back down to the heart of the ranch on its own.

"No heroes," Ellie said. "If you see fire or meet up with any smoke jumpers, get the hell out of the way and head back."

She and Brady turned to follow the rocky outcropping along a ridge. Night and ash began to fall, and the horses spooked with every snap and explosion in the distance. The air grew thick and stinging.

Brady swung to the ground near a line of fencing strung across the vee of a hillside gully. He tossed his reins to Ellie and tugged his tools from his saddle pack. "This is as good a place as any to start," he said.

THE WINDING CANYON ROAD through the Hollywood hills was tricky under the best of circumstances. Fitz thought trying to negotiate the curves while fending off Sam's clumsy, clutching attempts at seduction seemed suicidal. She pouted, she fumed, she ranted. And, when she didn't get her way, she grabbed the steering wheel.

The world spun, screamed, jolted and shattered in an explosion of glass and thudding pain. Fitz had some trouble sorting it all into a logical sequence at first, but the throbbing in his head and his arm gradually helped bring things back into focus. That, and the grim voice of the highway patrol officer who stepped into the path of a sequence of colored strobing lights.

JENNA STARED AT THE MONSTER in the distance Friday night—a boiling column of smoke with hell at its feet and an inversion layer at its head. She could taste the threat of it on the evening breeze, acrid and ominous and nauseating. It had already smothered the sunset, sucking the sun down in an unnatural glow of amber and amethyst cloaking the mountains. She imagined the crackle and roar of it as it swallowed acres of Harrison timber and scorched miles of Harrison pasture.

She rubbed her hands up and down the sleeves of her sweater

and paced her front porch as ash drifted in like snowfall. The drone of a helitanker machine gunned through the floorboards before its black, drop-nosed silhouette swooped past, whipping the ranch dogs to a frenzy. Behind her, the radio crackled to life, and she listened to her neighbors' voices below the static. Checking in, passing rumors, trading facts, reassuring each other. She fingered the cell phone in her sweater pocket, though she knew the relay tower might already be gone.

The dogs' barking frayed her unraveling patience. "Rufus! Chowder! Hush now!" They disobeyed her and leaped from the edge of the porch to dash down the drive. Someone was coming—probably the district official delivering the evacuation order she dreaded.

A familiar, battered truck sped up the main ranch road. It rattled past the barn and swung onto the drive leading to the house, and then jolted to a stop at the foot of the front porch steps. The dogs danced in delight as the driver's door opened.

Jenna ran to the edge of the porch and was caught up in a longed-for embrace. "*Will.*"

She wrapped her arms around his strong, warm neck and rubbed her cheek against the stubble on his chin, and then his mouth closed over hers, feeding from her, sustaining her, loving her. Her mind was empty of everything but the feel of his body against hers and the echo of his name. *Will. Will.*

He dragged his lips from hers and skimmed them over her ear. "Where's Ellie?"

"She took a crew out to cut the fences."

"Did she take Brady with her?"

"Yes."

"Good. He'll know what to do." Will shoved his way through the door and stalked over to check in on the radio.

Jenna followed him, soaking up the sound of his voice—the deep rumble, the calm tone—and felt his strength seep into her.

"And Jody?" he asked.

"Maggie took her to town."

He nodded. "That's the best place for them."

"Are you heading up after Ellie?"

"No. I'm staying here."

She read the reason on his face—the fire was headed their way.

"Make coffee, and plenty of it," he said. "Pack the coolers and that big basket of yours with as much food as you can—sandwiches, anything. I'm going to round up the men Ellie left behind, and then I'll be back."

She followed him to the door. "I'm glad you're here."

"Did you think I could stay away?" His voice was a harsh rasp, his eyes rimmed red from the smoke and dark with emotion. "Did you hope I would?"

"I never wanted you to go."

He stood there, waiting. The decision was hers, and only hers to make. "I never thought you'd stay away," she said, "but now I understand why you had to."

"Why, Jenna?"

"I needed to figure out for myself that your absence from my life was worse than anything I could ever imagine your presence in my life could possibly be."

His eyes narrowed in a squint. "Sounds like a welcome back. Feels like one, too." And then his mouth twisted up at one corner in the beginning of one of his slow smiles. "Or did I miss something in the translation?"

She struggled not to smile back. "I think you got the gist of it."

He moved so quickly she didn't have time to take a breath

before he caught her up in a dizzying kiss. His big palms cradled her head, holding her prisoner as his tongue swept into her mouth, teasing her pulse to a tango. Then he dropped his hands to her waist, dragging her against him as his lips trailed from her jaw to the base of her throat, sending her mind spinning.

She sighed and pressed closer, but he straightened and shifted away with a moan. "We'll continue this discussion later," he said.

"I'll be waiting." She tossed her hair back and gazed up at him, letting him see her heart in her eyes. "I'll be ready."

"God, woman." He brushed his fingertips along her cheeks. "We'll discuss your timing later, too."

"You'd better go."

"Right." He crushed his lips to hers for one more needy, giddy moment, and then he bounded down the steps and into his truck, and sped toward the barn with the dogs yapping in his wake.

Jenna turned to prepare for the coming battle in her kitchen, hoping it wouldn't be the last time she knew the joy of working in it. But before she could fill the first thermos with coffee, the evacuation order for Granite Ridge crackled and hissed over the radio.

ONCE THE AUTOGRAPHS HAD BEEN distributed, celebrity didn't count for much in a hospital's emergency room reception area. Fitz cradled his aching left arm against his stomach while he waited his turn for treatment. He'd already survived the clerical triage—identification, vital statistics, insurance carrier—and had been rewarded with a cold, droopy bag to press to the lump on his head.

There wasn't going to be much of his hide left for Ellie to work over this time; he was doing a thorough job of stripping it off on his own. What an idiot he'd been to think he could control Sam and his car at the same time. He was grateful the accident hadn't injured anyone else.

Sam had been treated by the paramedics at the crash site for the tiny air-bag scrape on her forehead and released to the care of a cab driver. Fitz's arm required more serious attention.

He dropped the icy bag on the table beside him and slanted his slightly concussed head against the pale yellow wall, closing his eyes to shut out the ice-pick glare of the lights and the curious stares of his fellow inmates. They were all in this together, locked in an institutional time warp. But he was making plans for a breakout.

As soon as he could get Burke to answer his phone. His assistant would have to choose tonight to escort his latest lady to some highbrow concert. Another five minutes and he'd try the pay phone down the hall again. Maybe he could catch Burke between symphonies.

God, what a mess. If his arm was broken—and that was the general consensus—he'd end up in a cast, and that meant a major delay in the filming. Van Gelder would howl over the schedule and Kagan would stress over the expense. And Nora's waistline would continue to expand.

On the television suspended from the ceiling, a cable news broadcaster reported on life in the world outside. Twenty-four seven, disasters on a global scale. He wondered how long it would be before the first of the tabloid vultures descended to pick over his sorry carcass.

"...two counties in southwestern Montana," the voice droned from the ceiling. "Authorities are evacuating an area—"

"What?" He turned and stared at the television. On the screen, a mountain of flame boiled up into the night sky, outlining a stand of doomed firs. "What was that?"

"Wildfire," said Dyana with a Y and one N in the corner. She shifted the whining toddler on her lap and pulled a plastic toy out of the canvas bag between her legs. "In Montana."

"Where in Montana?"

Dyana shrugged and handed the toy to the toddler, who threw it to the floor.

"Mr. Kelleran," called the clerk at the window.

"I've got to make a call." He sprang from his seat, aiming for the pay phone. The waiting area whirled around him in a sickening starburst as he struggled for balance.

"If you'll just follow the yellow arrows on the floor and step through the blue double doors, the doctor will see you now."

He stumbled into the hallway and pulled some coins from his pocket, the same coins he'd been feeding into this machine for the last twenty minutes.

An orderly opened one of the wide blue doors and tipped through the opening. "Mr. Kelleran."

"In a minute." Fitz narrowed his eyes and punched at the boxy chrome numbers, the breath constricting in his chest, the blood rushing in his ears.

"Mr. Kelleran, follow me, please." The orderly swung the door open and gestured toward the wide corridor beyond.

Fitz held up his injured arm in an awkward signal, grimacing against the pain. He focused on the electronic trilling. Five, six....

"Mr. Kelleran."

He slammed the receiver into its stand and battled back another wave of nausea. "I need to make another call."

"After the doctor sees you."

Fitz's hand slipped from the black plastic. She'd be all right. They'd all be all right. They had to be.

CHAPTER TWENTY-ONE

STALE SMOKE FILTERED the sun's rays over Granite Ridge on Saturday, banding the evening sky in jeweled hues. Jenna was so very grateful to be enjoying the view from her kitchen window. The blackened skeletons of the cottonwoods down by the creek told her how close they'd come to losing everything.

Behind her, Will and Ellie slumped over their coffee mugs at the kitchen table. She knew they were dreading tomorrow, a day they'd spend assessing the damage and counting up losses. Though it appeared most of the main buildings in the northern sections of the ranch had been spared, an ominous gray pall draped the foothills and summer pastures to the south and east.

Jody clomped down the back stairs, her new cell phone in hand. "Mom. Fitz called. *Again.*"

"I'll call him back later."

"When?"

Ellie stood and swayed against the back of her chair for a moment. Bruise-colored skin outlined her puffy eyes. "When I'm ready."

"What you need is some rest, little girl." Will's voice was hoarse with exhaustion. He'd spent the night seeing to the transportation and care of the stock—what stock they'd managed to round up. "Go on up to bed now. I'll call Hank to check on the heifers we penned at the fairgrounds."

"No. I'll do it."

Jenna pinned Ellie with a glare. "Eleanor Louise, it's been years since I sent you to your room, but at this moment, I'm sorely tempted to give the order."

Jody shoved the phone toward her mother with a straight, stiff arm. Will raised an eyebrow.

Ellie donned her mulish face and marched to the stairway. Angling past her daughter, she climbed out of sight.

Jody headed toward the back porch. A few seconds later, the screen door squeaked open and slapped shut.

"Ellie's dead on her feet," said Jenna. "And she's got another mountain of trouble coming at her from Fitz's direction."

"I'm sure he'll make it right in the end," said Will. He stood and carried the mugs to the sink. "That man would walk barefoot through the cinders in the fields out there if he thought it would make her happy."

"What's going to happen with those two, Will?"

"That's up to them." He tugged her into his arms. "I'm more concerned about another couple at the moment."

"This isn't the time or place," said Jenna. She cast a furtive glance toward the spot where Jody had disappeared and knew she was blushing like a schoolgirl.

His smile spread, as slow as the sunset, across his face. "This is the only time and place we've got."

"You know what I mean."

"Maybe I do. But I'm thinking this is a brand new start for us, Jenna. The old excuses aren't going to work anymore." He stepped back and held out his hand. "I want you to come home with me."

Her pulse thudded, warm and weighty with desire. "Now?"

"Yes."

She scooped her hair back with a nervous laugh. "I must look a sight."

"Yes," he said, and what she saw reflected in his face made her feel beautiful. "You do."

"We've both been up since early yesterday."

"Then maybe we should both head straight to bed."

Her heart rolled right over. "Oh, my," she whispered.

"Take my hand, Jenna."

She reached out, with no hesitation and no regrets, and did as he asked.

ELLIE BRAKED HER ATV Sunday morning near the charcoaled remains of a fence post and pulled a notepad from her shirt pocket. Miles of fencing, acres of feed. Gone. Along with the stables, the calving barn, eleven storage sheds and cabins, and the south pump house. She didn't need to tally up the details and sums on the insurance forms to figure out the bottom line.

She turned her face to the sky and dragged in a deep, shuddering breath as ammunition against the sting behind her eyes. No time for tears or self-pity. No time to waste on thoughts of a Hollywood superstar who thought he could pick her up, toy with her a while and then toss her aside when something more interesting came along.

Well, hell. She'd promised herself she wasn't going to think about Fitz Kelleran today. Besides, just about everyone else in America—including her own daughter, the preteen traitor—was doing that job for her, anyway.

Okay, so he'd crept back inside when her defenses were down. No big deal. Her defenses were down over two thirds of her ranch, so what was one more miserable breach while she was adding them up?

She just wished it didn't hurt so much, that was all.

But oh, my, it hurt, much, much more than she'd figured it might. Seeing those pictures of his car crash on the news… It was eating her up inside. What a fool she was to believe that tabloid nonsense when she knew better. And what a coward she was for not taking his calls.

She didn't like the way those labels looked on her in the mirror. And the foolish, cowardly woman looking back wasn't half as pretty, or polished, or desirable as Samantha Hart. That hurt, too.

Wayne Hammond's tan pickup nosed over the edge of the horizon, spewing a comet's tail of dust and ash. Ellie tucked her notepad back in her pocket as the truck rattled closer. The last thing she wanted to deal with right now was a man. Will had taken Jenna off to his cabin and neglected to bring her back. Fitz had taken his ex-lover out for a joyride and nearly gotten them both killed. No telling what Wayne might pull.

Too bad she didn't have her shotgun handy.

"Hey, Wayne," she said when he pulled to the side of the road next to her. "What brings you out this way?"

He put the truck in Park and killed the engine before leaning his elbow out the open window ledge. "Just wanted to see if there was anything I could do to help."

She stared past his truck, past the ugliness of scorched fields and the mirage of black and blue mountains hovering on rivers of heat. "Appreciate the offer. Not exactly sure yet what we need."

"Looks like you lost some of your alfalfa crop."

She pulled off one of her gloves and rubbed at a blister. "Most of it."

The truck's door whooshed open and thumped closed, and Wayne's shadow fell across her feet. "That's rough," he said.

"Winter feed's going to be scarce now that half the local supply's been wiped out. That means expensive."

"I know." She shoved her hair out of her eyes and rose from the four wheeler's seat. "I'm shipping out most of my stock in the morning. I'll have to sell on the short, but it can't be helped."

"Ellie." He reached out and raised her chin with one of his big, wide fingers. "Let me help."

She looked up into his eyes and then let her gaze roam over his face—his familiar, weather-worn face. A face that rarely cracked a grin but didn't lie.

"I can't, Wayne. I can't accept the kind of help I think you're offering."

"You haven't heard my offer yet."

"All right." The tiny smile she managed was weak and wobbly on the ends, but she reached up and circled his wrist with her fingers so neither of them would let go. "I'm listening."

"Ellie." He stepped closer and tilted his head toward hers, and then he hesitated, just a moment, just long enough to have her hitching her breath and bracing her back as his callused palm spread along her jaw.

She forced herself to look up into his soft, sweet brown eyes. Kind eyes. Gentle and warm, and steady on hers. She told herself not to look for more—for heat, and humor, and yearning. "Yes?"

"I'm not the kind of man who can dress something up with fancy words. But I don't think I need to do any more talking, not about this. I think we both know what I have in mind. And why it would be good for the both of us if you could find a way to consider it."

"If that was a proposal," she said, "it wasn't much of one."

He dropped his hand from her face. He didn't seem insulted and he didn't seem amused. He didn't seem anything but patient and reasonable—and that was a disappointment.

"I said what needed saying."

"All right." She sighed and pulled her glove back on. "Yes, you did. And I appreciate it."

"I don't want your appreciation."

"You don't?" She tossed up her chin at him, and a foul brew of emotions trickled through her. "What is it you do want? Come on, Wayne, spell it out."

He set his mouth in its stubborn ditch and stared over her head.

She sucked in a deep breath and wondered how to go about sabotaging a misbegotten courtship while salvaging a priceless friendship. "Why did you start coming around this summer, Wayne?"

"Because I wanted to." He flicked a bland glance down at her. "Because I've been wanting to. All those years, when Tom was away at college. And after that, when he stayed away, when you and I…"

He colored and shifted his eyes to that distant spot over her head. "I wasn't ready to come around back then. And then Tom came home, and you got married."

"Oh, Wayne." She stepped forward and slid her arms around his waist. "I'm so sorry."

"Nothing to be sorry for." His hands settled over her shoulders in a heavy, awkward embrace. "You didn't know."

She burrowed her head against his shirtfront, smelling steer and soap and a woodsy aftershave. *What if.* "Maybe I wish I had known," she said.

"I wouldn't have had the good times I had with Alicia. And you wouldn't have Jody."

He tightened his grip and set her away from him. "I can wait."

She laughed, a choking laugh that had to hitch its way through the gaping crack in her chest. "Just how long are you going to go on waiting, Wayne?"

He gazed out over the blackened earth. "Till winter."

And then he looked at her with a calculating glint in those steady eyes of his. "And maybe I won't have to wait that long."

FITZ SLOUCHED WITH A SIGH in his sleek metal deck chair and watched the Pacific dump yet another wave in his backyard.

"Here." Burke reached across a table set for lunch to hand him one of the painkillers the emergency room physician had prescribed. "Take this."

"I don't want it."

"Take it, or I'm leaving."

Fitz slanted him a grumpy glance. "Your bedside manner leaves a lot to be desired."

"I could say the same thing about your company."

Fitz snatched the pill out of Burke's hand and chased it down his throat with a slug of water. "There," he said. "Satisfied?"

"Maybe if you eat the lunch I fixed."

Fitz stared at the soggy grilled cheese sandwich grown cold on his plate. "I'm not hungry."

"You have to eat something."

"The pills make me woozy," he said, raising his good hand to test the knot on his forehead. "I can't eat when I'm woozy."

"If you'd eat, the pills wouldn't make you woozy."

"Got an answer for everything, don't you?"

"I don't have an answer for Barton yet."

"Well, you're not going to get one." Fitz pressed the bruise too hard and winced. "Not today, anyway."

"You can't put this off any longer." Burke rose from his chair and walked to the edge of the deck to stare at the sand below. "Barton might lose interest, and I think you'd regret that."

Fitz closed his eyes and let himself drift, waiting for the medication to take the edge off the pain. If only he could take something for the cramping, panicky ache around his heart.

God, it hurt.

"She won't talk to me, Burke."

"What would you say if she did?"

Ellie had told him once she couldn't trust anything he said, anything he did, because he was an actor. He'd played the honesty part well enough to get her into bed—and lots of other interesting places—but then what? He'd walked away with her daughter's cell phone number, her favorite horse and some vague talk about a visit—and then he'd climbed into his sports car with his former lover and headed off into the Hollywood hills and the latest scandal.

Why hadn't he told Ellie he loved her before now? Before this? After all that had happened, how could she ever trust him? "Nothing I want to say over the phone," he said at last.

Burke straightened away from the railing and took his seat at the table. "Then call Barton. And Clarkson, and Malakoff, and Robbins. And Greenberg—who is genuinely concerned about your health, by the way."

"I'll bet." Fitz's stomach was queasier than ever. "All right. I'll call them. *All* of them."

He frowned down at the food on his plate and shoved it away. "What's for dinner?"

Burke shoved the plate back. "Leftovers."

WE HAVE TO SELL THE RANCH.

Ellie tossed her pencil on the papers and ledgers heaped on her desk and slumped back in the old oak chair in her home office. "We have to sell the ranch."

There. She'd said it out loud. She'd have to say those same words, repeat them over and over again, until they took on a life and meaning of their own, separate from hers.

Across the room Jenna stood silent and pale in the doorway, her eyes on Will where he sat slumped in his chair. He stared at the floor, his face gray and drawn from lack of sleep. Bank documents were piled on his lap, and crumpled papers dotted the faded carpet at his feet.

He'd worked with Ellie through the night and deep into Monday morning, adding and subtracting and manipulating the figures in all the columns, but the bottom line was always the same. Insurance funds wouldn't cover the repair costs. Recent improvements and film-padded payrolls had increased expenses. Film delays in California would postpone studio payments. No unencumbered collateral remained to secure any more debt. Too many overdue bills and a credit line stretched beyond the limit—no way, no time, no hope.

"God." Ellie swung to her feet and paced to the window, and lifted a hand to fist against the glass. Her fingers were shaking—how could her fingers be shaking when everything inside her was numb and half dead already? "*God.*"

"You shouldn't set too high a price," said Will. "It has to move fast."

She couldn't force a response through the tightness in her throat, but she managed a nod.

"But you can't set it too low," he continued. "You need to

cover the debts. And you need to move fast—an auction, I s'pose."

She shut her eyes against the image of strangers bidding on her home. "How am I going to keep Jody here?" she said. "In school, close to her friends? The last thing I want for her is—"

The kind of life I had, before I came here.

Will's chair creaked and then his hand fell, solid and heavy, on her shoulder. "I've got a job waiting for me near Dillon, and I'll be taking Jenna with me. I want you to know, little girl, that you and Jody will always have a home with us."

She reached back and squeezed his hand, and then he let it fall. Suddenly she needed to escape this room with its strewn papers and atmosphere of failure. She turned and shoved her hair back from her face. "Is there any more coffee?"

"I'll get some started fresh," said Jenna, and then she slipped from the room.

"Couldn't drink another drop." Will rubbed at the back of his neck. "Think I'll go help the crew finish up the morning chores."

Ellie wandered into the entry, trailing her fingers over the smooth top of the oak newel post rubbed nearly black by Harrison hands over the past hundred years. In the dim second parlor, the grandfather clock Henrietta Harrison had purchased in St. Louis during the 1904 World's Fair somberly marked the noon hour.

Jenna had already moved on to some other chore, but the coffeemaker gurgled and hissed, and the aroma of her blueberry spice muffins lingered in her kitchen. On the bright yellow tile, a bowl held apples ready to peel and slice for pie, and beside it, a bright red film mug with the little horse logo.

Ellie fingered the mug and let herself drift for a few stolen moments on memories of a teasing voice and a wickedly charming grin, of blue eyes gazing into hers with such a sweet intensity that her body tightened with the daydream.

Fitz would have to be told about the sale, of course. There were still a few threads dangling between them. Hannibal, and Disneyland, and...

Her thoughts began a familiar spiral, racing through well-rehearsed territory, faster and faster, looking for a detour or a way out of the box canyon at the end of the road.

She'd come full circle, hovering with the ghost of her twelve-year-old self. She was here at Granite Ridge Ranch, but she didn't belong, not anymore. She wanted desperately to stay, but she had no claim.

She had no claim because she'd lost the right. Lost the gamble, lost the land, lost her home and all the memories and treasures that it held.

Maybe things had been set in motion long ago, by Ben's stubborn resistance to change and by Tom's eagerness to change too fast. But the last nudges over the edge were hers. Her choices, her responsibilities.

There was one way out, one way to keep her family together at Granite Ridge. It terrified and shamed her to think of using another man to secure her place here, but she couldn't escape the driving need behind the thought, or the way it merged cold and calculated practicality with a hot and heady fantasy.

She would ask Fitz Kelleran to buy Granite Ridge.

She knew what would happen if she picked up the phone and dialed his number. He'd offer a loan, most likely, or he'd jump at the chance to buy the ranch. He cared enough about Jody—she thought he might even care enough about her—to let them stay, and she was desperate enough to consider any option.

But if he offered, and if she took him up on it, could he ever again trust the motives behind her affection?

Why hadn't she told him she loved him before now? Before this?

Their affair was over, stone cold and ready for the burial. There would be too many complications to consider this time around. If he bought the ranch, he'd be her employer. She wouldn't risk her place here, or Jody's, to satisfy those kinds of needs. And Fitz wasn't the kind of man to take advantage of the hired help.

She trailed her fingers down the side of the mug, one last time, and then she headed back to her office to make a phone call.

CHAPTER TWENTY-TWO

BEHIND A CURTAIN OF HAZE, the monotonous surf roared in and sucked itself back out. Seagulls whirled and scolded overhead, fighting over scraps, and the cold, dead air reeked of beached kelp and rotting fish.

Fitz stretched his legs over his beachfront deck and absently lifted a mug of tasteless, lukewarm coffee to his lips. He stared at the tiny cell phone tucked close to the cast on his arm and willed it to ring.

Ellie. Burke. Greenberg. The local law enforcement's fund-raising committee. Someone.

They probably thought he was resting and didn't want to be disturbed. As if he could sleep with his wrist twinging in its prison and his head throbbing in its lumpy case. And his conscience revving up for an overtime torture session.

He'd seen the reports of his car crash on the local and national news. Lots of material to slither and slobber over, lots of conjecture about drinks and drugs, a lovers' reunion gone wrong, a lovers' tiff gone awry. Lovers, lovers, lovers.

Prrr. Prrr. He grabbed for the phone with his injured arm and fumbled the play, but he managed to make the pass to his other hand and hit the button before the buzzer. The seagulls in the stands went wild. "Kelleran."

"Hey, Fitz."

"Ellie."

He squeezed his eyes shut. Even though he dreaded facing her disappointment in him, he'd been craving this contact every moment for days, so he could say something…something…

Something coherent would do. "I was hoping you'd call. It's been—"

No. Nagging at her was not a good idea. Not when her ranch was a disaster and her opinion of him was probably worse.

"It's been a while, I know," she said. "How's the arm? And the head?"

"Getting better. Listen, Ellie, about all that—"

"Your accident's big news, but I figure most of what I'm hearing isn't the real story. Guess my little taste of that kind of attention taught me a thing or two."

He winced. Anger would have been easier to play off than this breezy indifference. And because he was feeling a fresh pang of guilt over whatever role he'd played in dragging her into the tabloids, he decided to change the subject. "Speaking of news, I heard about the fire. Jody told me things look pretty bad."

He heard her deep intake of breath, and he sucked up one of his own, hurting for her and struggling to find a way to say the things he wanted to say. How very sorry he was that her precious ranch was damaged and how much he wanted to help, in any way he could. How very sorry he was that he'd betrayed their *friendship* in such a public manner, and how much he—

How much he loved her, damn it.

He wished he were there with her to wrap his arms tightly around her, to warm her clear through with the heat they could generate between them. She'd like that, he thought, if he held her close and propped her up until she found a little peace in his arms. He hoped so, anyway. God, he hoped so.

And God, he hated trying to talk with her on the phone. "Ellie, I wish I—"

"I have to sell the ranch, Fitz."

He slumped against the cold concrete wall behind his back. His heart pounded hard and fast and filled his ears with a roar that drowned out the sounds of the surf. He needed to think, and fast.

He suspected the cast on his wrist had provided a convenient excuse to duck the location payments—payments that would supplement fire insurance funds. Maybe that would give her some breathing room. "I'll talk to Kagan," he said.

"That's not—there are lots of reasons for selling, and it's—"

"How much do you need?" He knew her pride was mangled, that she might try to salvage the pieces by locking him out, but he wouldn't let her do it. There'd be no moving Jody from the only home she'd ever known, no scrounging for work on someone else's place. "I want to help."

"I figured you might." Her rusty laugh was a little shaky, a little thin. "I'm just not sure I can afford it. I sure as hell don't want to take it."

"But you're going to." He set his jaw and bore down on them both. He couldn't stand up to her—stand up *for* her—and be charming about it. "You know it's your best option."

She paused, and in the taut silence that stretched between them he felt the tenuous thread of their relationship twisting and knotting into something unrecognizable.

"It won't come easy," she said at last, "and it won't come cheap. I know how much you want this place. And I'm going to take advantage of that to attach a few conditions to the sale."

"Going to make me pay, huh?"

"Through the nose, Kelleran."

That's my girl. Still giving as good as you get.

"You get the ranch," she continued, "but we get to stay. All of us, including the crew. You're going to need someone to manage it for you, anyway, since you won't be here much."

So that's how she was going to play it—strictly business, cold and distant. He could handle the business, too, for now. He'd work on that ice-princess attitude later. "Wishful thinking, Ellie?"

There was another pause, briefer than before. "I can't afford wishes these days, either," she said.

"Good thing I can afford enough for us both," he said. "It's a deal."

He asked the name of her lawyer and rushed through the goodbye and disconnect before she could gather all the reasons he shouldn't do this to her. Once she got over the shock and the grief, once she started in on the paperwork headed her way, she was going to hate him for a while. He could only hope they'd both live long enough for her to get past it.

He staggered to his feet on legs gone as stiff and achy as the rest of him, and then he stormed into his house and slammed the big glass doors shut behind him. He wasn't built to play the martyr, and a relationship could only stand one injured party at a time, so he'd have to work through his own bitterness before he faced hers.

He couldn't take over a ranch in Montana, court a woman, and produce or direct a film at the same time. Something had to give, and he knew which items had just been shoved to the number three and four spots on his list of priorities.

He stalked down a dark hall and into his office, dropped the cell phone on his desk, swept up his precious optioned script and spun around to launch it into the corner waste bin. But he froze in the middle of his windup as his personal fog cleared and everything inside him clicked into place.

So that's what Barton had been getting at with his notes on *The Virginian*, with his subtle changes to the heart of the story. It wasn't about the action, and it wasn't about the characters, or the sets or the scenery. It was about love, about what love cost. Love was messy and demanding, it toppled the best-laid schemes and hungered for sacrifice. Love was damned hard work.

He'd just never realized before how hard it could be.

He loved Ellie. He loved Jody, and Jenna. He loved Granite Ridge. He loved those people and that place far, far more than anything this role, or this film, or this step in his career could possibly bring him.

He gazed down at the tattered pile of papers in his hand, papers that represented a fantasy world waiting to be conjured from talent and imagination, and he weighed that dream against the reality of Granite Ridge and the warm and wonderful woman waiting for him there. He hefted the lightweight bundle in his hand with a smile on his face. No contest.

Kruppman would have a coronary.

He pocketed the phone and swung by his wet bar to snag a Corona. Then he stretched out on his sofa, with his feet stacked on some pillows and the script on his lap, and set his mind loose to sift through his options. A half hour later, he pulled out the cell phone and punched in a familiar set of numbers.

"Hello, Myron." Fitz's mouth twisted into a resigned smile. "How the hell are you?"

ELLIE SHOULD HAVE BEEN prepared for the relentless speed and efficiency with which Fitz took ownership of Granite Ridge. The day he'd taken Nora to the hospital, Ellie had witnessed how he could pull himself out of his casual slouch to seize command of a situation and save the damsel in distress.

But oh, how she detested playing that role in this drama.

So she worked a punishing schedule, supervising repairs with Will and making a thorough inventory of ranch assets. She plowed through a mountain range of paperwork and took dozens of complicated phone calls from dozens of complicated consultants—and she nearly succeeded in blocking out the noxious mix of grief and anger bubbling through her system. But beneath it all, beneath the body-numbing exhaustion and the mind-fogging details, beneath the sickening taste of defeat, lurked a fear so powerful it threatened to bring her to her knees.

Soon she would be dependent on a man who lived a larger-than-life existence on movie screens and tabloid pages. A man who would drop by for the occasional visit, with the press trailing him like slug slime to distort and cheapen their world. A man who had sliced up her heart when he'd climbed into his sports car with his Bond lady and brought all her secret dreams crashing to an end.

Yes, she'd been dreaming of seeing him again, of traveling to California to store up another set of memories. She'd wanted to feel, one last time, like the woman she'd been with him, that passionate and joy-drenched woman. But now she'd have to bury that woman deep beyond his reach. She would allow Fitz to provide her daughter with a home; she couldn't allow him to come after her with his carving knife. She couldn't let him do that to her again—and again—and expect to survive.

But she wasn't sure she could stop it from happening.

TWO WEEKS AFTER HIS ACCIDENT, Fitz drizzled his homemade vinaigrette over two plates heaped with fresh baby spinach and crumbled Gorgonzola and carried the salads to his seaside deck.

Burke sipped from a glass of merlot and hovered over corn cobs steaming in their husks and bacon-wrapped filets hissing on the grill. "I like mine rare, remember."

"I've got it under control," said Fitz. He ducked back into his kitchen for a basket of bread and a tray filled with assorted dinner items, and then slipped the food from the grill to their dinner plates. "Have a seat."

Burke watched him touch a match to the worn stub of a citronella candle in the center of the table. "What's the occasion?" he asked.

"A celebration." Fitz raised his wine and gestured for Burke to do the same. "To *The Virginian*. To all the players who've lined up. And to one key producer who's about to, if he'll accept the offer."

Burke nodded with obvious pleasure and sipped. "Things are falling into place, then."

"You could say that." Fitz set his wine aside and picked up his fork. "Greenberg and I have reached a new and improved understanding."

"You've been spending enough time at his office lately."

Fitz held up his cast-encased arm. "I've got some time on my hands these days. If I can't act, I might as well do lunch."

"You hate to do lunch."

"I have to eat. And doing lunch is what executive producers do."

Burke smiled and held his glass aloft for another toast. "I knew you'd come around."

"As you yourself pointed out, I'm already doing everything an executive producer does, anyway. And to handle the things I don't want to do, I've taken on a partner. Myron Greenberg."

Fitz tipped his glass toward Burke's. "Here's to Big Sky Entertainment."

Burke shook his head as he clinked his glass against Fitz's. "Hollywood's newest odd couple."

"Sounds like a headline in the next issue of *Variety*."

"It's perfect, now that I think of it." Burke twisted his glass stem between long, lean fingers. "Greenberg gets to do more of the wheeling and dealing he enjoys—and the lion's share of the work. And you'll get to do what you do best—smiling for the camera, and as little work as possible."

Burke set his glass back on the table and cut into his steak. "In fact, it sounds like a lot of extra work for me. Maybe I should ask for another raise."

"Don't bother." Fitz took a sip of his wine. "Because you're fired."

Burke's fork froze halfway to his mouth. "What?"

"I'm firing you, Burke. I'm kicking you out of the nest. It's time for you to take your talents for organizational detail elsewhere. You are no longer my personal assistant."

"What?"

"It's for your own good, believe me."

Burke carefully set his fork on the edge of his plate. "I don't understand."

"It'll make it easier for you to accept the job of associate producer on *The Virginian* when the executive producer offers it to you."

"Associate producer?"

"Don't worry." Fitz dug into his salad. "You'll get that raise after all. A substantial one."

"You want me to be your associate producer on *The Virginian*?"

"Starting Monday morning. You've got a nine o'clock meeting with Greenberg at bungalow twenty-one on the Paramount lot." Fitz leaned to one side and reached into a pocket. "Here's the key."

"Paramount?" Burke stared at the key dangling from Fitz's fingers. "A bungalow?"

"Greenberg and Malakoff worked out an exclusive three-year production pact. Two films. I star in both. Barton's signed on for *The Virginian*, which will be our first project, but I've agreed to do Barton's film first."

"Barton's directing?"

"I came to the conclusion, at some point during the last few weeks, that *The Virginian* is essentially a love story about a charming man and a reluctant woman." He fingered the stem of his glass with an ironic half smile. "Barton's vision is essentially in sync with mine, and Greenberg's drooling over his bankability."

He set the key ring on the table and shoved it in Burke's direction. "Take it."

Burke glanced at the shiny gold key and then looked up with a frown. "Who's going to take care of you?"

"I am, for a while." He stripped the husk from his corn and reached for the butter tray. "I'm heading back to Montana in the morning. I bought Granite Ridge."

Burke slumped in his chair with a groan. "You don't need an assistant. You need a keeper."

"I'm hoping I'm going to need a best man."

Burke grinned and lifted his glass. "You're right. This is a celebration." He waited for Fitz to join him in his toast. "It's a wake," he said. "To the memory of Fitz Kelleran, may he rest in peace."

"Ha, ha."

"You just bought the only thing in the world that Ellie Harrison loves as much as you think she loves you," said Burke, "and you're about to waltz right back into her life and propose? She's going to cut you into little pieces and feed you to those mangy ranch curs. She's going to skin you alive and spread you out like a rug on the bunkhouse floor. She's going to—"

"I get the picture." Fitz clicked his glass against Burke's. "Going to come and visit?"

"You know that phrase 'every chance I get'?"

Fitz nodded.

Burke sipped his wine. "It doesn't apply in this case."

FITZ DROVE THE PICKUP he'd bought in Butte—one with no-nonsense, non-leather upholstery and the bare basics of a sound system—along the familiar route from town. At the ranch turnoff he braked and let the truck idle as he stared at fresh fencing stretched over charred ground—and the empty spot where the sign noting the entrance to the Harrison ranch used to hang.

Not the Harrison ranch. His ranch.

No, he thought as he made the turn. He'd make sure folks still called it the Harrison spread. First official act of ownership: get that sign replaced. He'd already instructed his attorney to leave Granite Ridge to Jody in his will.

He sped along the dusty track, past swaths of missing fencing and blackened fields, past groves of toothpick timber and patches of ruined crops, fighting a belly full of nerves. It would have been a hell of a lot less complicated to convince Ellie to agree to a loan. He had a regular payroll to meet now. Health insurance, state and federal employee regulations, equipment upkeep, building maintenance, livestock markets, timber harvests, crop rotations, environmental agencies—it all gnawed at his gut. He couldn't shove it off on Burke, now that he'd gone and promoted him. And though he had a ferociously competent ranch manager, the ultimate responsibility for these several square miles of timber, river and pasture now rested squarely on his shoulders.

He hadn't considered that, not really, not until he saw it flashing by his window, spreading out in sad and silent glory to stretch to the horizon, something bigger than even his fertile imagination could get a grip on. Much, much bigger than putting together a movie deal. One of the biggest challenges he'd ever tackled.

And a few minutes later, when he pulled into the open space beside the tall, rambling white house and saw Jenna, Will, Maggie and Ellie step out on the front porch to greet him as if he were their lord and master, he knew he was looking at the biggest challenge of all: his future family.

CHAPTER TWENTY-THREE

THERE HE WAS, STEPPING OUT of a shiny new truck and strolling toward them as if he hadn't a care in the world, his white cotton shirtsleeves folded back to reveal a fiberglass cast on his left wrist and his fingers shoved into his pockets: Fitz Kelleran, the new owner of Granite Ridge.

Ellie thought she'd been prepared for this moment, but she'd been wrong. She simply couldn't stop the emotional mayhem wreaking havoc on her system.

He seemed taller than she remembered, and a bit thinner. He was even more handsome—and that should have been an impossibility.

But the reality of the Fitz Kelleran climbing the front porch steps was that no man should possess such an instant, potent power over her mind and heart. Surely it was impossible for one weary, crooked grin to rattle her resolve and weaken her resistance. Surely it was impossible for two blue eyes to lock on hers and make her want to weep for the pain of her loss and the joy of his presence.

And it was impossible not to stare right back, not to study each detail of that beautiful, wonderful face. She tried not to stare, and she swore she'd defy his threat to her heart.

But then he said, "Ellie." Just her name, just the one word, the way he'd said it when they'd made love. And in that final, helpless moment of reunion, she knew she had never stopped loving him, and she never would.

She knew it was wrong, she knew she'd suffer for it, but the emotion just floated up through the denser atmosphere of resentment and grief. It shattered her defenses and left her utterly vulnerable to him.

She hated him the most for that.

"Fitz," she answered with a businesslike nod. "Welcome back to Granite Ridge."

She noted with wicked satisfaction the tiny ripple of muscle along his jaw and the slight narrowing of his eyes. She was glad he was annoyed, and she hoped he felt some small piece of her grinding ache. And in the next instant she wished she could take it all back, feeling mean and low and ungrateful for everything he'd done for her and her family.

"Yes, welcome," said Jenna. She stepped toward him and hesitated for one uncertain moment before kissing Fitz's cheek.

Will extended his hand. "Good to have you back."

Fitz gave it a solid pump. "Good to be back. And congratulations. When's the wedding?"

Will's wide smile and Jenna's blushing answer punched another hole through Ellie's sorry, self-centered haze, and he seized on their vivid joy to dam up the misery flooding through her. It had taken a disaster to force Will and Jenna to face what had been there between them all along, but the result was worth the wait and beautiful to see.

Jody, off the phone at last, burst through the front door. "Fitz! You're here!"

She flung herself into his outstretched arms, and they wrapped themselves around each other, laughing, shutting out the tension hovering around them.

"How's your arm? Did anybody famous sign it?" Jody

asked as she squirmed back to check out his cast. "Did you bring me a present?"

"Jody!" Jenna clucked and shook her head. "Shame on you."

"Yes, shame on you, you greedy thing." Fitz gave her a noisy smack on the lips and set her on her feet, and then tossed an arm around her shoulders as she clung to his waist. "Yes, I brought you a present. I brought presents for everyone."

"Everyone?" Maggie raised an eyebrow in skeptical amusement.

"Everyone."

"Oh, Fitz," said Jenna with a sigh. "You didn't have to do that." She waved a hand toward the door. "Well, come inside and cool off. You must be awfully hot and thirsty."

"I can leave my things in the truck for now," he said, "unless you want to show me to my room first."

"Oh, you're…you're staying here, then. I'm so glad." Jenna clasped her hands in front of her and squeezed until her knuckles turned white. "I thought you might be more comfortable up at the guesthouse, but there's a room here you can use."

God. He'd be sleeping right down the hall. They'd share a bathroom. Ellie felt herself start to tremble, and she locked her knees the way she used to in school when she'd had to deliver an oral report.

"Will can get your things out of your truck," Jenna continued, "and carry them in for you."

"No need," said Fitz. "I can get them myself."

"But your arm—"

"I'm not helpless, Jenna."

"Of course not." She pasted on her brightest company smile. "Well, then, let me get you some lemonade. I made some fresh, just this morning."

Fitz grinned and rubbed his good hand up and down Jody's arm. "I don't suppose you have any of those sugar cookies to go with it, do you?"

"Oh!" Jenna flushed with pleasure and swept her hair back from her forehead. "I suppose I just might at that."

"I'll take a couple, then. Unless I'm setting a bad example and spoiling dinner."

"You're company. You can do whatever you want," Jody said. She quickly realized her mistake, and she slowly slid her arm from around his waist. "Well, you're not really company, I guess. I mean—"

"That's why I've got to obey Jenna's rules," he said, staring at Ellie. "Don't want to get in trouble my first night here."

"How long can you stay?" asked Will. "There are some decisions to make about replacing the stock and some of the outbuildings."

"Let the man have a few moments to eat and drink a little something in peace," said Jenna. "Jody, help Fitz carry his things in while I get the tray." Jenna and Will disappeared into the house, and Jody skipped down the steps and raced to the truck.

"Maggie," said Fitz without shifting his gaze from Ellie's, "why don't you go see if Jenna needs any help?"

Maggie shot her sister a questioning glance before lifting a shoulder in a careless shrug. "Yes," she said, "why don't I?" She slipped through the door and left them alone.

Fitz shoved his fingers back into his pockets and continued to stare at Ellie. His hot and hungry gaze traveled the length of her, from her mud-caked boots to the wisps of hair coming loose from her braid. She held herself as still as she could and let him look, burying her pain and her yearning until she was as stiff and cold as marble.

His expression smoothed and hardened to something just as cool and lifeless, and then he turned and jogged down the steps to help Jody unload the truck.

Her supply of bravery ran to empty, and she fled to the barn.

AN HOUR LATER, AFTER A GLASS of Jenna's lemonade and talk of wedding plans, after he'd settled into a guest room and distributed his gifts, Fitz cornered Ellie at the squeeze chute behind the main barn. He shoved one shoulder against a corral gate post to watch her help Chico dose an ailing heifer, and he readied himself to launch the biggest and most important battle of his life. "Jenna sent me to fetch you for dinner," he said.

"I'm not hungry."

Chico shot him a warning look and made a fast exit.

"Are you going to avoid sitting down at the same table with me for the rest of the week?"

"Is that how long you're staying?"

"Answer the question, Ellie."

"Yes, sir." She flicked him a barely polite sideways glance. "No, I'm not going to avoid it."

So, she'd cast him in the role of absentee landlord. He bit back his frustration and picked up on his cue. "What's wrong with the cow?"

"A case of lungworm. She'll be back out to pasture in another couple of days."

"Is that common?"

Ellie pulled a lever to release the heifer into the corral, and then she faced him with a carefully bland expression, kicking his pulse into overtime. If she knew the effect her cool and disinterested routine was having on his libido, she'd shut it down in a heartbeat.

"It can be," she said. "That's one reason we rotate the herds to different pastures so often. This one managed to slip through the latest roundup. She's lucky we found her when we did."

"I've got a lot to learn."

She nodded, slow and solemn and oh, so maddening. "If you want to."

He cocked his head to one side. "You tell me, Ellie. Do I want to?"

"That's not for me to say."

"I'm here to tell you that it is for you to say. It's your decision, same as always."

"It's not the same," she snapped, and then she bit her lip and turned away.

All right, then, he thought. There's a little heat under that frozen exterior, after all. But just because she was still the same old Ellie firecracker didn't mean this was going to be easier than he'd figured.

He was struck by the realization that nearly everything in his life had been easy up to this point. He'd been handed good looks, natural talent, career breaks, fawning women and piles of cash. Now he was undertaking, all at once, the launch of a production partnership and the long-distance ownership of a working Montana ranch. And the courtship of the one woman in his personal universe who was immune to his charm.

Gramps had always said the real test of a man lay in how he dealt with adversity. Fitz figured if he simply survived the next few weeks he'd earn a high score on the exam.

"I know what this looks like," he said. "Like I swooped in here, with my millions in hand, looking to satisfy my latest whim, and simply took it all away from you. And I did, okay? But not just because I could, and not just because I wanted to, but because you needed my help. You and Jody both."

"I didn't let you take it."

Her chin angled up in defiance, but it hurt his heart to see it didn't come up as high as it used to.

"I sold it," she said. "And I would have asked you to buy if you hadn't offered."

"And you could have changed your mind, at any point in the process."

"I didn't have a choice."

"We all have choices, Ellie."

He held up his injured arm when she opened her mouth to speak again. "I bought this place, even though I knew it would hurt you. Even though I knew I was risking any chance I might have with you. I did it in part because I felt guilty, about this," he said, waving his cast, "and I wanted to try and make things right."

Her eyes narrowed to slits. "I'm so relieved I could sell you a little peace of mind in addition to my home."

"Okay, I had that one coming." He nodded, accepting the hit. "And let me point out that I could take that line and put another spin on it. Hell, I could come out the hero here, if I wanted to. It wouldn't be much of an act—everyone would buy it when I was finished, maybe even you."

He stepped closer to her. "But the truth is, you didn't need my help, not really. You're the strongest woman I know, Ellie Harrison, and I need that strength from you. I need what you can do to me. I need to feel the way you can make me feel."

He reached out before she could move away. Even though his wrist twinged a bit, he grabbed both her arms and hauled her against him and gazed down into her cool, shadowed eyes.

"Don't you see?" he asked. "I'm the needy one here, not you. I'm the one doing the begging, and I'll beg for as long and as hard as I have to, because I want you. More than I want this place, more than I've ever wanted anything."

She softened against him as he spoke—not much, but enough that he knew his words were gnawing their way through her stubborn skull. She swallowed, and her eyelids fluttered, and for one blessed moment he thought she was going to surrender.

But then her chin came up again, nosebleed high, and she twisted away and swatted at her sleeves where his fingers had wrapped around them. "I don't come with the ranch, Kelleran."

He stood where he was and watched her hips swing in that sassy swagger of hers as she stalked into the barn.

End of round one. His mouth was dry, his heart was racing and his hands were trembling. But he was still standing.

TWO HOURS AFTER A TENSE DINNER with Fitz in Ellie's place at the table, Jenna perched at the foot of Will's bed. "Do you think those two are ever going to find a way to work through their problems?" she asked.

Will sprawled on his side of the bed, the sheet pulled up to his waist and his head resting in his hand as he watched her pull a comb through her hair. "They have to be in the same place at the same time to start with."

Jenna sighed and lowered her hands to her lap. "Ellie can be so stubborn."

"She's got to eat. Maybe you could padlock the pantry and the refrigerator and flush her out."

"I'm tempted to do just that."

"Let me try to help you put it out of your mind for a while." He stroked her hip with his foot from beneath the sheet. "Come and lay with me, Jenna."

She glanced over her shoulder at him and caught her breath

at his handsome face and form. What a wonderful lover he'd turned out to be. She'd known he would be gentle, and patient, and thorough. The passion had been a surprise.

He was a young and energetic man, an enthusiastic and inventive lover, and he craved her touch—oh, how he craved her. His eagerness for her was a powerful aphrodisiac, and her doubts about her ability to please him quickly dissolved as she abandoned herself to the intoxicating intensity of this new love affair.

She set the comb aside and stood to face him, pushing her gown over her shoulders. It slipped down her length to pool around her ankles on his bedroom floor.

He caught her hand and tugged her down beside him. "You'd think twenty years of pining for you and the prospect of a wedding would give me the patience to wait just a little while longer. But now that I've had a taste of you, I don't want to let you go."

He curled her hand in his and turned it, using her own knuckles to skim over her breasts, and her breath caught at the erotic feel. But she could feel the tiny puckers in her skin beneath her fingers, and she bit her lower lip. "I've got stretch marks."

"A woman's battle scars."

He lifted her hand to his lips again and moistened her fingertips with his tongue, and then used them to draw a wet circle around her nipple. She gasped as the cool evening air in the cabin washed over her and puckered the tip.

"Do you want to touch me, Jenna?"

"Yes."

He guided her hand to her mouth, and she licked at her fingers, as he had done. He slid his hand to circle her wrist, and waited, watching her. "Where would you like to touch me?"

She raised her hand to his face, and his fingers fell from

her arm. She traced the shape of his mouth, his perfectly bowed upper lip and the generous lower one, spreading her moistness over their satiny surface. "I'll start here," she said. "Who knows where I'll end up?"

He moaned and rolled her beneath him and shoved a long, warm legs between hers. "Just promise me you won't get lost."

She slipped her ankles around the backs of his knees and arched her back to slide against him. "If I do, you can help me find my way."

CHAPTER TWENTY-FOUR

ELLIE LIFTED ONE OF HANNIBAL'S wide front feet the next morning to check for stray pebbles. She'd escaped the house at dawn to groom him in the barn, figuring Fitz would take him for the afternoon's surveying ride with Will. And she wanted to steal some private moments with the big red horse before he got shipped to California.

"You skipped breakfast."

She pressed her lips together to hold back a sigh at the accusing tone in Fitz's voice. "I had coffee."

"That's not breakfast."

She moved to Hannibal's other side to put the horse between them. "That's all I wanted."

"What are you doing?"

"Getting the big boy here ready for the day's work." She patted his solid rump and ran her hand over his smooth summer coat toward his rear foot. "It might be a good idea to try out his travel wraps a couple of times this week and get him used to them."

"He's not going anywhere." He walked around the horse's hindquarters to stand before her. "I want to keep him here."

She shrugged against Hannibal's leg. "Suit yourself."

"I intend to."

"That almost sounds like a threat."

"Pardon my inflection."

He uttered a vile curse and swung away. "We sound like a couple of playground brats."

She started to make a smart remark, but he was right. She sighed and tossed the pick into Hannibal's brush tray, suddenly exhausted by the combination of no sleep and no food, by the constant pummeling from her conscience and the constant ache in her heart.

"I'm sorry, Ellie. For everything."

"You've got nothing to apologize for."

"Are you sure? Because I came here prepared to grovel." His mouth twisted up in a self-mocking grin. "I'd hate to see all that rehearsal time go to waste."

She could feel his charm chipping at her resistance, and she backed away. "You don't have to grovel," she said. "You don't have to say anything, or do anything. You don't owe me—owe us anything."

He stared blankly at the barn floor. "I've gone over that evening—that evening with Sam—a hundred times. I put her in my car because she was too drunk to drive herself home."

The cast on his arm caught as he shoved his hands into his pockets, and he frowned as he wriggled and wedged it in. "I couldn't have known she'd try something as stupid as grabbing the steering wheel. And though I've gone over and over it in my mind, I still can't see how I could have done anything different."

She'd gone over it, too—imagining him in his elegant tux, tucked into the intimate confines of his sporty car beside another woman. Her jealousy was far less logical than his explanation, but it was just as real. She didn't know who she resented more—Fitz, for his knack for ending up in the tabloids, or herself, for her failure to deal with it.

She stiffened her resolve to keep him at a safe distance and folded her arms across her chest. "You've already paid your penance, Fitz. An impressive one, too. A spread like this doesn't come cheap."

He raised his head and stared at her. "It wasn't any penance to buy this place."

"Not if you have millions to spare, I s'pose." She tilted her head. "Convenient, too. You won't have to pay the location fees if you film *The Virginian* here."

"Ah, yes." His lips thinned in a grim smile. "*The Virginian*."

A nasty trickle of ice wormed through her as she began to suspect the true price he'd paid for Granite Ridge. "*The Virginian*," she whispered. "What have you done?"

"What needed to be done." He narrowed his eyes at her. "And I don't want your pity, or your gratitude, any more than you want mine."

"But your plans. Your—"

"All right," he said. He tugged his hands from his pockets and threw his arms wide, making Hannibal blow and jerk at his lead. "Do you want to hear exactly how much I had to give up? Do you want to know which scraps I managed to hold on to? How much detail do you—"

"Stop!" She sucked air into her lungs and fought back the panic surging through her. "Just stop."

"A movie may not be much, it may not mean a hell of a lot in the larger scheme of things, but it was mine. My dream. I wanted to show you what I could do."

"I wanted to see it." She tried, but failed to dam up her sympathy—and her love, curse her traitorous heart. "I wanted to see your dream come true."

"Well," he said, and he jerked his head in a stiff nod.

"You'll get to see part of it, anyway. It seems I have a hell of a lot more inside of me to pour into that role than I did just a few weeks ago."

He stepped toward her. "But there's a more important project I'm working on right now, Ellie. I think it might make more of an impression on a certain woman I know, even if it is a little singed around the edges."

She retreated another few inches, and her shoulder bumped against a support post. "What do you mean?"

He trapped her between the beam at her back and his hard, uncompromising gaze. "I think you know what I'm getting at here, Ellie."

She did, but feeling her secret dream drift within grasp filled her with a terrible, dangerous hope, the kind of hope that could leave her crushed beyond cure. He wanted her, but did he want her forever? Could he love her the way she needed to be loved, the way she deserved to be loved? Could she be a Hollywood kind of wife? Could he be a Montana kind of husband?

It didn't matter—he still hadn't asked the right question, the one she wanted to hear. But what if he did? What answer would she give—and why would she give it? Any answer that came bundled with her concerns for her family and home wouldn't be fair to him.

Not fair, not right, not possible, not real, not good enough—the reasons swarmed in that same tight, exhausting spiral, threatening to drive her mad.

She tossed up her chin and grasped at her crumbling resolve. "I gave myself to a man once for a place to call my own. If I give myself to you now, how can you be sure I'm not doing it for the same reason?"

He lifted his injured arm and rested the cast along the

beam above her head. "You go ahead and keep repeating that touching little speech, as often as you need to hear it. Just don't make the mistake of thinking that I need to hear it, too. Because it pisses me off."

She turned to slip away from him, but he grabbed her with his one good arm and pinned her in place.

"You wear your obligations like a badge of honor, and damn," he said, "I can't help but respect you for taking responsibility for your actions and the people you love. But when you twist the purpose of your life around so that it's based on what you owe others, pretty soon you lose yourself, and then you've got nothing left."

He lowered his other hand and wrapped his fingers around her arm. "You already passed the point of drowning in your debts, Ellie. All of them, everything and everyone you think you owe. You've gone under for the third time."

"Let go of me," she said. She knew he could see the flush rising into her face and the way her chest rose and fell with every tortured breath. She struggled to hold on to her anger and her pain, to focus on them, but the pitiful defenses crumbled as shame flooded in. She wanted to run and hide and curl up in a ball of misery, but she couldn't do any of those things because she had chores and a daughter and Jenna and Will and—and she had to find a way to deal with this man who was making her life too confused to live the way she needed to live it.

He looked at her, looked right inside her. She wanted to turn back the hurt and drive him away, and she wanted to cling to him and find oblivion in his kiss. She thought she might split in two, just like her pathetic heart.

"I thought maybe, just maybe," he said, "with all that's happened, you'd changed enough to be able to see how things are. But you're still sizing me up based on what I can give you, aren't you, Ellie? Figuring how many acres come with the deal? Isn't that the way you calculate a potential husband's worth?"

He pulled her against his chest and lowered his mouth toward hers so that his hot breath rushed over her face with his words. "Who's better husband material, the rancher next door or the one right here? Who's got the bigger spread, the better stock?"

"That's not true." Her voice quavered, and she hated the weak and mewling sound of it in her ears.

"Isn't it?" He twisted her closer and ground his fly against her belly. She was already wet and ready for him, already frantic and wild for him, and she hated that, too.

"Have you once given a thought to who's going to slip inside you and make more children with you?" he asked. "Who's going to put up with your stubbornness, and your cussedness, and your tiresome insecurities, and stick like glue to you every day for the rest of your life?"

"Fitz, I—"

He crushed his mouth over hers, and she wrapped her arms around him as he dragged her up and shoved her against the wide post. Hannibal snorted and shied at the end of his lead rope, and Pete nickered behind a nearby stall door. Dust and alfalfa shreds rose up in a whirlwind to spin around them.

The kiss was brutal and punishing, and tender and pleading, and painful and filled with defeat and despair—and then it was over, and he snatched his arms away from her so suddenly she nearly tumbled to the floor.

He stood over her, tall and beautiful and defiant, and his features twisted with pain. "I'm asking you to look at *me*, Ellie. To look past your wounded pride, to look beyond the film screen and the tabloid pictures. Beyond the acres of Granite Ridge. To look at *me*."

She did, and she saw a man who could stand up to her and offer her support at the same time.

He whirled away and stalked out of the barn. She sank to the floor then, relieved he hadn't stayed to see her collapse.

She huddled there, while the dust settled in the manure-scented gloom and Hannibal snuffled at the tears cascading down her cheeks, and she reminded herself that she'd sold him the ranch because she trusted him. She trusted him with her home, and with her family, and with her daughter's future.

It was long past the time to trust him with her heart.

ELLIE TRUDGED UP THE ROAD just before noon and frowned at the strange white sedan parked next to the front porch steps.

Jody blasted through the door. "Mom! You gotta come in here and see this!"

Ellie staggered to a stop and closed her eyes. She didn't think she was prepared for whatever Fitz might have done to the house, now that it was his. On the other hand, he'd have to go through Jenna if he wanted to make any changes, and she didn't think he had enough charm or ruthlessness to win that battle. "I'm on my way."

Jody took her hand and tugged her through the front door. "Just look at them, Mom. Did you ever see anything like it?"

Ellie stared, open mouthed, at a forest of roses. Hundreds of them, perfect and long-stemmed, filled the front parlor with their perfume, bursting from vases crowding every available horizontal surface. And blush-pink, every last one of them.

"Oh, Fitz," she whispered as she pressed her hands to her heart. "What are you doing?"

"Ellie? Is that you?" Jenna walked in from the dining room, twisting her hands at her waist. "There are some gentlemen here with a package to deliver."

"You gotta see the dress first," said Jody.

"The dress?" Ellie moved forward, as if in a dream, and reached out to touch one of the roses set on the tea table. It was powdery soft and smelled like heaven.

"It's the most beautiful thing I've ever seen in my entire life," said Jody as she took Ellie's hand to tug her along. "And the lady who brought it set it up on a stand. Gran wanted to put it in your room, but I told her we should keep it here, with the flowers. Look."

The lace curtains in the second parlor's bay windows framed an ivory gown borrowed from a fairy tale. Pearls and crystals edged the satin bodice in delicate swirls, and miles of tulle netting flowed over Martha Harrison's antique Persian rug.

Maggie stooped to arrange the cloud-like train. "I hate to admit it, but I'm impressed," she said. "I sure as hell don't want to be, but I am."

"It's an impressive dress," said Ellie.

"That's not what impresses me." Maggie straightened and skewered her with a sharp look. "Most men would assume that a woman like you wouldn't go for a cream-puff gown like this. This man obviously knows you better than most. He's been paying attention, Ellie. And when a man pays that kind of attention, the woman he's paying it to better pay close attention right back."

Yes, he'd paid attention. All along, through everything, he'd been tuned to her every mood and motion. It wasn't just some freakish actor's talent—it was an eloquent kind of caring. The hope she'd been damming up inside burst free and flowed through her, warm and smooth, coating all the sharp and empty places.

"Fitz asked me to look in your closet and tell him what size you wore," said Jody, "but I never thought he'd come up with something like this."

"Didn't you?" Ellie reached out to brush a fingertip over a tiny pearl. And then she looked down into Jody's hopeful face.

There were two women being courted here. The fact was, Fitz had captured Jody's heart from the very first moment. And Ellie knew that her daughter had taken hold of his long ago.

"Ellie?" Jenna gestured toward the kitchen. "They're waiting."

"This is the best part," said Jody as she dragged Ellie through the dining room. "Wait'll you see this."

Two large men in dark suits rose from the kitchen table as they entered. "Ellie Harrison?" one of them asked.

He lifted a large black velvet box from the yellow-checked cloth and handed it to her. "For your approval, ma'am."

Jody crammed up against her side, and Jenna and Maggie moved to peer over her shoulder as she took the box.

"Open it, Mom."

She didn't need to open the box to understand that Fitz was trying his best to make all her dreams come true, and she didn't have to blink back the tears filming her eyes to see what was inside. But she lifted the lid so the miracle of her Miss Longhorn crown could dazzle them all.

ELLIE HIKED TO THE BARN and followed the sound of cursing to find Fitz wrestling a bale of alfalfa onto a stack in a storage stall.

"What the hell do you think you're doing?" she asked.

He flipped the bale on its end and shoved it into place. "Can you be a little more specific? If I'm about to get another layer of hide stripped off, I'd like to know what it's for."

She flung an arm back toward the main house. "The dress. All those roses. That crown thing."

"It's called a tiara."

"It came with a couple of guys who look like they're from the Mafia."

"Close enough. Harry Winston."

He grabbed a dolly and shoved past her on his way out of the stall. "I've brought my elephants over the Alps, Ellie, and I'm ready for battle. Unlike the real Hannibal, though, I'm not going to lose the war."

She followed him to the flatbed truck parked at the main barn entrance and watched him struggle, mostly one-handed, to yank another bale down on the dolly. "I told you once I had some big moves," he said. "All that stuff up at the house is just a sample."

"I have to admit it was a pretty impressive one."

"Ready for another?"

She shot him a wary glance and slowly nodded her head.

He moved to stand before her, solemn and sweaty and studded with bits of feed. "I love you, Ellie Harrison. I've loved you since the first time you busted my butt. And I'm going to love you until the day you scrape so much of my hide away there's nothing left for a decent burial."

"My, my. I don't quite know what to say." She slapped a hand against her chest. "That was so poetic my heart's thumping a mile a minute."

He worked his jaw for a few seconds, and then his face eased into one of his shifty smiles as he leaned in close. "Is that what you want? Poetry?"

"It wouldn't mean anything." She waved her hand under his nose. "You've probably got dozens of lines you could trot out at a moment's notice."

"Hundreds."

"Lucky me." She batted her eyelashes. "Maybe your lines would be an improvement on some of the stuff that's been pitched my way lately."

"What lines?" His eyes narrowed to slits. "What do you mean, lately?"

She edged up next to him and poked her finger into his chest. "Changing the subject?"

He pasted on one of his most innocent grins, obviously preparing to change the subject. It wasn't one of his biggest moves, but it was one of her favorites.

"So," he said, "what line comes next? Or do we cut to the happy ending?"

"I don't know." She frowned and tilted her head. "I think maybe there should be a proposal in there, somewhere before the end. It would be a shame to let one of your big moves— not to mention all those roses—go to waste."

"As long as we're on the subject of missing lines, isn't there something you want to say to me?"

"Hm." She wrinkled her forehead and took her time. "Thank you for the presents."

"You're welcome," he said. "Anything else?"

"It's time for lunch."

"Okay, I'll be there in a minute." He frowned. "Anything else on your mind? Anything at all?"

"You mean, like, the fact that I love you?"

The mix of expressions and emotions that flickered across his face made her toss back her head and laugh.

"What's so funny?"

"You." She tucked her head beneath his chin and squeezed him tight. "I do love you, you know."

"Yeah, I know." He squeezed her back, and it was the most wonderful feeling she'd ever known. "God help me."

"Now," she said, pulling back a bit. "About that proposal…"

He settled his hands on her shoulders and cleared his throat. "Ellie, I know we have a lot of things we need to work out. My work and my life can get crazy sometimes. But I love you, and you love me, and I'm sure we can—"

"Fitz?"

"Yeah?"

"Shut up and kiss me."

He smiled a warm and wonderful smile, a smile no one would ever see on a movie screen or a magazine cover, a smile he smiled only for her. "Yes, ma'am."

* * * * *

*Watch for Wayne's story
in Terry McLaughlin's next Harlequin Superromance,
coming in February 2007.*

Set in darkness beyond the ordinary world.
Passionate tales of life and death.
With characters' lives ruled by laws the everyday world
can't begin to imagine.

Introducing NOCTURNE, *a spine-tingling new line from*
Silhouette Books.

The thrills and chills begin with
UNFORGIVEN by Lindsay McKenna.

Plucked from the depths of hell, former military sharpshooter
Reno Manchahi was hired by the government to kill a thief,
but he had a mission of his own. Descended from a family of
shape-shifters, Reno vowed to get the revenge he'd thirsted
for all these years. But his mission went awry when his target
turned out to be a powerful seductress, Magdalena Calen
Hernandez, who risked everything to battle a potent evil.
Suddenly, Reno had to transform himself into a true hero and
fight the enemy that threatened them all. He had to become
a Warrior for the Light....

Turn the page for a sneak preview of
UNFORGIVEN by Lindsay McKenna.
On sale September 26, wherever books are sold.

Chapter 1

One shot...one kill.

The sixteen-pound sledgehammer came down with such fierce power that the granite boulder shattered instantly. A spray of glittering mica exploded into the air and sparkled momentarily around the man who wielded the tool as if it were a weapon. Sweat ran in rivulets down Reno Manchahi's drawn, intense face. Naked from the waist up, the hot July sun beating down on his back, he hefted the sledgehammer skyward once more. Muscles in his thick forearms leaped and biceps bulged. Even his breath was focused on the boulder. In his mind's eye, he pictured Army General Robert Hampton's fleshy, arrogant fifty-year-old features on the rock's surface. Air exploded from between his lips as he brought the avenging hammer down. The boulder pulverized beneath his funneled hatred.

One shot...one kill...

Nostrils flaring, he inhaled the dank, humid heat and drew it deep into his massive lungs. Revenge allowed Reno to endure his imprisonment at a U.S. Navy brig near San Diego, California. Drops of sweat were flung in all directions as the crack of his sledgehammer claimed a third stone victim. Mouth taut, Reno moved to the next boulder.

The other prisoners in the stone yard gave him a wide

berth. They always did. They instinctively felt his simmering hatred, the palpable revenge in his cinnamon-colored eyes was more than skin-deep.

And they whispered he was different.

Reno enjoyed being a loner for good reason. He came from a medicine family of shape-shifters. But even this secret power had not protected him—or his family. His wife, Ilona, and his three-year-old daughter, Sarah, were dead. Murdered by Army General Hampton in their former home on USMC base in Camp Pendleton, California. Bitterness thrummed through Reno as he savagely pushed the toe of his scarred leather boot against several smaller pieces of gray granite that were in his way.

The sun beat down upon Manchahi's naked shoulders, grown dark red over time, shouting his half-Apache heritage. With his straight black hair grazing his thick shoulders, copper skin and broad face with high cheekbones, everyone knew he was Indian. When he'd first arrived at the brig, some of the prisoners taunted him and called him Geronimo. Something strange happened to Reno during his fight with the name-calling prisoners. Leaning down after he'd won the scuffle, he'd snarled into each of their bloodied faces that if they were going to call him anything, they would call him *gan*, which was the Apache word for *devil*.

His attackers had been shocked by the wounds on their faces, the deep claw marks. Reno recalled doubling his fist as they'd attacked him en masse. In that split second, he'd gone into an altered state of consciousness. In times of danger, he transformed into a jaguar. A deep, growling sound had emitted from his throat as he defended himself in the three-against-one fracas. It all happened so fast that he thought he had imagined it. He'd seen his hands morph into a forearm and paw, claws extended. The slashes left on the three men's faces after the fight told him he'd begun to shape-shift. A fist made bruises and swelling; not four perfect, deep claw marks. Stunned and anxious, he hid the knowledge of what else he was from these prisoners. Reno's only defense was to make all the prisoners so damned scared of him and remain a loner.

Alone. Yeah, he was alone, all right. The steel hammer swept downward with hellish ferocity. As the granite groaned in protest, Reno shut his eyes for just a moment. Sweat dripped off his nose and square chin.

Straightening, he wiped his furrowed, wet brow and looked into the pale blue sky. What got his attention was the startling cry of a red-tailed hawk as it flew over the brig yard. Squinting, he watched the bird. Reno could make out the rust-colored tail on the hawk. As a kid growing up on the Apache reservation in Arizona, Reno knew that all animals that appeared before him were messengers.

Brother, what message do you bring me? Reno knew one had to ask in order to receive. Allowing the sledgehammer to drop to his side, he concentrated on the hawk who wheeled in tightening circles above him.

Freedom! the hawk cried in return.

Reno shook his head, his black hair moving against his broad, thickset shoulders. *Freedom? No way, Brother. No way.* Figuring that he was making up the hawk's shrill message, Reno turned away. Back to his rocks. Back to picturing Hampton's smug face.

Freedom!

Look for UNFORGIVEN by Lindsay McKenna,
the spine-tingling launch title from Silhouette Nocturne™.
Available September 26, wherever books are sold.

Introducing...

nocturne

**a spine-tingling new line
from Silhouette Books.**

**These paranormal romances will
seduce you with dark, passionate tales
that stretch the boundaries of conflict,
desire, and life and death, weaving
a tapestry of sensual thrills and chills!**

Don't miss the first book...

UNFORGIVEN

by *USA TODAY* bestselling author

LINDSAY
MᶜKENNA

*Launching October 2006,
wherever books are sold.*

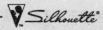

SPECIAL EDITION™

**Experience the "magic" of
falling in love at Halloween with
a new *Holiday Hearts* story!**

UNDER HIS SPELL

by KRISTIN HARDY

October 2006

Bad-boy ski racer J. J. Cooper can get any
woman he wants—except Lainie Trask.
Lainie's grown up with him and vows that
nothing he says or does will change her mind.
But J.J.'s got his eye on Lainie, and when
he moves into her neighborhood and into her
life, she finds herself falling under his spell....

SAVE UP TO $30! SIGN UP TODAY!

INSIDE *Romance*

The complete guide to your favorite
Harlequin®, Silhouette® and Love Inspired® books.

- ✓ Newsletter ABSOLUTELY FREE! No purchase necessary.
- ✓ Valuable coupons for future purchases of Harlequin, Silhouette and Love Inspired books in every issue!
- ✓ Special excerpts & previews in each issue. Learn about all the hottest titles before they arrive in stores.
- ✓ No hassle—mailed directly to your door!
- ✓ Comes complete with a handy shopping checklist so you won't miss out on any titles.

- -

SIGN ME UP TO RECEIVE INSIDE ROMANCE
ABSOLUTELY FREE
(Please print clearly)

Name _____

Address _____

City/Town   State/Province   Zip/Postal Code

(098 KKM EJL9)   **Please mail this form to:**
In the U.S.A.: Inside Romance, P.O. Box 9057, Buffalo, NY 14269-9057
In Canada: Inside Romance, P.O. Box 622, Fort Erie, ON L2A 5X3
OR visit http://www.eHarlequin.com/insideromance

IRNBPA06R   ® and ™ are trademarks owned and used by the trademark owner and/or its licensee.